SENTINEL

Blue Blooded Brothers

SOFIA AVES

First Edition
Published by Little Quail Press
Cover Art by JS Designs Cover Art
Editing Services provided by A. Strom - Edits with a Coffee Addict
www.redpensandcoffeebeans.wordpress.com/
www.facebook.com/redpensandcoffeebeans/
ISBN 978-1-922448-14-9

CONTENTS

BLUE BLOODED BROTHERS SERIES

VII

DEDICATION

To Tony.
For letting me have
book cover Christmas ornaments.

CHAPTER ONE

BLACK

The fight was over in seconds. I ducked the man's sloppy blow and delivered a sharp one of my own. My opponent wavered, dazed in the aftermath. I spun low, knocking his feet from beneath him, and knelt to plant my fist firmly in his face.

My breath increasing, I ignored the applause from the crowd and the emcee — rattling on about Theo Black, the new *King of the Cage* — and collected my winnings. I headed for the decrepit trailer Liam had rented for me in silence. Music pounded my exit, but I ignored that, too. If I wasn't fighting, I was working. Ego had no place here.

Stay in character.

Though my personal apartment could be described as spartan, the dingy trailer was still a step-down. I'd left the door open; in a place like this, a locked door only invited unwanted visitors. I pressed my palm to the face of the burner phone Liam had given me, checking it remained in the same place I'd left it.

I surveyed the small space, but nothing appeared to have changed, though I'd left it looking ramshackle. Clothing hung in what appeared to be a haphazard disarray from the bed and a small, pull-out table. Bowls of cereal I hadn't touched sat on the benchtop. All indications that said this was my existence.

Except it wasn't.

The phone vibrated beneath my hand; I jumped a mile, swearing, and snatched it up. Only one person had that number.

"Liam."

"Don't talk," he snapped, then sighed, "listen. I want to be brief."

That's not unusual. You're harder to get information from then a damned clam.

I exhaled sharply, muscles beginning to ache after the few moments of my fight. Though I'd had no real contact, the stress of the event weighed heavy on me. I needed to keep warm or stretch. Shouldering the phone, I tucked my other arm behind my back, relishing the strain of lengthening bunched muscles already tight and cold.

"Find a way to get into the business. I want to know how this is all working out. If you can get me something tangible, Selena will make sure it gets seen in court."

I nodded in response, then shook my head in disgust at myself. It wasn't a vid call. If I kept on like this, the case Liam spent hours trying to put together would be toast.

Focus — A word I had used with the team over the years, but rarely on myself.

"Good fight, by the way."

"You were there?' I asked in surprise, forgetting to not speak.

"Always." Amusement coated Liam's voice, though I knew he was a hard bastard. "If I put a man under, I'll never leave him behind. You know that."

I did know. Liam had lost a troop of men in the desert nearly a decade ago — well before his police career as head of our elite task force — and still had not forgiven himself for it.

"Right. So." I cleared my throat. "What's next?"

"Next...stay with it. We'll sort Logan from this end. I need you to work Samson. Find out his transactions, and who's bankrolling him."

I snorted. "You know it's Logan. I stay in the cage?"

"For now."

"Then I have another fight to get my ass to."

"I'll be watching." Liam ended the call.

I gritted my teeth. From anyone else, that would be creepy as hell. But from Liam...it was a consolation. My greying head matched his, but he was the better pick to drag me from the cage, should things go south.

Which was likely.

We'd been trying to pin Wayde Logan for years, and Operation Predator had given us a lead. Bank robber, murderer, kidnapper. The growing list of charges became an ever-evolving beast. Just when we thought we had him, he slithered free. If he was financing an illegal cage fighting racket, then we had a way to get to him; for now, it looked like I had to stay King of the Cage.

Metal from the cage dug into my back where I slid down into a low crouch. I kept my grimace off my face as the other fighter — some young gun they thought would either make a good show or go down easy — slammed his fist where my head was meant to be.

Coming up underneath, a clean uppercut dropped him to the floor. I stepped over his jittering form and out of the cage before the ref — from outside the cage, the slimy bugger — counted my opponent out. The bookie passed me my winnings with a crooked grin.

"Samson wants to see you."

I ducked my head before he could see the smile I couldn't hide.

Samson's office was the typical rundown space I associated with small-time crooks who thought they rated much higher in the ranks. Cramped and overly cluttered, it stank of weed and bodily fluids. Perched on the edge of his grimy desk was a bimbo in a red dress. If I dusted for fingerprints here, I'd get enough to book half of Melbourne.

The woman flicked hair away from a pair of breasts that jiggled precariously within their enclosure. She eyed me with interest, though I was likely twice her age.

Fucking a girl who wanted to call me *Daddy* was not on my to-do list.

Samson reclined in a worn chair, his feet sticking out the side of the desk. I half expected him to be smoking a cigar.

"You won. Again." His combined gaze with the bimbo had me wishing for the showers.

"Disappointed?"

"Far from it."

Good. I wasn't sent here to disappoint you.

"What do you want, then?" I tipped my head back, my eyelids heavy. The epitome of bored, I sent him a *don't-waste-my-precious-time* glare.

"I want you. More fights, more perks." He leaned back in his chair. Thick, rounded arms that had never done a day's labour perched on the armrests.

I tilted my chin down in time to see him nudge Red and raised an eyebrow.

"Fine. You want more money? Here." He snorted, digging about beneath the desk to scatter notes in my direction.

I ignored the cash. "Give me a cut."

"Of your fights?"

I sneered at him, taking a step forward. My hand cupped Red's knee, then slid upward. She arched back, her legs sliding apart. I didn't bother looking at her as my hand skimmed beneath the hem of her short dress.

Play the part.

"Of the fights. All of them."

Samson stared. "You're not that good."

I grinned. A soulless, nasty thing that closed Red's legs in a hurry.

"Then test me."

I fought for him every night for a week. Small fights on weekdays, bigger fights on weekends. Liam was present every night.

Sometimes in his typical black shirt and jeans, blending into the crowd to the point of becoming noticeable; just another face. Others, he wore a suit. Those would be his networking nights. I knew to expect him at the table the next time I negotiated with Samson.

The neverending roar of the crowd was muted from outside the pop-up stadium. My muscles cooled far too quickly between fights. I circled my trailer, and when the text came through to head back into the warehouse, I sprinted on the spot for a moment, swinging my arms to get the blood flowing. When I stepped outside into the frigid evening air, I found Liam leaning against my trailer, dressed in charcoal-black.

"Nice look."

"You'll need these tonight." Liam slipped metal into my hand, and without looking down, I knew they were my throwing knives. With an indecipherable look that penetrated something deep inside me, he disappeared into the night. However, I knew he'd be in the stands.

Just in case.

The crowd became raucous. I watched the prior participants as they were both carried from the cage. The winning fighter — I assumed — gave me a thumbs up before slumping back, blood running freely from several deep wounds around his body. I frowned, my hands clenched tight around my knives.

I didn't bother slipping the blades into my boot.

My opponent was short. Lithe, too, though I wasn't bulky, and I had a few years on him, at least. He'd be fast, I judged, watching him bounce on his toes. Maybe he could hook up with Red after the fight, though I guessed she only took winners.

I didn't intend to lose.

He stamped about the other side of the cage, encouraging the crowd through the chain-linked wire, pointed metal tips protruding from between his fingers — a crowd-pleaser. I suppressed a grin. This would be short and quick.

His first toss was an easy dodge. His second, not so much. Most knife fighters didn't throw as well as this guy, and although I wanted to glance over to where I knew Samson would be, I didn't dare take my eyes off the pocket rocket racing toward me.

My first knife thudded into the top of his thigh. I couldn't aim for a bodyline this close; while I didn't mind ending his fighting career, I didn't want to risk his life.

I sidestepped his blade and hit his other thigh with my next throw. He went down howling. I kicked his last knife aside, sending it skittering across the ring. Pocketing my last blade, I waited until the medic collected him, and nodded to the ref.

Samson caught my eye, jerking his head toward his office.

I didn't bother to collect my winnings.

"Get in here," he grunted, hauling the door shut behind me.

He crabbed his way around his desk, avoiding Liam, who leaned against one wall, immaculate in a crisp, charcoal suit. I didn't look at him.

"Who's this?"

"The man who might want to give you a future," Samson answered shortly. He shook his head at the impossibility of the task and seated himself with a gusty sigh.

My friend, you have no idea.

"Right. So, what we talked about—"

"Your cut." Samson twiddled the pen between his chubby fingers.

"Yeah."

Samson eyed me, then turned to Liam. "How do we best explain this?"

I held back a laugh but let the scenario play, if only for my personal amusement.

Liam never took his eyes off Samson, playing his part in return. "Let's call it an investment in your future. A part of your earnings goes into the pot, and you get to win that back."

I nodded. "That's what I get right now."

"Now, you get a piece of other fights, too."

This was too easy. I kept my eyes on Liam, knowing he had Samson in his pocket. What was I missing?

"But you also pay out on their losses. If they leave, then you...deal with the situation."

"You want me to be muscle for hire, beat the guys I've already taken out?" I backed up, my hands raised. Why was he getting Liam to say all this? Doubt that shouldn't have existed bloomed in my stomach.

Logan is infamous for screwing with your head.

"No," Samson agreed. "It's not. But you get this one opportunity. Do it. Or you won't get any further...career opportunities." His eyes gleamed.

The temptation to answer him in a nineteen-thirties New Yorker accent was tempting, but I resisted. Just.

"Fine," I spat through gritted teeth, "I'll do your small jobs. For a week, Samson. Then I'm gone. No more jobs. No more King of the Cage shit." A make or break moment; it came in every job. If I couldn't get Samson across the line, I'd completely lost control. That wasn't happening.

Samson leaned over his desk, his jowls sagging. "You want into my circle, Theo? You earn it."

I pressed my lips together, thinking furiously, then gestured to Liam. "He's here to what, finance you?"

Samson chuckled. "I already have that backing, son. In spades."

I nodded, pretending to consider his offer. My chance to push him harder drifted away.

"Alright. So tell me, *boss*. How long will it take for me to earn my way in?"

Liam walked out of the room, passing behind me. He patted my back lightly before he left.

Samson refused to give me an answer. We were in the long game now. Liam had disappeared off the radar; he might be active in the background, but I noted his absence with disquiet.

I frowned, cooling down from my final fight for the night. He'd sent me up against five fighters; typical, as Samson knew I'd pull in the goods. Cash overflowed from my small coffer, none of it mine. I took on some small jobs, handed out some beatings, but still nothing that would put Samson away or lead me to Logan. All it accomplished was to further stain my soul.

Selena would use the activities in court to set up these small timers. But I still needed to get to Logan. He hadn't made bail, but there were rumours of a corrupt judge, though I'd thought we'd eradicated those; locally, at least. The thought of having him free bothered me in more than one way. My thoughts strayed to Jenny.

Would she be asleep on the couch, surrounded by a host of unicorns? More likely she'd be waiting up. The corner of my mouth curled up. I fought it back with effort. Jenny shouldn't be in my thoughts at all, but she crept in, all the same. Hovering at the edges. I desperately wanted to grab the shade of her and pull her into the light.

My chest locked tight, but I buried it deep.

There would be time for that, after this case closed off.

A heavy knock rattled the door as I unravelled stained tape from my clenched fists. My skin was clear of cuts, but the fights were getting dirtier.

"What?" I grunted through the thin metal.

"Boss wants ya."

I shrugged; my standard reply, but I couldn't not turn up in Samson's office.

"You wanted me?" I leaned against the door frame, arms folded over my chest. Samson hunched over paperwork behind his desk.

He didn't look up. "You wanted in." He kept writing on a dog eared pad beneath his pudgy fingers.

"Yeah."

"So. One more job." He slid a photo toward me, pushing it over loose papers cluttering his desk. I tried not to breathe as I entered the room, sliding the offering from the desk. Liam's picture lay heavy in my hand.

"What do you want me to do with this?" I asked, letting disdain lace my words, though my heart raced.

"He's a cop. I don't want to see him again. Ever." Samson finally looked up. "You understand me?" Bloodshot eyes bore into mine.

You're a hired grunt. Don't show you have brain function.

"I don't kill," I said idly.

Samson snorted. "After what you did tonight in the cage? Bullshit. Get it done."

I nodded sharply, turning on my heel. The hall extended into the darkness of the closed warehouse, my lungs craving fresh air. My breath boxed in by cold walls, I burst from the building, my long strides eating the short distance to my trailer.

If I wanted to get to Logan, I had to kill my boss.

CHAPTER TWO

JENNY

I cuddled my coffee and moped. It wasn't my usual status, but without Black, the house had an emptiness about it. Though he provided security to Ashley and I, to us, he was far, far more. I collected a herd of listing unicorns left outside their playpen. I placed them in their usual enclosure, wishing I could escape my prison as easily.

Our safehouse was a small cottage on the outskirts of town.

No neighbours.

No car.

No going outside.

I found more unicorns and added them to the cage. My coffee cooled in my hand. I sipped it, resisting the urge to gulp it back, make another and toss that back, too. But what was the point? I'd end up buzzing with energy I couldn't use and nowhere to put it.

My toe tapped the worn carpet of the rental as I stared out the opaque windows that should have been transparent. A little love could make the place pretty, but it had been dirty when we arrived, and apparently, that suited our situation, hiding us from the world.

It was amazing the simple things you took for granted, that you whined about, mattered so much when they were taken away. I could barely remember what my driver's licence photo looked like. Not a single thing in the house had my name on it. Jenny Smith simply didn't exist.

The world, according to Theodore Black.

And so it stayed that way.

A small head of blonde hair, not unlike my own joined me on my unicorn quest, though we weren't related. Anything to stop me peering out a window I'd been warned away from while I waited.

But we did it, anyway.

We stared at the empty street on a Wednesday morning until our first passer-by flitted past the window. Ashley waved at the crow perched on the fence outside. I ruffled her sleep-mussed hair, attempting to untangle the hair tie at the root of the bird's nest on her head with one hand and gave up.

"Eggs and toast for breakfast?"

"I want coffee."

I grinned. There was no way I was giving caffeine to this lanky bundle of energy, even if I had the space to let her burn it off.

"Hmm. How about a hot chocolate instead?"

Ashley's eyes lit up. "Yes, please! Wait. When did we get that?"

"I'm magic." I winked, giving her a little nudge and pulling the curtains over the grimy windows. "Go get washed up."

"Okay, Mum."

My heart lurched, and I gave her a tight smile behind her back. We'd been family for seven years, and I would never get tired of the love she sent my way.

I could only hope to return it tenfold to a little girl abandoned by a man who never deserved to have her in the first place.

Ashley stood on her tiptoes, her fingers skimming the tin of drinking chocolate Black had bought before leaving for his other job. I bit my lip. That *other job* both protected us and left us bare. For the time being, we were safe. Which meant no round-the-clock security detail. No company.

Just us.

I missed him like hell.

Ashley succeeded in getting the tin down without spraying the kitchen with tiny particles of freeze-dried chocolate and presented it to me with a proud smile.

"Thanks, popcorn." I smiled. "He shouldn't have put it up that high."

"Did Teddy buy it?"

I bit my lip. She was far too attached to the boys, but who else did the nine-year-old have in her life? The trust of my nine-year-old foster daughter reminded me how resilient children could be.

If only adults were the same.

First, Cal and Mila entered her life. They had been with her since the day Logan abandoned her. After a run around with foster families who couldn't deal with the policing aspect of a child with a psychotic, murderous father, to me and now Theodore Black.

He was well old enough to be a father figure; he probably had ten years on me in my early thirties. And with his hardened exterior but total sweetheart inside, the big, cuddly cop offered his protection and earned our loyalty.

"Yes, he did."

"When's he coming back?"

"When he's done his job. We're not his only one."

"Are we hard work for him, Mum?"

I closed my eyes as tears pricked at the corners. Cold coffee hit the back of my throat in a poor attempt to distract myself. I swallowed it anyway and made a fresh one.

"No, Popcorn. We're not hard work."

I closed my eyes against the lie and wished that one day it would be true.

"She's gotten so lanky." Mila sighed, settling into the saggy sofa left behind from the last occupants. She rubbed her hip, but no bulge showing on her tiny frame. Yet. Her eyes wandered to the scones I'd made, resting on the table. Freedoms were few for Ashley and me, but Theo always made sure we had plenty of ingredients to cook with.

Anything to pass the neverending time.

Ashley rolled on the floor, wrestling with her unicorn clan when it should have been a child her own age.

"It happens, or so I'm told. Was told," I corrected myself. "I haven't been in touch with the foster people since..."

"Since the bank incident?" Mila's eyes flicked to Cal by reflex.

"Yup." I squeezed my mug. It was my fifth refill for the morning, and the tiny buzz trembled my fingers. I knew I spoke too fast, but Mila didn't seem to mind.

We haven't seen anyone apart from the team for two years.

The thought shocked me.

Mila shifted in her chair, her hand brushing at her lower back.

"I'm sure I shouldn't be this uncomfortable yet," she grumbled good-naturedly.

"I'm not the right person to ask." My hand pressed to my abdomen automatically, my mouth drying. "You're not showing if it helps." I gave her a tight smile that Mila returned, kindness and understanding flashing in her eyes. At least it wasn't pity.

"It's okay. I can talk to Teddy about it."

I frowned. Theo didn't have extended family, as far as I knew. We might have spent a lot of time together, but I didn't know a lot about his life, nor him mine. Sharing wasn't a part of our relationship — if you could call living together and barely speaking that.

I sat in silence as Cal hefted Ashley into the air, groaning under her weight. She poked glittery fingers at the already-filthy roof.

"You ever wonder how all those handprints get up there?" Cal asked, shifting Ashley to his shoulder, then swung her downward.

Mila sighed, covering my squeak as blonde hair lurched toward the thin carpet, taking my stomach with her.

"You'll have to learn to be gentle, Cal," Mila admonished him. "Babies can't be swung around like nine-year-olds."

"Nine-year-olds shouldn't be swung around either," I grumbled softly.

Cal didn't hear me. Mila's tiny, fine-boned hand curled around mine. It was perfect for the portrait work she did. Had done, before her pregnancy. She'd put herself on a self-imposed hiatus until the baby arrived, though I suspected Cal had a lot to do with it. He'd been without a family for such a long time that now he had one, he'd hit the alpha-protective button.

"I'm so glad you wanted to come to see us." The words ripped out of my mouth. I winced. "Sorry, my desperation for human interaction is rising. Daily."

Mila's hand gripped my damp one. "It's fine, Jenny. I get it."

"I know."

Of everyone, Mila *did* know. She'd spent five years of self-imposed isolation hiding from a psychopath who'd robbed the bank she worked in, killing her friend and workmate in front of her.

Logan had haunted her, stalked her for five very long years, where she'd been trapped in her own home, unable to face people or crowds.

The same man left his daughter at the bank when Cal and Black had turned up and pursued him across the city.

Ashley's father.

Mila's only friend had been Theo — *Teddy* — her minder. Their relationship had developed into more of a sibling-type closeness, despite the twenty-plus years between them. He'd helped her deal with people, had pulled Cal into line when he approached it or stepped over it in his eyes.

The ever-protective alpha male.

Now, we were in his care.

But witness protection wasn't the same for us as it had been for Mila. After the debacle at the bank, she'd changed her name, her home, her appearance — a totally new person.

Ashley and I simply ceased to exist.

18

No car, no income or bank account. No details on our lease, no licence, no bills. No vote.

No life.

Until he was convicted which, now Wayde Logan had been caught, should be soon. The thought of testifying against him terrified me.

Alone. Somewhere Black couldn't help me. A gap in my life where my husband should have been. I wished I missed Paul, but in all of this, my husband rarely crossed my mind. He'd left us before Logan had resurfaced, snatching Ashley the first time.

Theodore Black had been there, had our backs the entire time.

Back on her feet, Ashley pushed her hair off her face, the ends flying stray. I'd spent half an hour working on a fishbone braid with a youtube video while she read off tips to me. The girl looked like no one cared for her. A snort bubbled behind my nose, and I covered it with a cough. I'd have to watch the video again later.

At least it would give me something to do.

Nothing moved outside the window. Barely a handful of cars had come through this way all afternoon, leaving us in a semi-silent state while Ashley ate her way through the fresh berries Cal and Mila had brought with them.

I'd been tempted to join her; indulging in comfort eating would pass the time nicely. But I refused to become a product of my incarceration, a shadow hidden away from the world. Some choices and power remained with me, and what I ate was one of them.

A small win.

Standing back from the window, where Theo had directed, I watched the road in the direction he'd come from. If he came back tonight at all.

Liam's invite to watch Theo fight still rattled me. Even though Micah was happy to mind Ashley, the betrayal of Theo's trust, however small, sat heavy in my stomach.

Cal had only mentioned the slightest hint of Theo's absence, and I wondered how much his ex-partner knew about his activities. Liam insisted on bringing Micah in to watch Ashley under strict orders not to say a word to anyone.

The house sat in darkness — Theo's rather forcible suggestion, but my choice. He made that clear from the outset; they were his thoughts on our safety, but it was my choice what we did with them. It gave me a strange ownership and heightened responsibility I didn't need but was sure I'd want if I didn't have it.

Outside, the single streetlamp dangled sadly over the cracked road. Theo hadn't wanted the area lit, and he and Micah had hung off the streetlight in the small hours of the morning until it resembled a toddler's mangled drinking straw.

Shattered glass coated the bitumen in a glossy sheen of brittle shards. By the end of the week, it would be nothing but powder from the small amount of traffic.

Twiddling my empty mug in my hands, I studied the faint city lights. Not one part of me wanted to be in there, cluttered with the people, any of whom might be *his*. Just because Logan waited in jail didn't mean he couldn't reach us.

Cal and Theo's team had learned that the hard way.

He'd come for his daughter, and I'd stood between them. It hadn't been a conscious decision; heroics hadn't played any part. My actions had been based purely on terror and desperation. I'd never been near a gun in my life before that, and my body had come close to losing all control.

But the scariest thing about Logan had little to do with any physical weapon he wielded. His eyes showed a dead, emotionless soul, and I knew he'd pull the trigger faster than I could comprehend. Talking him down wouldn't work. And so I closed my eyes and waited.

Every time I closed my eyes, I waited.

Waited for the click or bang or whatever would happen, and wondered if I would open them again. In the darkness, his breath brushed my face. His presence never came close enough to touch, just enough to move the air there, cool tendrils of impatience brushing my cheek before he'd clubbed me with the thing, and tied me to a bomb.

Every time I closed my eyes.

Shadows moved outside the window. I squinted, staring at the black Lexus rolling its way silently across the crossroads outside the house, trying to hold back the knot of anxiety and elation bubbling in my chest.

Theo was back.

I stood in the lounge room, staring out the window knowing he'd come to check on me before he had a shower and washed away someone else's blood.

The air moved behind me as he entered the room. But with him — and *only* with him — I wasn't afraid. My skin flared, reacting to his presence, but fear had nothing to do with it. Not that kind of fear, anyway.

I squeezed my cold mug harder.

"She's asleep?" His voice strained with exhaustion. It matched my antipathy, but I hoped he would sleep tonight.

"Yes. Hours ago."

"That's good." He took a step further into the room and stopped.

I swivelled on my heel to face him, assessing his wounds as best I could in the dark, trying to work out which were his, and which were splatter from someone else. He stood in dark relief, a sliver of light reflected from the city beyond the window illuminating a shadow of his face.

Theo's dark hair striped with silver was sluiced back over the top of his head, looking wet. Which meant he'd either had a shower, and gone back to it, or it had been a lot messier than it looked. His beard needed a trim, if he'd let me. His arms bulged from the black singlet he wore, his leather jacket hanging off one arm as he stripped it off. Hard, carved muscle defined his physique, honed from decades of physical demands.

Tattoos curved over his biceps to his wrists, with more on his back I couldn't see but knew were there, along with scars that decorated his skin in their own way. What to say to a man who isn't your husband or lover but lived with you silently, day-to-day? I couldn't ask where he'd been, what he'd done, who he'd hurt.

After the bank incident with Logan, he'd wrapped his arms around me, holding me secure against him. His mouth against my hair, his breath brushing my cheek, he'd held me tight, and I'd sunk into him.

For a single moment, his mouth brushed over mine.

I'd come so close to releasing the tears that often threatened but never emerged, and been grateful for it. If they started, maybe they'd never stop, and I needed to be stronger than that for my daughter.

Since then, he hadn't touched me but often stood near me, close enough his body heat mingled with mine in the darkness, while the world forgot us. I treated wounds he wouldn't otherwise fix. Letting my hands rest on his skin longer than necessary, the hard muscle bunching beneath them until I managed to make them relax.

Unlike a wife, a girlfriend or a sister, I had no rights with him whatsoever.

Stepping forward, I studied the new shadows around his jaw and above his cheekbone. Here, I was so close to dark eyes that surveyed me with a fathomless depth that I knew should be intimidating. But it wasn't. Instead, the swelling skin drew my eye. My stomach clenched.

"Let me get an ice pack."

"Appreciate it. I'll shower. You don't need this shit on you." He held my gaze for a long moment, turning silently to head down the hall.

Once he left the room, breathed again.

I laid out our three ice packs — he refused to buy more — in their respective tea towels, knowing he'd forgo the latter, regardless of how I snarked at him.

He re-entered the kitchen a few scant minutes later, shirtless but clean. His torso travelled into black sweatpants, the tight vee disappearing beneath the soft material. Fine, dark hair smattered across his broad chest, barely covering his ink.

A double-headed phoenix bathed in black flame coiled around a snake eating its own tail. An ouroboros. Infinity times infinity. I ached to ask him about them, but the words stuck in my throat, tracing the dark shading with my eyes alone.

Fuck not being inappropriate, I just didn't want to get caught.

His gaze weighed on me while I faffed with the ice packs, stacking them in unnecessary piles. Theo slid one from beneath my fingers. His breath brushed the curve of my neck, slipping beneath my shirt.

"Thanks, Jen."

He sank into the chair I'd pulled out with a soft groan, pressing the pack to his jaw. The chair looked like a matchstick compared to his bulk, but it hadn't broken in the three months we'd been in the house, so I supposed it would stand up for another few.

Bowing his shoulders forward as he hunched, he leaned his elbows on his knees, muscles stretching tight. Some knots were evident, standing out beneath his skin, the pattern of the wire cage he fought in imprinted across his back.

Which I wasn't supposed to know.

"What happened here?" I asked, tracing the diamonds etched in his skin with light fingers. He groaned, a sound I wanted to hear from him but in a very different context.

Get your head out of your vagina, Jen. You're clearly starved for attention.

I was, but I really *did* need to keep it hidden. Ashley had to be the priority. My only priority.

The body of a raven curled at the base of his neck, one wing fully extended across his back and shoulder, the feathers stretching down his side to curl around his ribs. The skin there puckered with three small, round scars that pinched his skin, tearing into the wing. Places he'd taken hits, and walked away.

Had the wing been real, he would never have been able to fly.

I traced the line over his ribs. A muscle jumped beneath my fingers, and I stopped.

"What happened here?"

A grunt. "Got kicked."

"Were you on the ground?"

Theo swivelled to face me, an incredulous look emerging from behind the ice pack. "You think I'd let someone get me on the ground?"

I raised an eyebrow, and he turned back with a huff. "Apparently not."

Holding back a smile, I spread tiger balm over the area. Menthol and camphor mingled in my nostrils, reminding me strongly of Christmas and mothballs. Not an attractive combination. Another area bruised lightly already below his ribs. I slid a pack wrapped in a towel between Theo and the chair, tugging him back to lean on it.

That lasted all of a second.

"Take the wrapper off," he spoke to the fridge in front of him. I left my hand on his shoulder in a silent match of tug-o-war, until he turned to face me again. "Please."

"Better," I said tartly, tugging the towel free. Breath hissed between his teeth, his skin jumping beneath the sensations of the pack. "Did you...get the guy?" I winced, closing my eyes. I'd nearly said *did you win?* But, then he would know.

And Liam and I would both be in deep shit.

Theo didn't answer for a moment. I pressed a pack to his other shoulder, sliding it around the join of his neck to cover the diamond shape of the grill impressed there. Had he been slammed against it?

"Fence?" I asked softly, tracing the shapes absently on his back. When I ran my fingers over the raven wing on his shoulder, he grabbed my hand, holding it still pressed against hard muscle.

It was about the only thing because my heart wanted to jump out of my chest.

"I thought I saw you. Earlier this week. Did I?"

"At where you work?" I said carefully, running the words over in my head so I wouldn't trip myself up.

A pause.

"Yeah."

"No, Theo. I have no idea where you go each night. Or day."

His hand released mine, bumping the pack, so its icy touch replaced the warmth of his. How many times would he ask me to trust him when I could only lie?

CHAPTER THREE

BLACK

"Well, that's not gonna fly." Cal snorted, leaning his elbows on his desk. "It'll take a hell of a lot more than you to take him out."

I nodded my agreement from my customary place against the back wall of the incident room, my arms crossed over my chest, and sent my ex-partner a wry grin. "Yeah, he wouldn't be an easy target."

"Who wouldn't be an easy target?" Liam asked mildly, leaning around the open doorway. Cal jumped like a school kid caught perving on the teacher, but I knew Liam had heard every word.

"You." I held the steel-grey gaze he turned on me. "You'd be tough, but..."

"But?" Liam's voice remained soft, but a query lit in his eyes, reminding me of a crocodile sizing up his next meal.

"Apparently you're my next job." I nudged the file with his picture in it his way. Liam's eyes dropped to study the photograph then they returned to my face.

Not another inch of him moved.

"Are you going to do it?"

He could have been asking me if we needed milk.

I shrugged. "If it gets the job done. I mean, we want to sort out all Logan's loose ends, right? I need to retire one day."

Sooner, rather than later.

"Of course. Would you like me to turn my back, or is that too easy for such a...veteran?"

Liam straightened and walked slowly across the office to the elevator, his back to us the entire way. I stared at the back of his immaculate charcoal suit jacket, willing myself to take the dare.

Fucking hard bastard.

"We need Nerf guns." Danny emerged from under his desk.

I stared; the thing barely covered his bulk. "Were you fucking hiding?"

He gave me a wicked grin. I rolled my eyes.

"Nah, just fixing some cords down here." He held up a tangled mess of coloured plastic I swore he'd pulled out of the wall when Liam arrived.

"Yeah, right." I eyeballed the younger man with dislike. He might have redeemed himself in Cal's eyes, but he looked like an irresponsible twat to me. I focused on Liam's picture on the desk. "He should never have been involved. Now he's on their radar."

"If we're investigating it, we're all on the radar. Instead of under it. Where you're meant to be." Cal glared at me. "You abandoned the job I gave you, the responsibility of lives I wouldn't trust with anyone else. I want you just on Jen and Ash."

His intensity might lack Liam's badass factor by a few degrees, but he was still my old partner. And technically, my boss. I was supposed to care.

I stared at Cal, my dislike momentarily transferring from Danny to him. "The fuck?"

"Use your words, Black," Danny called over my shoulder.

I curled my fist, but after the weeks of fights, the knuckles were bruised and tight, and I had little energy to waste on punching anyone. "You can't take me off an investigation I'm halfway through." I hardened my expression while I searched for a loophole. The corner of my lips curled — in a smile or a sneer, I didn't much care. "Especially one that's not yours."

Cal shook his head. "I can if you've been made. They clearly know who Liam is. Do they recognise you?" He leaned back in his desk chair, tapping his pen on the arm.

"That's what he said when I asked, too. Remember how well that turned out?" Danny yabbered behind me.

"I remember driving a motorcycle into a house to save your juvenile ass." I didn't bother looking at him. The seed of doubt Cal planted did its job well enough. "Now shut the fuck up, and let the adults talk."

Danny grumbled behind me, clacking at his keyboard.

"We need to organise Selena to interview Jen. For the trial."

"If we get that far." Cal tossed the pen on the desk. It rolled off the other end, but I couldn't be bothered lunging for it.

I sucked in a breath "Is there a doubt?"

"It's Logan. There's always a damned doubt. I'll organise it. You're not going back in." Cal actually pointed a finger at me. I sighed, staring at him. He didn't budge. "And that stopped working on me eight years ago."

"Yeah, well. Maybe it's time for a change. There were tyre tracks outside the house when I came in last night. I think we need a new safehouse." I pressed my lips together.

"Well, it's a road."

"These weren't on the road."

"I was there yesterday. With Mila." Cal looked at me with exasperation.

"You park in the dirt? Right beside the house?"

Silence greeted me as Cal pursed his lips. "No. The grass."

"'S'what I thought. Now, if you're not going to let me do one job, let me do this one."

"They'll get sick of moving. And Ashley needs stability," Cal said quietly.

I pulled a chair from my desk to face Cal's and straddled it. "I know, man. But keeping them alive is more important. Especially after..."

"That was my fuck up. And I've apologised for it." Cal's spine straightened. "And it nearly cost me all of you."

"We've all had our share of mistakes."

"Yeah, but mine with Logan..." Cal brushed his hand over his shorn hair. "They're adding up."

"He's a mindfuck," I agreed. "We have to be vigilant. I'm going to move them," I said, closing the conversation.

Cal's mouth thinned, but he nodded. "Fine. What do you want to do?"

I shunted a file across the desk I'd printed the night before once Jen went to bed. She'd stayed up as late as she could, fixing my back, but eventually, the exhaustion of doing nothing with a silent companion had worn her down, and she'd said goodnight.

The urge to ask her to sleep on the sofa while I watched the remainder of the night out for them grew every night. My hands itched with the desire to wake up with her head in my lap, to run my hands over her hair, see those amazing eyes look up at me, and kiss her good morning...but she wasn't mine, could never *be* mine.

I couldn't get close to her; I'd seen what happened to the boys when they had relationships on the job. It nearly cost us Mila, and if that had happened, I would have had more than a few weak smears of blood on my hands.

Jen and Ashley were far too important — both as under my protection for my job and on a far-too-personal basis. I refused to risk ruining the faux family unit that had developed between us, but their safety was paramount.

What I wanted couldn't come into it.

Cal read through my proposal. His hands flattened on the desk, and I knew he didn't agree with it, but he could see sense.

"You've bookmarked the ones you want to use? The houses?" He glanced at me, then shook his head. "No. Of course, you haven't."

We'd worked together long enough to know each other better than family.

"Every time we use a safe house, someone connected with Logan turns up. Or someone connected to him. Somehow."

The asshole had people everywhere.

I pressed my feet firmly on the floor, under the pretence of stretching. It brought a real yawn from the exhaustion of pulling double shifts. I'd slept on the couch, sitting up, and woke with a blonde head across my knees. And as cute as Ashley might be, she wasn't the female I wanted to wake up to with my arm around.

When Jenny's daughter stirred just after sunrise, I'd turned the TV on to morning kid's shows and let Jenny sleep. She'd earned it, wasting her hours waiting on me when I couldn't give her what I wanted, what I suspected *she* wanted. I hoped.

A fine layer of glitter adorned my jeans, but I'd become used to it after two years of looking after the girls. We all were.

"You know I can't approve this." Cal found another pen and resumed tapping. "So you'd better get your sales pitch right."

"Why?"

"Because you'll have to sell it to Liam."

I presented a signed and approved file to Cal after lunch. Liam had worked out a shift roster with Danny behind Cal's back to keep me in the cage fighting ring while the younger man covered me with the girls. He lived only a few blocks from the inner city cottage, Cal a few minutes away on the other side. Both placements were completely intentional. Micah's warehouse covered the southern side, closest to the interim set up of the fighting ring.

We had it covered from most angles.

My father's house sat on the other side of the river, but I'd abandoned both it and my spartan apartment two years ago to move in with Jen and Ashley full time. I hadn't been back to either for some time, though Liam had sorted a gardener for Dad's house while I monitored the girls' safety.

The file landed on Cal's desk with a light slap. It didn't warrant a harder toss, largely because Liam had removed most of the case details from Cal's version.

"That was fast?" Cal assessed me with a speculative glint in his eye.

"Yeah, don't take it personally. It only cost me a blow job."

"Should've been a lot more than that." Cal didn't look away, seeing far more than he should have, and didn't crack a smile. I pushed food at him as a secondary distraction.

He opened the bag, still looking at me, and pulled out the lunch I'd bought. A bottle of tablets tumbled onto his desk, and he read the label with a frown.

"Jen says they're the bomb for pregnant women. Her sister-in-law used them, apparently. Before Jen...." *Before she'd been pushed into a house where she's isolated from everyone in her prior life because we fucked up. Again.* I coughed, pushing on. "She said Mila will need them."

"Tell her thanks." Cal dug into his food.

"I need to take time to see Dad." The words sat bitter on my tongue.

"It's fine. Take what you need."

"Yeah." I returned to my desk, finding it full of paperwork that didn't belong to me. "Can I move this?"

"Oh, that was me. Sorry." Danny gave me an impish grin, hefting the tall pile of files.

"These are cold cases." I flicked through the top one. "What the hell are they for?"

"Practice, for me." A shiny white bag drifted past me to the back corner desk. Micah waved at our newest team member from his desk at the other corner of the room, his eyes glued to his terminal.

More white obscured my vision. "Jesus. It's like the fucking Sahara."

I didn't apologise for swearing. If she was going to work with us, she'd have to get used to it soon enough. Ally straightened her pristine suit, extracting a white laptop from her blinding bag. She'd performed well over Christmas in the small undercover job she'd been set when she transferred from her job upstairs. Danny seemed to be impressed with her, but I still hadn't forgiven her for screwing around during the last job we'd worked as a team.

"You'll get used to it." Her voice rolled around the room, sugary sweet. I stared at her, but her eyes turned hard and cold. Somewhere to my right, Danny snickered.

"I won't be here to worry about it." I turned back to Cal scraping food from his desk back into the bag. "Feed yourself, yeah? And come 'round for dinner once we've moved. It'd be good for the girls to have some better company than me."

"You're a right sorry prick." Cal grinned. "Let me know what you need."

"Sleep. Look after– Mila." I cleared my throat, nearly calling her his wife. She was six weeks pregnant, and Cal hadn't proposed yet. It pissed me off to no end. "When will you...?"

"When I feel like it," Cal said shortly, opening a new file. "Just let me know what you need."

What I need is for you to make an honest woman of the girl who's family to me.

"What's it like?" Ashley asked from the backseat of my coupe a day later.

Liam worked ridiculously fast, but efficient and the only one I'd really rely on when the girl's safety came into it.

"It's clean, and it has a garden with a really high fence. Which we should probably tend to?" Jenny looked briefly at me before she promised her daughter anything more. I gave her a small nod. Breath whooshed softly from her lips. "And maybe Mila might bring us some garden herbs or strawberries to plant. She likes flowers. What do you think?"

"Ohh, yes. And Mila can paint them!"

"She's not painting, popcorn. Remember? The baby."

"Oh. Could she draw them?"

"I'm sure she could."

Listening to the girls talk about their new home gave me hope I'd made the right call in moving them. I'd parked at the old house next to litter that shouldn't have been there. It could have come from a passing car, but it lay right next to the tyre tracks, and that was too much coincidence for me.

Jen had blessedly reined back anything she wanted to say and hurried Ashley along. Relief swamped me. I didn't want to fight with her, but my gut told me it was time to go. Packing their meagre belongings into two small bags took less than an hour. They fit tidily next to my gym bag in the boot of a car never meant to hold a family.

Their entire life.

I shook my head, wondering at their combined ability to flit from place to place at our whim, and when it would break.

The driveway led up a steep incline, covered by shrubs that stood as tall as the pailing fence around the older house. The degree of privacy and aspect from the street front made it a safe space in a medium-density suburb.

We might have neighbours, but we'd likely never see them. The front of the house was fully glassed-in, covering the verandah at the front. I pressed the square remote, which opened a set of black metal gates. They closed behind us silently.

The drive turned at the top, and another button opened the garage. I drove straight in and closed the door behind us. Lights sprang on, illuminating the internal of the garage brightly. I'd changed the bulbs, so there were no dark spots. An internal door led directly into the house.

There were no houses above us to see into the yard with its tightly laid palings that stood seven feet tall and obscured the yard from the road below. Not even headlights would make it through the fence, which meant the girls would be protected enough to go outside — if I was with them.

It had cost me half of the department's remaining budget for the year. Still, Liam had covered the rest out of his seemingly bottomless bucket of funds for our needs. After nearly two years of not being able to set foot outside their safe house, this qualified as a need.

Ashley squealed as I passed over her bag, decorated with unicorns and coated thickly with glitter. Jenny took hers with an odd look, following me wordlessly through the house. I'd picked out their rooms when I collected the keys, placing a small flower on each of their beds, and a book for Ashley.

Moving them around constantly while they were in witness protection to such a stringent degree lay heavily on the team, and I was determined to make it up to them in the few ways I could.

A woman in her late thirties with a foster kid engaged in homeschooling shouldn't be stuffed in a dingy box of a house that smelled of a decade of previous occupants. This was my apology for them being stuck there, and being stuck with me.

The best I could do now was to do my job damned well.

I pointed the hall out to Ashley. "Go find your room." Her eyes widened as she stared at me, then she disappeared in a flurry of blonde hair and pink sparkles. Glitter fluttered to the tiles in her wake.

I snuffed out a laugh.

"At least she's marked her territory," Jenny spoke behind me, way too close.

I tensed and tried to relax, my stance awkward. "Least I could do," I said tightly.

"Seriously, Theo. Thank you."

I turned to find her right in front of me. She rose on her toes, arms around my neck in a hug that moulded her curvy body against mine. I drew her into me automatically, pulling her closer. Something illicit — lily or night jasmine — hung in the air around her, wrapping my skin in it. In her.

Her lips brushed my cheek, touching the corner of my mouth before she sank back, a flush creeping across her chest beneath her black tee, into her cheeks.

I breathed deeply again, catching the last hint of her scent as she dropped away from me.

"You're welcome?" I looked down at her, my hands empty without her in them.

What the hell is wrong with you? She's a job.

"Thanks." She grinned, energy bouncing off her as she slid past me, much closer than she needed to, I was sure.

My hand brushed her arm before I could think. She glanced over her shoulder, a small smile at the corner of her lips, her eyes sparkling. Then she trotted away down the hall, her feet padding on the hardwood floor, calling out to her daughter.

I stared after her, watching her curved hips sway gently as she chased Ashley down the hall.

Maybe the flowers on the beds hadn't been the brightest touch, after all.

I sighed, running my hand over my hair, a cool sweat prickling my skin as I adjusted myself in my pants and grabbed my own bag.

Damn.

This could be a long live-in stint.

CHAPTER FOUR

JENNY

"It's so beautiful." I peeked out my bedroom window from the side, the way Theo had taught me, so I wasn't standing in direct light. Logan appeared hell-bent on his vengeance, and as Ashley's foster Mum, I stood between him and what he wanted most.

"I hope you– that it suits you." Black stumbled over the words, catching himself quickly and giving me a heart starter.

I spun, my heart thumping. I hadn't realised I'd spoken aloud, let alone that anyone who wanted to listen to me. Theo stood in the doorway, leaning against the frame with his arms crossed. His familiar bulk posed in the position I associated him with unless I was fixing something on him after the fights.

Fights I didn't know about.

"The change is wonderful. And being able to go outside is healthy for Ashley. And me. Thank you." I gave him a small smile, the spiced scent of him still on my skin after my impromptu hug. It felt like a good idea at the time, but now the divide between us had widened, with me on the opposite side.

He shrugged one massive shoulder, the muscles of his chest rippling. "I wanted to make it seem like a home."

"You've done a fine job." I picked up the small frangipani flower on my pillow, twirling it in my fingers. White and yellow streaked petals spun in a heady scent of the tropical flower. "Did you have to go far to pick this?"

"There's a tree in the backyard. Ashley got one too. Don't go thinking you're special." He snorted, but his smile belayed the harshness of his words.

"She'll be thrilled. She's a little in love with you, you know."

She's not the only one.

"We can sort a school for her, after the trial and everything's settled down."

Hope bloomed in my chest. The thought of returning to a normal life, that Ashley might have friends, develop how a girl her age should...Until it died a quick death when I realised the impossibility of the dream.

Don't placate me. Don't feed me lies.

I blinked, the image of Ashley in a school uniform filling my vision.

"Will anything ever settle down?"

His head turned slightly, he took a hesitant step into my room. "It will, once all the court proceedings are done."

"And how long will that take?" I stared at the flower, tracing its soft petals. I knew the answer.

"A few years, maybe." Theo stepped into my space, hooking his knuckle gently beneath my chin. "You'll get through, Jen. You've survived tougher than this."

"This is different. Wait. What did I...oh."

"Yeah, oh. That moment where you stepped between me and the asshole when it's supposed to be *my* job to protect *you*."

I swallowed against a closed throat. "I wasn't thinking."

"That's what makes you so damn badass."

"I couldn't do it again." I knew I couldn't do it again. It had been a fluke that it had happened in the first place and that I hadn't gotten everyone I loved killed.

Theo snorted. "You could. And you would, Jen. It's in you. You're so full of love and sass." His mouth curled up in a wry smile, his thumb brushing along my jaw.

Blinking back sudden claustrophobia — not of him, but the four walls my life was constantly boxed behind. I dropped every barrier I had up. Dropped every part of me that pretended each day ran like a normal one, and let the abject terror I lived with daily overwhelm me in a rush. My skin prickled, my fingertips numbing. Little puffs of short breaths parted my lips as I swayed, too many memories swamping me.

Theo's fingers dropped from my chin, and he swore, engulfing me in his huge arms. I sank into his chest, his heart beating a rapid rhythm against my cheek. A single tear tracked down my face to mingle with the salty musk of his sweat and something deeper...dark chocolate and coffee.

This man smelled of mocha and salt, and *that* made an excellent distraction from the anxiety that threatened to overwhelm me over absolutely nothing.

I tilted my head back, looking up at him. His beard brushed my cheek as I moved, close enough that his breath mingled with mine. Dark eyes, an intense clash of steel and charcoal, bore into mine. A tiny shiver ran through me as I raised up onto my toes.

I hesitated for a moment, then pressed my lips to his: only a brief brush, but enough to convey what I wanted.

Theo stood stock still. I began to sink back onto my heels with a sigh, disappointment winning over the embarrassment, my mind already running to the awkward *what do we do now* moment I knew would come after.

Instead, his hand curled beneath my hair, halting my descent. His eyes never left mine as he drew me back to him, dipping his head only a little to kiss me.

Slowly moving his lips over mine, he tugged my head back gently, deepening the kiss I'd craved for so long. I arched into him and let the pressure of his mouth against mine push the fears back into their corner until all I could do was feel.

Just feel.

Him.

The warmth of Theo wound around me; it seeped into my skin until sweet, gentle kisses became something more. Jolts and sparks tore over my skin, electrifying the places we touched — everywhere. His arms moulded me to his broad frame, tucking me into him until he engulfed me within the protection his embrace offered.

I sank into him with a sigh, surrendering my fears for a single moment as his arms tightened around me. His tongue traced the lines of mine, a slow dance where he held the reins, angling my head to take what he needed. The intensity of his touch, his slow demands brainwashed me until he was all I could focus on. I nipped lightly at his bottom lip, my laugh turning to a moan as he kissed me harder, crushing me against him.

Theo drew back with a groan, pressing his forehead to mine. Storm-dark eyes filled with lust and controlled a rage that seared me stared into mine, and I fell damned hard right then.

"Jen." His mouth brushed mine again, tingles shooting to my fingertips. I gasped as he kneaded my back with strong fingers. "That shouldn't have happened."

"You live with us. You're all I see."

You're all I want.

I tilted my head back, willing the words to stay inside my head. Theo dropped his hands. I stared at him, my mouth still tingling from where his beard had grazed my lips.

"Is that all? Lust and loneliness?"

"You make it sound like a movie." I grinned, but those eyes stayed on my face, unwavering. My confidence dissolved beneath them. I bit my lip hard, just to feel the pain, to bring myself back from the numbness that had coated me in his arms, like an addiction. His eyes tracked the movement.

"It's not a game, Jen. I have work to do."

He spun on his heel, half out the door before I could speak.

"Yes. Us."

Theo paused, one hand on the doorframe before he disappeared into the hall without looking back at me.

Ashley loved the house, as Theo had predicted. He might have gotten the place for both of us, but really, it all centred around the needs of a no-longer-so-tiny girl in a unicorn headband trailing glitter in her wake.

And that was just fine with me.

I made lunch for us, all three of us, though Theo didn't speak, even when I placed a plate of toasted sandwiches next to him. Ashley loved cleaning up, and I put on Junior Masterchef replays in lieu of her regular Iron Chef reruns. Mila had made me promise to leave those for her, but the little girl loved cooking so much, I didn't mind her watching a program that gave her something to dream about.

Dreams a regular kid her age should have.

Theo resumed his post in the shadows, his eyes heavy-lidded as he watched us. I often wondered if he slept with his eyes open, going by the scant hours of rest he actually used. My phone filled quickly with notes of things I'd like to do or add in, in the hope we'd be in one place for long enough to make it a home. The phone was well beyond the policy for situations like ours, but Theo had argued my case. They let me as my few friends were connected with the unit, and having contact with Black and Cal gave us an extra layer of protection.

The unit provided me with a stipend every week to pay for essentials I couldn't leave the house to get for us myself. I generally sent them as a message to Theo's phone, and he bought our things, alternating shopping duties with Mila and Cal. That way, there wasn't much of a pattern, but I needed an excuse to talk to him, and this was the best I could come up with.

I stopped beside him in the dim light. From this height, we had a good view of the street below and the city beyond. I promised myself I'd take Ashley outside to play soon and discover the garden.

"Would you be able to get us some things, please? We're running out of staples like milk, coffee, and toilet paper."

"Only one of those is a staple to you." He said it without looking at me, but I heard the grin in his voice and smiled. Maybe he'd forgiven me for pushing him before when I had no right to. Maybe I was just a lonely person, looking for entertainment or release. But to have something like what Cal and Mila had...I studied my feet.

Clean but bare, next to Theo's well-worn combat boots. Or motorcycle boots. I had no idea of the difference, but they looked black and tactical and suited him. Black jeans were tucked into them, his stretchy black shirt the boys all wore over that. It clung to every curve of muscle, enhancing the work he'd done to his body. Dressed in my regular faded blue jeans and tee, I felt small and frumpy beside the finely honed behemoth of a man.

"It's fine. I'll get whatever you need."

My skin prickled, a fine shiver springing goosebumps along my arms. I looked up at him, trying not to fidget. His eyes tracked over me, seeing far too much on a day when the edges of my walls were frayed beyond fixing. The energy it took to hide everything I wanted to keep to myself depleted, I pressed my hands down my sides, holding his gaze. My stomach curled back on itself.

"Thanks." I took a step back. Theo's hand whipped out, catching mine. His gaze shifted briefly over my shoulder, towards the living room, then back to my face.

He tugged me toward him, my heart slamming blood through my body far too fast.

"Before." That one word quietened everything. His eyes settled on mine, pinning me in place. "You're in a high-stress environment. Your — *our* — reaction to each other is understandable."

"It's okay," I said quickly before he said something I didn't want to hear. "It's just a job."

I stumbled over the first word, nearly saying *I'm just a job*, but his gaze held firm over mine, and I knew he'd caught it. Theo was faster on the uptake than I'd expected, and I loved having a companion with intelligence and a quick wit.

He stood, unspeaking for a long moment. "I have to go back to the c– to my investigation tonight." His head cocked to the side. "My way of offloading some of the stress."

Apparently, I wasn't the only one stumbling over my own lies. I nodded, sucking my bottom lip into my mouth as I thought about his words.

"I'm sorry we're such a drain on you."

He grinned. It changed his whole face, crinkling lines around his eyes, bringing life to the hardened man.

It was also sexy as hell.

"You're not. Logan fucking is. I want you — both of you — safe before—" He cut himself off, the grin sliding from his face. "Selena is coming by later. I'll leave as soon as she's gone."

"We'll be fine."

"You are tougher than you think, Jen. Remember, I've seen you in action."

I remembered the way he'd mouthed off to Logan, bound and bruised, with a gun in his face and laughed. "No, I think you get that label."

"Nah, I'm just a bored, middle-aged man with no life."

"I *think* we can say you're a bit more than just middle-aged." I poked his bicep and nearly bent my finger back. He smirked. "I'll send you the list; if you can get things on your way ho– back, tomorrow. Whenever." I tugged my hand from his grip, anxiety rippling over my confidence.

Theo just watched me with eyes alight with something cheeky, darkness burning beneath. A darkness he kept locked away, but I had an idea what he was capable of. After all, I'd seen him in action, too.

I backed away beneath his gaze, bumping into the kitchen divider and fussed with cleaning an already spotless benchtop. Theo turned back to his place at the side of the window, positioning his reflection to stare back at mine.

Part of me found it reassuring.

Part of me found it something else.

Finally, I managed to stop fussing and joined Ashley on the sofa, not really listening to the TV. Lost in my own thoughts, I repaired all the barriers I put up and tried not to let memories of Logan intrude.

That would happen soon enough.

I greeted Selena when Theo let her in, his hand at the small of his back as he opened the garage door, despite having opened the gate via remote for her. He locked it methodically behind her, two shiny deadlocks securing it.

They looked strong enough, but I knew that if Logan wanted to get to us, they wouldn't be anywhere near enough to stop him. Or whoever he sent. I had the impression he'd bide his time, brewing something beneath the layers that made up the psychotic layered mess of his mind.

Selena hugged me, another distraction to be grateful for, and I kept my thoughts to myself.

"How's Liam going?" I asked softly though her mass of hair.

Selena gave me a wry grin. "Oh, you know. Being his usual workaholic self. Busy." She gave a one-shouldered shrug, laughing when I raised an eyebrow at her.

"Mhmm," I murmured.

Their best-friends-living-together relationship was an odd one. For all the man's hardened exterior, Liam seemed incapable of committing to a woman who clearly adored him.

Theo leaned around me to kiss Selena on the cheek. "Total prick then?" he winked. She laughed again, wagging her finger.

"Only you will *ever* get away with saying something like that about him."

"Not even from Cal? I'm flattered." He grinned again.

"Especially not Cal." Selena's glossy dark curls flung out like a model. I stepped out of her way, pressing my hands into my pockets.

Theo leaned against the doorframe to scratch his back and shrugged. "What can I say?"

I rolled my eyes at Selena. "All that muscle and not an inch of flexibility," I muttered.

"I'll give you flexibility," he grunted.

"Promise?" I flipped him a grin over my shoulder as Selena started organising herself. Theo's eyes lit, a dark light that looked *almost* like a promise. I shivered, the corners of his mouth turning up in appreciation as he watched me.

"Okay, we need to go over all the information you have on Wayde Logan." Selena turned on solicitor mode as soon as we entered the dining room. She placed files of case notes across the oval dining table.

"I've already done this," I protested as a slow flush crawled up my neck, my shirt constricting around me. Theo frowned, his eyes flicking between Selena and me. Ashley raced through the hall. I caught her, taking the unicorn bible offered while she set up her stables and a drawing pad on the living room floor, almost as pedantic as Selena in her display. The book disappeared from my grasp too fast. I squeezed my fingers together, knowing Theo watched me, my anxiety spiking.

"Yes, but I need to make sure I have all the information possible." Selena pushed two files apart to make space for a final one, straightening them all in a specific order known only to herself.

She straightened, pushing dark waves back that shone in the meagre afternoon light afforded us inside the house. I tugged at the hem of my oldest shirt, wondering if I mightn't be out of line asking Theo to buy me a new one, then decided it was a vanity I didn't need. After all, where would I go or see?

Selena motioned me to a chair, seating herself on the other side. Theo reached for the chair back, holding onto it as I sat, squeezing my shoulder.

I appreciated his support, but I knew the gorgeous solicitor missed nothing. Ashley placed her hands on my waist, wiggling herself up, a unicorn clutched in each hand. I stopped her.

"Popcorn, would you do some of the spelling app I found for you? This might get a little um...and I want you to be..." *Happy* didn't seem to be the right word. "Safe."

She gave me a look of a nine-year-old who knew way too much and flounced to the sofa, collecting her iPad mid-skip. Theo had given me his apple login, as I had no real income of my own anymore or access to my bank accounts.

I waited until Ashley's attention became engrossed in a spelling game and turned back to Selena.

"Alright, let's start."

Terms flew over my head, and I asked her to repeat the same things several times. I apologised half a dozen times before she held up a hand.

"Stop apologising. I have clients who never fully grasp all the details, and that's fine. It's not their job, it's mine. As long as you understand what we're doing and why, for your own rights and safety. Those are the important things."

I nodded, my hands covering a photo of Logan she'd put in front of me. My palms prickled as though he was looking at me through the picture, the thought ridiculously illogical.

"What happens next?"

"I might be jumping the gun a little, but I want to start preparing you for a trial. Maybe run through your interactions with Logan again, giving me as much detail as possible." She slid her phone to the centre of the table. "Just speak normally, and it will catch everything, so we don't have to do this very often."

My stomach hit the floor. I gripped the edge of the file, crumpling Logan's photo.

"Okay."

"Jenny, you're safe. He's not here." She looked over my shoulder, focusing on the man at my back, then across at me for a long moment. In the silence hairs on the back of my neck rose. I'd drawn Theo's attention too.

"It's okay. Just— let's get this over. Please."

"Where do you want to start?"

With me running away as far from all this as I can.

Which was the end of the hall.

But a little head of blonde hair peered over the top of her iPad, and I knew I'd do anything for her.

I started talking about Ashley's adoption, the information I'd been given on Logan as a baseline, trying to warm myself up. My mouth dried as I thought about the day at the safe house — Theo dropping in front of me, his head hitting the deck with a thump. Looking up at Logan as Theo's name left my mouth in a whisper when it should have been a scream.

It was the only time I'd called him Black.

"It's okay, Jenny." Selena's voice was soft and soothing, but it came through a long funnel from a great distance to me.

I nodded, and she kept talking, but my eyes found the same scene in my head, over again. Sprinting through the house, my heart bursting in my chest, knowing he wouldn't bother to chase me because he didn't need to. Watching as Ashley was ripped from my arms, her hands stretching for mine, tears coating her face crumpled in terror.

Mum. Save me.

But I couldn't. Watching her being taken away, bile and salt mixing in my mouth as I screamed and thrashed in the arms of a man who had the same eyes as my daughter.

What the fuck is wrong with this family?

I swallowed back bile, blinking at Selena. She stopped, peering at me.

"Are you okay?"

I pressed my hands on my knees, pushing the chair back as I stood. It scraped across the gorgeous hardwood floor, but I didn't care. Theo took a step at my back, but I couldn't deal with even him touching me right now.

"I can't do this." I swallowed back the same bile, my phantom hands still reaching for my child—

She's not yours. She was never yours.

—and ran for the bathroom, vomiting the contents of my stomach and the vitriol Wayde Logan had put there.

CHAPTER FIVE

JENNY

Cool tiles pressed against my overly-hot cheeks where I lay on the bathroom floor. My breaths puffed so softly I mightn't be breathing at all. A knock bounced the door against my legs. I squeezed my eyes shut, knowing my moment of indulgence had ended.

Back to real life, and facing the demons.

"Mum? Are you coming out?"

Fresh, hot tears cascaded down my cheeks as I tried to answer. The next knock wasn't as polite.

"Jen? Move away from the door."

My mouth sandpaper, I pushed myself up with a momentous effort. I scooted back, tucking my legs beneath me to make enough room for Theo to open the door. He took one look at me and barred the doorway with his bulk.

"Ash, can you go make your Mum something to eat or drink. Please?"

Ashley spoke softly on the other side of the door, Theo twisting back to answer her. He looked away as her footsteps faded along the hall then turned back to me.

His eyes fathomless, he lifted my boneless body from the floor. I mumbled meaningless apologies as he set me on my feet, cleaning my face gently. It began to register the warm cloth he'd prepared. I blinked mechanically as he turned my head from side to side, then checked my arms and legs.

"I don't hurt myself," my voice came out hoarse, "if that's what you're checking for. But I'd like to clean my teeth."

"I'll wait."

He leaned in the doorway, his eyes on me in the mirror. I brushed my teeth, clearing the taste of bile from my mouth and splashed cold water on my face. This time, I felt it.

I pressed my face into my towel, hiding for one last moment, and took a breath.

"Is Selena still out there?" I asked, the towel muffling my voice.

"I sent her home. Told her to keep it to herself, only tell Liam what he *needs to know*." Sarcasm coated his voice at that last comment.

When has he said that to you?

Arms wrapped gently around my waist as he pried me from my small haven, folding himself around me.

"He can't hurt you. He won't, Jen, not ever again."

I pressed my cheek to his chest, breathing in time with his heartbeat, slow, long breaths.

"You can't know that. You know what he's like. I remembered that day at the other house when you passed out."

"Bastard shot me with fucking tranquiliser. But that's not here, Jen. He's not here. It's just us."

I pressed my lips into a thin line, lifting my head to look at him. His knuckle grazed my neck. A flash passed across his face, and he pulled my head back to his chest.

"I can't do it," I mumbled the words into his shirt, instantly wishing I hadn't spoken.

I can't do any of this without you.

That one, I kept to myself.

He was silent for a long moment. "I have to work this case, but I'll call Liam. I can do it another night."

"But don't you have to fight?"

My eyes flicked to his, caught the moment of recognition, and I knew I'd made a huge mistake.

That same knuckle caught beneath my chin, raising my eyes to meet his. But instead of burning with the fury I'd expected, he grinned.

"I knew I'd seen you there. Got punched because I was looking for you."

"You saw me?" I frowned, then shook my head. "I'm sorry. I should never have gone."

"No, you shouldn't." Theo considered, still holding my chin as his eyes bore into mine. "Who– ah, fucking Liam." He cut himself off with a snort.

"Liam," I agreed with a small smile. He dropped his hands to close them around my arms.

"We've got you, girl. Can't you see that? You're safe with us." His eyes turned serious, but I refused to let my tiny, happy moment fade so fast.

"I'm nearly forty, Theo. Well, thirty-eight. Hardly a girl."

"Which means you're seven years younger than me."

"Is that all?' I asked, unable to hide my surprise in time.

Theo's eyebrows rose. "All?" he echoed, drawing back a fraction from me. "Do I look that ancient?" He craned over my shoulder, peering at himself in the mirror.

"Could you wait until I leave the room before you check yourself out? That's a love affair I don't want to be a third wheel to."

Theo turned back to me, his hold on my arms gentling. His thumbs made tiny circles on my skin, and I wondered if he knew he was doing it.

"Let's get you fed, girl." My eyes narrowed, the corner of his mouth twitching. "Let's see what your daughter's concocted."

He let go of me, backing through the door to give me room and held out a hand. I hesitated then took it, letting his broad palm close around mine. It should have felt restrictive, but it didn't.

"You know she's not really mine," I mumbled to cover my embarrassment, staring at where his roughened fingers intertwined with mine.

"Stop that," Theo ordered.

I looked up from our joined hands, my brow furrowing. "What?"

"She's yours, Jen. God knows what Logan is, but he's got no claim to her."

"Neither do I," I said helplessly. "I have a piece of paper with a stamp on it and a whole lotta fine print I've read once."

"You have a daughter who loves you and calls you Mum. That's worth more than any DNA or a piece of paper."

I stared at him, willing myself to believe it, but one day, the state system would say our situation was far from optimal, too much of a danger to her. Or that her time to move on had arrived, and I would lose her.

My heart cracked a little more at the thought.

Maybe Logan should have pulled the trigger.

"Stop it."

"Stop what."

"That. The doubt. Self-sabotage. Whatever it is. Don't you *dare* give in to it," Theo snapped savagely. "You are going to stay strong for that girl because you're all she's got, and wallowing in fear and worry won't solve a damned thing."

Self-loathing swamped me. I did what I knew he wanted; take that energy and put it to use.

"Then get out of my fucking space and let me parent," I snapped back, letting it out.

Violent force, meet immovable object.

But which one was which?

"That's better," he said softly, leaning forward. My breath hitched, too many emotions swirling around us with me caught in their vortex.

I glared at him, my fear turned to something I couldn't put a stopper in. "It's better that I resort to swearing at you, full of rage and could argue all night?"

"I won't be here to argue with you."

"Whatever." That's right. Dammit.

Now I wanted to argue, and he took his freedom to bash his own issues out on someone else. I stormed past him along the hall, his lips curling in a half-smile as I passed him.

"It's better that you want to fight."

I was glad he couldn't see my own smile.

I ran Ashley a bath after Theo left, his fingers brushing my cheek briefly on his way through the garage. I couldn't work out what I wanted more: the emotionless boulder of a man who barely spoke, or this one. The one who kissed me, who talked me back from climbing onto the proverbial ledge before I realised I had gotten on it.

Ashley flapped around in the tub, pretending to be a mermaid. I set a timer on the microwave and prepped dinners for the next week, just to have something to do. Theo always managed to find fully-furnished rental places. Usually, ones that had a kitchen stocked with enough tupperware to entertain an adult woman who needed far better distractions in her life than making meals in advance.

The timer went off, and I extracted Ashley from her mermaid playground. I let her stay up with me to watch Star Trek reruns, because what did we have to get up for in the morning? It might be selfish of me, but I had no idea when Theo would return, or if I'd see him again for a few days, now we were settled in a new limbo.

Cal would message me if I needed to let Danny or Micah up, in order for Ashley to prepare a makeup station or other appropriate torture. He took perverse pleasure in sending the younger men up as duty, though I knew he would spend as many hours with Ashley as possible with his job, one of the reasons he kept us close to his unit.

To someone else, it might seem selfish, but their unit had quickly become our adopted family. Which might very well be better than the family I had.

My phone vibrated over the kitchen bench. I flipped it over, expecting some snarky retort from Theo about shopping after today's fiasco, and froze when I saw my brother's name.

I'd given him the number Theo had provided me, lying through my teeth when I promised I wouldn't give it to anyone. But I needed someone to talk to, someone I knew. My friends had disappeared over the years when I hadn't had kids when they had, when Paul had passed away.

Chad: When do I get to see my baby sister? It's been so long I've forgotten what you look like.

Me: Rather like you in the mirror, only prettier.

Chad: Nah, I'm the pretty one.

That earned a laugh. Chad stood at the same height as me, stockier and with a bit of a babyface. He could easily be a pretty boy, especially in comparison to Theo. My smile faded at the thought of him. I hated that I went behind his back; the whole thing felt like cheating on him, in its own way. A breach of his trust.

Which shouldn't be possible, as I wasn't even in a relationship with him.

I pushed the phone away on the benchtop, face down anyway. It vibrated again, but I ignored it, this time, joining Ashley on the couch.

I finally carried a very dozy girl to bed and tucked her in. The nights cooled early in the autumn months after a hot Christmas. I considered falling asleep with her, but I'd only be restless, waiting. Listening for new sounds in a new house, working out if they were footsteps. Theo hadn't gone over our usual escape or contingency plan with me yet, and it heightened my response to every little creak the house gave.

I made a note to ask him about it whenever I saw him again, curling up on the sofa with the lights out and a book I never intended to read.

CHAPTER SIX

BLACK

The man across the ring tilted on his feet in a drawn-out collapse, his bulky form hitting the mat with a thud as he toppled backward. It might have looked fake, but I knew it wasn't; my fist still stung from the blows I'd delivered to my opponent before an almost silent crowd.

I hadn't been lying to Jen when I'd told her this was my outlet.

The ref unlocked the cage and climbed inside with a hesitant glance my way. I turned my back to him, letting him rev the crowd back up after the violence of my fight that had silenced their combined voice. Ducking out of the cage, I loped back along the dim corridor that led to the offices below the temporary arena.

It had to be temporary, as the crowds were getting bigger every night, the busses bringing them packed beyond their usual capacity. But when your destination included an illegal fighting ring, traffic violations were the least of your problems.

I passed the bookie, my hand open but he shook his head. "Office. He wants to see you."

I grunted, pulling my hoodie over my head to block out the new uproar of the crowd. Once I entered the office hallways, I dropped it back, my head still ringing. Though it wasn't clear which came from the deafening music they played, or the hits to the head I'd taken while thinking about Jen.

"You do what I asked?" Samson spoke before I made it through the doorway. My mouth opened to reply when my brain caught up. He couldn't see me; he addressed another person in the room.

"Bit of this. More of that." Something hit the desk, meat slapped down on the butcher's table.

I winced, retreating into the shadows, then edged to the side of the door. I seemed to be spending more time hidden than I did in the light — a place well-suited to the stain on my soul. Voices floated out of the office, words garbled in a mix of mutters and curses. I shifted, my back aching, and I knew I'd let Jen tend it again tonight.

The thought of her hands on me, dampening back the need to touch her, kiss her, consumed me.

But that wasn't where I needed my head to be right now.

"Messy. Fine, pay him," Samson spoke to someone else in the office. "But be faster next time."

How many does he have in there, packed in like sardines?

The door creaked. I backed into the blackest part of the shadow, crossing my arms and ankles. With luck, they wouldn't see me. If they did, I was just another dumb grunt, waiting on Samson's time.

Which wasn't worth enough to spit on.

Three pairs of shoes passed me, Red clicking white patent heels that reminded me forcibly of Ally. But even with her platinum blonde hair, our newest recruit outclassed Samson's secretary by a long stretch.

I peered out of the shadows to catch a glimpse of the unknown exiting Samson's office. A grimy blonde head, shorter than Samson's already diminished stature, headed away in the opposite direction. Though it could be because Samson's girth currently equalled his height.

Slipping around behind them, I checked the office was empty, first. Clothing hung from random places, all male shirts and pressed pants.

For a grot of a man, Samson's vanity was preserved in his collection of hideous shirts and outdated slacks.

I flicked through haphazard mounds of paperwork, working my way around the desk as I waited for the rotund man to return. Red fluid congealed around one corner of the desk. I peered over the edge, staring at the contents of a waste paper basket and wished I hadn't.

Part of a hand lay in the bottom, its fluids soaking into Samson's refuse. Paper stuck up around it in a macabre bouquet. The cut had sliced through the palm at an odd angle, part of a wrist hacked at one end. Whoever had done the job was no expert. I shook my head at the mess; at least Samson was consistent.

A roar echoed faintly along the tunnel, and I glanced up. They must have a sixth fight for the night. My second one should have been the last; they always left the worst fights for the end of the night to draw the biggest bets.

Frowning, I continued around the far corner, taking pictures of written ledgers the bookie provided.

Samson might be overweight, but he did have some degree of intelligence; computer records could be hacked.

Danny did an excellent job of it. But as this job required more old fashioned values, Liam had put me in. So here I stood, with a shitty story to offer about why I couldn't do the job Samson had offered me.

Unless I could get the information I needed tonight.

That meant I could close up the case and get home to the girls. I hadn't set them up with an evacuation plan, which Jen and I had always done when we'd moved. She'd impressed me on her first night. She quietly asked questions, working through the routes and offered a stack of suggestions I hadn't thought of, despite having built a career on protecting people like her, and Mila.

My thoughts remained on Jen as I hunted for information, with no real idea of what I needed to look for. Anything that connected Samson and Logan. A name, banking details, drop points...Jen's hands on my cheek, her lips on mine.

I shook my head free of the distraction she offered, all too tempting and all too easy to lose myself in.

Ears pricked for Samson, I delved into his drawers, pushing aside a half-devoured, aged sandwich. Beneath, lay more ledgers and a little black book. I stared at it, the familiar clip of heels on the concrete floor outside the office bouncing back to me. Slipping it into my pocket, I shut the drawers, making sure everything looked as it had when I'd entered the room. I circled the desk to lean on a bookcase behind the door, pretending to play on my phone as Red walked in.

Tonight, she wore a yellow tube dress that clashed horribly with her hair and shoes. It pulled up at the back as she bent to collect a black suit jacket from Samson's chair that clearly wasn't hers and slipped it on. I wrinkled my nose; there was no accounting for bad taste, but I wouldn't touch the fat man's clothes, let alone wear them.

I kept my head down as she turned. A tiny squeak let me know she'd spotted me.

"You shouldn't be in here!" she shrieked.

I winced. "Tone that instrument down, woman. I'm waiting for Samson."

Her eyes narrowed. "Samson isn't coming back tonight. I'm locking up."

I raised my eyes from my phone. "Bookie told me to see him. Didn't pay me."

She sighed, flipping her hair over her shoulder and circled the desk. Her hands went to the drawers, mine flexing as she pulled out a lower one I hadn't had time to examine.

"Here. Money. Take what you need." She scattered notes over the desktop. I ignored them, much as I had the last time I stood in Samson's smelly cave.

"He said Samson needed to see me," I repeated. She looked up, irritation removing any natural beauty from her makeup-encased face.

"Come back tomorrow."

"I might not." I moved closer to the desk, pocketing my phone.

"You will." She shrugged. "They all do."

"Right. I won't see you later, then."

I pulled my hoodie back up, turning for the door. She caught my arm, moving faster than I'd thought possible.

"Wait! Did you do— the thing he set you?"

I tugged my arm free of her red talons. "No."

"He'll be mad."

"Then you deal with his shit, honey."

"He wants you to fight for bigger money."

I paused, my back still to her. "He could have asked me that himself."

"He makes a lot from your fights. He wants weapons in there."

"And?" I tossed out a gamble because there had to be more. Otherwise, I was wasting my time. My shoulders throbbed again. "I've already done knives. Are the masses bored with their choice of entertainment already?"

Red pouted beside me, her unnaturally swollen lips exposing white teeth I almost expected to be pointed. "He wants to see how brutal you are. That's why he set you that task."

"He wants hits? What the fuck is this, the nineteen fifties? I'm not a fucking gangster, Red."

"Colette."

"Red."

"Well, he needs someone. You see the mess the other guy made."

"Yeah, that's pretty rank. You gonna leave it like that overnight? It'll fucking stink."

She shrugged. "I'll work from a trailer. Someone else can clean it up."

"One of the fighter's trailers?" I asked though it had no pertinence to the job.

She nodded, working her lip between her teeth. The same habit Jen had when she thought something through, or nervous. Her motion was sexy. Red's was like a kid chewing gum. I sighed, knowing what would come next and began to back away, my hands up.

It was the wrong move.

"Are you inviting me back to your trailer?"

Hell, no. I wouldn't touch you even if you were free.

I was pretty sure she didn't fit in that category.

Her hands drifted down her sides, her hips moving to the rhythm the crowd made above us, their feet pounding the wood over our heads. Red tipped back a shoulder reaching out with the claws at the tips of her fingers. A demon's invitation to help.

All I wanted was to be back home with Jenny. But first, I'd need to shower. I didn't want my stain to compromise the pure strength she had.

I pulled my hood up, ignoring Red's advance and slipped back out the door, sliding into the crowd. Just another man making his way back from a cage fighting ring with everyone else and no one to see me.

Outside the gates, I slipped between the busses where people congregated, still drinking. Part of Samson's money came from booze sales. But the bigger fights drew in far more. At the back of the line of busses, I broke into a jog, heading for Micah's place.

I used a different way back each time, adding to an unpredictable schedule. Being on foot gave me a hyper-aware sense of my surroundings. By the time I'd run flat out for a kilometre and a half, I'd hit Micah's block. His warehouse took up most of it. I circled it, jogging slower and sent him a message.

The knots in my back eased with the motion, though if I didn't stay warm, any effort Jen put in would be wasted. The first night she'd offered had been nearly six months ago. Our relationship had become strained after the bank incident; both of us circling each other, two magnets pushing each other away whenever we got too close.

I reached Micah's door and gave it a push, my heart rate already back to normal. The door opened under my hand. I closed it, flicking the lock behind me and walked into the short hall that led into a wide space, lit at the far corner. His blue monster truck illuminated by a black light dominated the space. Bright, white light flared from beneath the chassis. A thin pair of legs stuck out from beneath it in green jeans. I grinned.

"Thanks for letting me in."

"No problem," Jimmy yelled back from the guts of Micah's truck. "You want a lift home?"

"Uh..." I trailed off, not wanting to say that I didn't trust her rust bucket of a tiny car. For a mechanical engineer who spent her days improving fuel distribution and other systems on the pro monster truck circuit, her own vehicle was a disgrace. "Where's the big guy?"

"Upstairs."

"And will this be working any time soon?"

"Not before daylight."

I sighed. "Okay. I'll take that lift."

I found a patch of wall and waited for either Jimmy to be finished with her work or for Micah to haul his ass downstairs from whatever he had his head buried in. I didn't want to go up there without his invitation; the younger man took his privacy seriously, and being invited into his space wasn't a privilege to abuse.

Half an hour later, I stared at the inner guts of a truck and learned the finer points of fuel distribution systems. Jimmy talked endlessly; she had a head full of knowledge that my mine wasn't equipped to absorb. Micah didn't chatter unnecessary words, and it surprised me they got along so well. Perhaps he just liked to listen?

I rolled my shoulders where they were glued to the floor and pried my eyelids open. Jimmy lay flat on a mechanic's creeper that looked like she'd made herself. Which didn't work so well for me; my back would need a good walking on once I managed to extract myself from beneath the beast.

A foot kicked my ankle in a place that had already taken minor damage during my last fight.

"Ow," I grunted.

"Get your ass out here." Micah's voice echoed in the large space, barely big enough to cater for the man himself.

"Yeah, yeah." I wriggled my ass along the ground. It was the only thing working. My shoulders were frozen to the cold cement.

I emerged feet first, a caterpillar breaking out of its cocoon, without the magnificent metamorphosis. Despite Jimmy's constant chatter, I hadn't learned a damn thing.

Except that my pain threshold had a whole new level as Micah pulled me to my feet.

"Get someone to look at this thing before you break it, old man."

I winced, attempting to stretch and forwent the activity when something popped in my ear. Something that was attached to me.

"Yeah well. I'm trying to get home to that someone."

Micah cocked his head, a damp gym towel appearing in one hand. I took it with a nod, wiping someone else's sweat from my skin.

"You want to take the bike back?"

"What?" I paused in my clean up, peering up at the big man.

"The bike. You ran it over Danny's mark last year. I've got it behind the bookshelf."

"You keep a motorcycle behind your books?" I followed the bodybuilder, bemused. Although Micah was only in his late twenties, he approached life in a very different way from anyone his age. From anyone else at all, really.

"Shelves," he corrected, pulling a leaning case upright with one hand. I shook my head as he towed the bike — cover and all — out from behind it, wiping off the dust cover with one hand. "How was the fight?"

"Fight was fine."

Micah raised an eyebrow. "Investigation?"

I opened my mouth and closed it again, swearing softly. "Shit. I've lost whatever momentum I had." My fingers brushed the small notepad in my pocket that I hoped held information we could use.

The lurid green bike glowed beneath dangling fluorescent lights. I blinked. "At least I'll stay awake on the ride home."

"See you in the morning." Micah flicked the key he'd left in the ignition.

"It *is* morning," I grumbled, rolling my shoulders. Micah patted them none too gently.

"Use the tiger balm. It will—"

"Burn the shit out of me while I pretend not to be a pussy. Yeah."

Micah's gaze weighed lightly on me as I rolled the bike back. Not judging, exactly; I'd rarely seen the younger cop angry or even snarky. He observed the world from a standstill as it flowed around him. I often envied his perspective.

He tugged the chain to raise the enormous roller door that led to his back street. I gunned the engine, Jimmy emerging from beneath the truck long enough to wave before she disappeared in a flash of mermaid-green.

I pulled up to the drive and killed the engine, opting to roll the bike to the top and open the garage manually. Not for any security-based reason, but simply so I didn't wake Ashley. Or Jen, though she likely had stayed awake, waiting up.

I paused.

The routine of her waiting up had become an expectation — a dangerous one. I cursed softly, stubbing my toe through my boot on the garage door and pretended that was the reason for it.

The internal door gave at the slightest touch. I walked into the dark house, shrugging my jacket off and let it fall. Jen caught it before it hit the floor.

My lips pressed tight. I knew exactly where she stood in the house, heat emanating from her at my side. My hands clenched into fists, itching to grab her and kiss her, but with the way my body reacted after a fight, I was likely to fuck her on the kitchen floor instead.

Though I no longer thought she was as averse to the idea, as well.

Her fingers brushed my back. The tight muscles pulsed beneath her touch, and I was glad I'd taken the opportunity to clean up.

"Take this off," she murmured softly. My imagination went into overdrive, my fists clenched until my nails bit into my palms. "Just the shirt." Her voice held an amused note; I knew she'd caught me out.

I grunted, letting her lead me to a chair she'd pulled out. Sharp scents assailed my nostrils where she'd laid the horrid stuff out. Shucking my shirt over my head, I bit back a groan. The ride back hadn't helped the state of my back.

Her hands glided over my back, warming the sore muscles, her nails scratching over the ink covering scars I'd rather forget. Sensation tore down my skin. I tensed and then relaxed with a forced effort.

"You're tight. What happened?"

"I went for a run in the cold. And I brought the bike back."

"Hmmm. I saw you." I spun in the chair, facing her and raised an eyebrow. She shrugged. "What? It's practically dayglo yellow."

"Green. But...yeah. Maybe not the smartest move."

"You couldn't run all the way back across the city."

"But I could have caught a cab. Or a bus."

"What bus runs at three in the morning?"

I swore. "Damn, girl. Stop staying up for me. Get some sleep."

"What for?" Her hands wound around the knots in my back, working the muscles smooth with long strokes. "I've got nothing else to do, Theo. No one else to worry about, apart from Ashley and me."

"I'm glad I made the list." I grinned in the shadow while she cussed at my back.

"So sensitive."

I could hear the smile in her voice, ignoring her barb. "But she deserves to have you at full strength– ow, woman." I rubbed at my shoulder, but she batted my hand away.

"And don't you think we deserve that too?"

"Are you going to hurt me again if I say no?"

"Maybe."

"An answer given under duress isn't going to be a real one," I warned her.

"Are you going to lie to me that easily?"

I snorted. "Like you lied to me about not coming to the fight?"

"An omission."

"Thanks, Spock."

Jen huffed behind me, her hands resuming their work. I didn't bother concealing my groan, muscles loosening beneath her touch. I let her go on for a minute longer, then rose. Her hands lingered on my back, but she dropped them as I turned, stepping away from the chair. I yanked on a clean shirt she'd left out for me.

"Get some sleep, Jen."

She eyed me in the early morning light. "And what are you going to do?"

I shrugged my jacket back on, my hand already on the garage door. "I'm going back to work."

Her only reply was her silence. I turned back to face her. She stood still, her arms wound around herself in a hug. A sliver of light illuminated eyes that pierced me.

"Why did you come home?" she whispered, her brow drawn tight.

Because I needed your touch to make me feel human again.

I rolled my shoulders, unable to answer her.

"Get some sleep, Jen."

CHAPTER SEVEN

BLACK

I left the bike in the garage and took my car, opting for seat warmers that eased the muscles in my back, the warmth of Jen's hands fading quickly.

If that was how *home* would be each night, I needed to set up a target — anything to use up the energy that threatened to turn inward when I couldn't use it where I wanted to. The woman was amazing, and I wouldn't have her in anyone else's care, but living with her without touching her drove me slowly mad.

The sun rose over the city, lighting it in stark relief as I delved into its depths. I drove straight into the underground car park to where the unit generally parked and congregated at the southern corner. A single, sleek silver Audi sat in its usual spot.

It was far too early, and though I could have stayed with Jen, my concern was less of falling asleep than doing something inappropriate with my charge.

I took the stairs to our office, unsurprised to see Liam already there. The tiny black book made a decent thump as it landed on the desk beside him — a measure of its sins, perhaps.

"What's this?"

"All I got from Samson's drawer. I haven't had a chance to read through it yet."

"I can't use that."

"Yeah, I know."

"And now he's going to know you — or someone else — has been in his office nicking things."

"The investigation's dead. He knows who you are; they want a hitman for hire, and I can't get any further without killing or maiming someone."

"Worried about your soul, Black?" He raised an eyebrow. I ignored him.

"More than that, I'm going to get shot. And I can't look after my g– Ashley and Jen if I'm not getting any sleep."

"You came straight from the fight?"

"Sort of."

"Go home."

"And what? Sleep through guarding the girls?" I snorted, flicking my terminal on. "I'll get you a report later."

"Don't bother." Cal kicked the door fully open, slamming his laptop on his desk. "Get the fuck out of here, both of you."

Liam didn't flinch. Neither of us was moved by Cal's tantrum. I nudged his chair with my boot. "What's up your ass?"

"You are." He ran a hand over his short hair, slapping it to his desk. "I'm trying to put a full case together for Selena," he looked pointedly at Liam who stared back, "to get this all on track, and you two are having your own little undercover party on your own. Were you going to include the rest of us in this?"

"Nope." Liam stared straight through Cal. "My team," he reminded him, "I'll run the investigations as I see fit."

"Then get rid of me because I clearly have no fucking use."

"Get over yourself," I snapped. "None of us have had enough sleep. Or any at all. No reason to pull the asshole card, though I know it comes naturally to some."

Cal glared between Liam and me in a charged silence, his jaw clenched, then dropped his head to the desk with a thud. Liam and I looked at each other over the top of him. I was the first to give, more because I was too tired to work through his bullshit, but I knew Liam would be harder on his protege than I would be on my ex-partner.

I squatted onto my heels at the corner of his desk. "How's Mila?"

Cal raised his head, the circles under his eyes a deep grey, though that wasn't unusual for him. What was unusual was that since we'd caught Logan, they hadn't gone away, which I had expected.

"She's sick. Every morning. Every day."

"She's pregnant, man. It's not going to get any easier."

"Thanks...but we're worried something might be wrong. With the baby. Or her." His head banged onto the desk again. Emotion, rather than exhaustion, was crippling him. I nodded to Liam, who slipped from the room. "*I'm* worried. She won't see a doctor or ob-whatever." His voice came out muffled, but the strain in it was unmissable.

"Ob-Gyn." I rocked back onto my heels, stretching my back then my hamstrings as I rose. "I can give you the name of a good one."

Cal's head bobbed on the desktop. "Thanks, man. I remember when—"

"It's no problem. I'll message details to you." I paused, but he didn't move. "Forgiven, then?"

"Yeah." Cal sat back. "Fuck, this is killing me. She won't let me look after her. Liam's off on his only little vendetta and fuck knows what you're doing."

"The job. It has to be done."

Cal glared at me, but his energy ran dry before his fury could take ahold. "The only one I can rely on is Danny."

I coughed, covering my smile with my fist. "That's a change."

"Yeah. I won't give that up, but I'd like to know you've got my back if things..."

"Go south with Mila."

"Yeah."

"Go beat Danny up when he comes in. If you can keep up with him."

I knew that would rile whatever reserves of energy my boy had left. Cal's eyes flashed. I bared my teeth, reminding him I could put any of them on the mat if I chose to. Well, maybe not Micah.

But that was more weight over skill.

I turned back to my desk, and it took me a moment to notice that the little black book was gone.

The Ob-Gyn number was still in my phone. I sent it to Cal quickly, then deleted it. There was no chance I'd ever use it again. Memories of Angela's smile, so happy when we'd conceived, rushed over me. Then, nothing. And slowly, we fell apart. Angela on the outside while I slowly self-destructed on the inside. The sole occupant to my own private pity party.

I hadn't tried to make a family since.

By the time the younger men filled the office, I was ready to go home, but I managed to push through until after lunch, blinking at a screen which wouldn't stay still.

"Go home."

"To which one?"

Cal glared at me out the corner of his eye, but I refused to give him the satisfaction of looking directly at him. Petty, but there was little I had control of today, so I clung to the tiny measure. That, and to just piss him off.

The asshole-factor was contagious.

I nodded, scrubbing my face, stray hairs scratching my hands. Jen would want to trim it, but that was too intimate for me. And with how I was feeling about her, I didn't want to break what we had, even though I wasn't quite sure what that was, any more.

Bottom line, I cared about her in ways I shouldn't, and I needed to do my job more than I needed her love.

If I kept lying to myself, maybe that would fill the hole in my chest where a family was supposed to fit. But I'd been there before, and I still bore the scars.

I couldn't deal with the risk factor of it not working out a second time.

My visit to see Dad was well overdue, but it would have to wait. Today wasn't the day to face him, which left only one place left to go.

Home.

"You really should let me trim it," Jen argued, passing me a pair of cold sandwiches wrapped in plastic from the refrigerator. "It's out of control." She flicked her fingers at my face. I dodged, giving her a lazy grin and hefted the plate.

"It's not the only thing." I sank next to Ashley at the table where she was devouring the remains of a sandwich from a second plate and paused. "Have you eaten?"

She waved my comment away as Ashley rose, eagerly sorting dishes to wash. "She's such a responsible kid. I'm worried about her socially, though. Being so cut off. It's not healthy. Is it the investigation?" Jen changed subjects so quickly I was surprised I managed to keep up in my sleep-deprived state.

"I can't talk about that." I bit into my sandwich, "God, that's good."

"Will you be here less?"

I swallowed a bite far too large and attempted to chase it with the lemonade she'd set out. Spluttering, I stared at her through a sheen of salt and tears. "Why would you ask that?"

Do you want me to go?

"I just thought you were getting busy...and—"

"I can get the younger boys to cover my shifts." I pushed back from the table. "But I'm not bothering Cal on a whim. He's got enough to deal with."

"That's not what I mean. Wait. What about Cal? Is it Mila?" Urgency laced her tone as her hand crept unconsciously to her stomach. I tried not to follow her movement with my eyes.

"Pregnancy. I can't tell if he's overreacting or if there's something wrong."

Her eyes narrowed, she planted balled fists on her hips. "Why would you know anything about that? You don't have kids."

"I was married once, Jen."

"Oh."

"Right. Oh. You don't know everything about me," I spat the words, pursing my lips. She hadn't earned that; it wasn't like I'd been particularly forthcoming in the two years we'd shared a living space. For the first time, I fully considered what it must be like from her point of view, and realised it was a well overdue thought. "Sorry. You didn't deserve that. I'll get the boys to cover. You do deserve better than me, though."

"Don't. Please. Unless you really wa– have to." Her mouth opened to say more. I held up a hand, looking sideways at Ashley. She cleaned the kitchen as she bopped around, humming.

"It's not a normal childhood."

"No." Jen stepped closer to me, though I saw her hesitation.

"Mum, can I play outside?"

"Sure, popcorn."

Ashley grinned. "I'll get my unicorns."

"I'll go out with her. You don't need to watch us. We're a burden to you." Jen brushed past me, but I grabbed her arm.

"You're not a burden to me," I said in a voice too low and too rough, tugging her closer to me though I knew I shouldn't. "I'll stay unless you want me to go."

Her eyes held no clue to the answers I sought. Two days ago that wouldn't have occurred to me, but we'd crossed a line, and I had no idea how to go back.

If I wanted it to go back to the way it was.

I smiled; I'd told Cal off for exactly this situation with Mila eighteen months ago.

"What is it?" Jen asked. I focussed on her with a wry grin.

"Nothing about this is normal. I can't expect you to be able to deal with me on a daily basis."

Not with the way my other job is going.

"It's good for Ashley to have some routine in her life. Someone constant."

"A routine where you sit up until dawn, waiting while I come home battered and covered in someone else's blood?" I winced at the thought; it sounded far too much like Logan.

"A routine with people she knows and trusts."

"Are we talking about your daughter or you?" I let go of her arm, but she didn't move away.

A puff of glitter announced the unicorn stampede as they passed through the living area on their way out the back door to the garden.

I looked down to find Jen studying me, a hint of panic in her eyes.

"Maybe both of us."

She turned and fled into the garden, leaving me in a cloud of glitter.

CHAPTER EIGHT

JENNY

Ashley literally rolled in the grass when we got outside. She lay on her back in the afternoon sun, soaking up actual, moving air. And sunlight. I realised how pale she'd become and looked up where Theo was positioned at the back fence where he had a clear view of the house and gate. He glanced down at her, his mouth thinning as he saw what I had.

When the air began to chill, I headed back inside, answering a few messages from Chad, but I soon got sick of his whinging about a boss who wouldn't let him handle bigger jobs. I slid my phone face down onto the bench, grabbing the tray of biscuits and coffee I'd promised Theo and Ashley, mulling over how best to approach my brother's issues.

How did one tell one's younger sibling the reason was themselves? Chad had never been particularly responsible, always attracted to money-making scams while I struggled to work less than fifty hours a week at my own accounting business.

Apparently, that much work was too boring and time-consuming.

But that job had gained me a family. No matter how short my time with Paul had been, we'd managed to adopt Ashley together, and the three of us had been a tight little unit for the first two years. I rubbed my ring finger, the indent fainter than it had been a few months ago. It was funny how something that was supposed to be permanent could fade so fast.

I thought back to Black's comment about marriage; it hadn't occurred to me that he might have had someone. He's never mentioned it. And I'd kissed him, crossing more than one line — a professional one as well as a personal one.

Sunlight warmed my back as I crossed the small patch of grass and laid the tray on the small, two-seater table in the far corner. I sank onto the freshly cut grass, soon surrounded by ponies. Theo stood above us, his arms crossed over his chest, watching over us without a hint of boredom.

I knew he was meant to be dark and imposing, but all I saw was a man who worked hard and valued loyalty above all else. The guilt I expected didn't come as I studied him, knowing I couldn't have what I wanted.

A pony clambered over my leg, perching on my knee. I became a restaurant stable, with a story unfolding around me that involved unicorns with water spouting from their horns to put out fires.

The sun had set behind the house, taking the warmth of the day with it as Ashley carted her herd back inside. I shook out my legs and tried to push myself up. Everything protested, my rear suspiciously absent. I sank back into the grass with a groan.

"Come on. You only put out three hundred and something fires."

"It was hard work. Damn. My legs are asleep. And my ass."

Theo guffawed above me, holding out a hand. I took it, his fingers wrapping around my wrists as he lifted me to my feet, steadying me when my legs wouldn't cooperate.

"You were down there for a while," he admitted.

I stared at him suspiciously. "Why aren't you numb and bored out of your brains?"

"Because I have two beautiful girls to watch over." He prodded me toward the house.

I gaped over my shoulder at him. "Since when did you become so easy to get a compliment from?"

I stepped inside, blinking rapidly to adjust my eyes to the dim light in the kitchen. Theo leaned in the doorway, grasping the doorframe over his head. Hardened muscle bulged from places along his arms and sides that I hadn't realised *could* bulge. I traced over the hard muscle built on muscle bunched along his forearms to where his biceps met his shoulders in a continuous line.

"Since I had two hours to think about how much I'd miss both of you if I got myself taken off the job. You sure you want me to stay?"

His eyes asked another question altogether, one I knew neither of us wanted to answer.

Did I want Theo to stay? To spend every day with a new officer assigned to us who wouldn't play with Ashley, who wouldn't speak to me and who would never go shopping for unicorn books? Was Theo who I wanted guarding us? The thought that this was my choice left me shaking.

Hells, yes. At least that way I have something cute to perv on.

Another lie I told myself. I thought back to the way he'd methodically checked my body for signs of self-harm. That he hadn't abandoned me or been embarrassed by me when I'd crashed.

But there *was* that aesthetic factor. My eyes began to retrace their journey over his shoulders and arms, lingering on the curves of muscle. I'd never been horny for a fit man like this in my life. Theo brought out something maddening in me, an addiction I couldn't kick.

His lips curled up, a dark fire alight in his eyes as he watched me. My mouth dried, and I couldn't get anything out.

"Mum! I'm going to have a shower!" Ashley yelled.

"Fine!" I yelled back. "Don't yell through the house!"

I turned back to Theo's grinning face.

"You know how contradictory you are, right?"

I waved his statement away, ignoring it completely.

"What do you want for dinner?"

I felt like a kid playing house. Now all I needed were some unicorns with water putting out fires, and I'd be set. Glitter sparkled on the bench. I tapped my finger over it absently.

"We'll get your life back, Jen. I promise."

Sensation flared at my back. I bit my lip when it began to tremble; why would I want anyone else guarding us? My fingers pressed the tiny shiny square into a ball. I flicked it over the kitchen bench, following its path as it bounced across the few rays of sunlight still slanting in through the window — anything to stop the tears from flowing.

"You can't promise me that." I turned, intent on getting food from the fridge, though I had no plan in mind. My brain was slowly dying from lack of use, day by day.

I came up smack against his chest. My palms pressed against the black tee he always wore, expecting him to step back. Instead, his hands reached past me on each side to grip the bench behind me. Theo bent to stare straight in my eyes. I blinked, both needing to escape him and wrap my hands around his neck to kiss him again.

Am I just a desperate woman in a ridiculous situation?

How greedy could I be? I'd had a strong marriage for nearly eight years, and been blessed with the most wonderful daughter in the world when I couldn't have my own. I was lucky Ashley hadn't been taken away from me after Logan's last attack, and I knew Cal or Liam had intervened on my behalf. Maybe both.

"Don't promise me what I can't have." I tried to turn his words back on him, but it came out as a plea instead. Something roiled in my stomach, igniting a fire all too quick to burn. "Don't promise me anything!"

I slapped both hands against his chest, again and again until my palms stung but he didn't budge. My tears never made it to the surface, sinking deep to simmer within me. Theo's arms closed around me, invading more of my space than he already had and drew me to him, weathering my rage and my desperation.

How can you be haunted by the dream of a normal life when you've never had one?

I didn't know if my anger was for Ashley as well as my own selfish desires, but I had an outlet to release into that appeared to be holding up under my onslaught, so I spent my energy against him.

Ahh.

I am the violent force.

But I did stop. Panting, I leaned my forehead against Theo's chest, my cheeks on fire. I sucked in deep, long breaths as he cradled my head to his chest, his ridiculously broad arms a barrier between me and the world.

"Are you keeping me in, or them out?" I asked with a small hiccup.

Theo's steel grip on me loosened a fraction. He looked down at me, his eyes unreadable. "Who?"

"Me. It doesn't matter. I'm sorry. You can write a report now, tell them I'm unfit to be a foster mother to an already-traumatised and abandoned child."

"Jen, look at me." His hand cupped my face, gently but firmly tipping my chin up. I held his gaze, letting him see the unhealed wounds inside me. His arm around me tightened for an instant, his thumb brushing my jawline. "I will never take Ashley away from you. I *will* promise you that."

I blinked back unshed tears, bowled over by the loyalty and determination our minder had for us. He released my chin, running his hand along my arm to wrap around my hand, towing me to the sofa.

"Theo, I need to be—"

"Doing nothing at all. Stop. I know what you're doing because I've watched Cal nearly kill himself with stress and sleepless nights over it for years. I've held Mila while she cried, shaking in my arms because after him, being around people was too much for her. And I see you attempting to find the best coping mechanisms you can."

Theo finished his speech. I gaped up at him as he tucked a blanket around my legs and placed my phone on my lap.

"That's the longest I think I've ever heard you talk."

The corner of his mouth crooked up. "Don't get used to it." Ashley ran into the room, bouncing across the room in a fluffy unicorn onesie. I laughed, doubled-over type laughing when nothing's really funny, the tears finally leaking from my eyes, but they weren't from the frustrations of before.

"Thank you." I gripped Theo's hand as he turned away. "Really. You're—"

"Teddy!" Ashley launched herself into the air at him. He caught her easily and lowered her to the ground.

"Got your iPad? Good. Let's go cook something spectacular for your Mum." He let Ashley chatter on, turning back once to brush his fingers over my cheek.

I put my phone on the arm of the sofa, snuggled beneath the blanket that smelled faintly of him and closed my eyes.

Theo murmured into his phone when I woke. His voice permeated my sleep, drifting into dreams I couldn't remember. I blinked, stretching beneath the blanket and wondered how long I'd been out. Not too long, I judged. Full dark had fallen, but in the autumn months, it really didn't take that long. Cold night air filtered through the windows, and I was glad of the rug.

Ashley cooked happily in the kitchen while he stood outside, monitoring her through the window. When I walked into the room, he gave me a curt nod, turning his back. His voice rose, bouncing back off the tall pailing fence surrounding the garden. I guessed either Liam or Cal were copping a load of the stress he tried to hide daily.

Ashley cooked well on her own, a zucchini slice with a side salad, and I was content to watch her, swiping grit from my eyes. The sleep had definitely been necessary, but I still felt like death. A meal made by someone you loved did a lot to fix it. Mostly.

"That was amazing, Ash." I kissed the top of her head. She nodded, yawning. "Can I read to you for a bit in bed?"

"Are you coming down with something, Mum?" Concerned grey eyes peered at me. The colour was where the resemblance to her father stopped. His emotionless stare held a promise of pain, of cruelty for his own enjoyment; hers held nothing but love and compassion.

"No, I'm just tired."

You're bored out of your amazingly creative and growing brain.

"Promise we'll find some things on Youtube to make or learn tomorrow, okay?"

"Like the history of mermaids?" She gave me a tired, hopeful grin.

"As long as the mermaids also do science and geography, absolutely."

"Awesome." She hugged me, trudging into her room and hanging from the door frame.

My phone buzzed again. I checked my pocket, but it was only Chad. I flicked back something inane to his question, my care-factor long gone for the day. I wished I could ask about his ex-wife, as I dearly missed my sister-in-law, but then it was just another person who knew something about us, and Theo had warned me against it.

Talking to Chad broke his trust yet again. Another lie to add to the growing heap.

That I shouldn't speak to my family annoyed me, but the only family I needed and protected right now was attached to the head of blonde hair reading in her bedroom.

Theo walked through the glass back door that led into the garden, locking it behind him. His jaw clenched, and he flicked the screen closed too hard. It banged against the doorframe, ricocheting back.

"Not good news?" I placed my phone on the benchtop. It vibrated, but I ignored it.

Theo frowned. "Just work." He brushed past me, checking the locks on doors and windows methodically throughout the house. Ashley's light turned off, casting the other rooms into darkness.

I went in and kissed her goodnight, but she was already asleep, her unicorn compendium open over her knees. I closed it up and checked her window myself when Theo blocked the light from the doorway, shooing him into the living area. The light flicked off, he took up his post by the window with his back to me.

I stood in the middle of the room, sucking on my bottom lip. "Do you want to talk to me about it?"

"No. Just– do whatever you do, Jen." He passed a hand over his beard — a beard I desperately wanted to trim — jiggling his shoulders and toes.

"If you're trying to keep yourself awake, maybe you should sleep?" I suggested softly. "Or I can make some tea or coffee?"

"I'm fine, Jen. Stay out of it."

His short words hit my chest like a physical blow. The afternoon had passed so well, and now this...the volatile nature of his work. Us. My lips pressed tight together. I knew I should stay out of it like he'd asked, but he wasn't the only tired or stressed person in the house.

"Thanks for the nap before."

"You're welcome."

I fidgeted. "Are you going back to the fights?"

"No."

"So we get you full time?"

"I told you to stay out of it."

He swung around, his frame blocking the light from the window, which wasn't much. No clouds filled the sky, but a dark moon shone down on us.

"Are you staying with us? Or are you passing us off to...someone else."

"The boys have better things to do with their time." He folded his arms over his chest, his feet shoulder-width apart. Even in the darkened room, he made an impressive silhouette.

"Hell, you really are in fine form tonight."

"That's– not what I meant. At all. I love spending time with you and Ashley, Jen. But the job has to be done. If they'll let me do it."

"You work hard," I said softly, stepping into his space. His gaze sharpened, but he didn't move. "But you can't kill yourself over it."

"If I'm not here to do it, I'm worried that's what will happen to you."

"What a lovely reminder." My stomach clenched, but I held his gaze.

"What do you want, Jen?" His voice was low, sending a shiver up my back.

"Honestly? To have a life. A real one. I want to leave the house, go somewhere. Anywhere."

"You know—"

"Yes, I know," I snapped bitterly, shaking my head. "I'll make that cup of tea."

His hand snaked around my arm, stopping me mid-whirl.

"Wait."

I looked down at his hand wrapped around my arm. It took up more space than it should have; his knuckles were well bruised and calloused. His touch was firm but gentle. My skin ached for his hands on more of me. I turned back to him.

"Are you supposed to be touching me?"

He cocked his head. "A little late for that, isn't it?"

"Is that an invitation?"

Please, God, be an invitation. One that involves a lot of muscle and no shirt.

Theo withdrew his hand. "No."

I stood in the middle of the room as he pivoted to face the window in the same place I'd been when this conversation began.

"Is that what you're going to do, close me out every time I get close to you?"

"You're my job, Jen. My responsibility. It can't be any more because that compromises your safety. Because I'm distracted."

"We're not a *job*, for Christ's sake, Theo! We're people who had lives!" I hissed in a whisper. It came out like a strangled cat.

"You're alive." He faced me with folded arms and a closed expression that brooked no argument. "And I intend to keep you that way. A fuck that means nothing won't fix your problems."

I gaped at him, knowing he was being crass on purpose, though my brain recognised that he was right. Mostly. Well, all.

"Then give me some freedoms. Find a school for Ashley. Something," I spluttered, slamming my hands into my pockets. I needed to hold something, but the only thing keeping myself upright was me.

His face closed. "I'll talk to Cal in the morning. The boys can come and watch you."

My mouth was open to say, *but you leave us alone all the time* when he turned his back, dismissing me as nothing more than a petulant child who had overstepped her bounds.

And just like that petulant child, I slunk back to my empty bed, lying on top of the covers, staring at the ceiling. I ached for the prickle of oncoming tears, but the dam remained closed as always, my heart hard. I studied the paint above my head until light crept into the shadows.

CHAPTER NINE

BLACK

Danny turned up five minutes before I was due in a meeting with Cal and Liam that I wasn't going to make. I'd avoided Jenny all morning, loitering in various corners of rooms at the greatest distance to her, checking doors and windows we'd both already done. Our morning routine.

When would these girls have any semblance of normal life?

"Could you be any damned slower?" I glared at the younger man who appeared to be growing a man-bun. Or trying to.

Could he be any more pathetic or less professional?

Jenny's words from last night rattled around my head. I winced inwardly, knowing that same badge could be applied to me.

"Cal's waiting for you." Danny drank something green from his thermos. My lip curled at the young cop. I needed back in the ring to take some of my energy out on an unsuspecting soul who'd already sold his. Or maybe I could challenge man-bun boy here. Cal said he was getting faster. I was willing to throw down and see how long it took me to knock him on his ass.

"Fine," I gritted out, swinging into the garage to find the door up and the gate unlatched. "Are you fucking kidding me?" I turned back to Danny. It looked like he might be getting that punch after all.

"Whoa, man. It was just because you were heading out."

"And left the plate's numbers exposed to the street?" I snapped, wrenching the remote for the gate from his hand. "Sit. Stay. Don't fucking move your ass until I get back."

"Woof." Danny grinned widely, but his eyes told another story. I knew the younger man was a hell of a lot smarter than any of us — Liam excluded. Maybe.

Grumbling under my breath, I took the bike out, figuring it was a good change of routine and made sure the garage door shut. Two, bright eyes peered between the fence posts though I would never have seen her if I hadn't been looking.

I gave Ashley a small wave, the cold fury inside my chest settling at the thought of coming back to her and Jen.

Hopefully, with some answers.

Cal and Liam were silent when I walked into the Incident Room, each holding up a different piece of the wall opposite each other across the table at the back of the room.

"And here I thought I'd be going upstairs to somewhere plush." I tossed my keys on my desk, looking between them. Neither moved or fidgeted. "Who died?"

"Selena's not sure there'll be a trial."

I blinked, the familiar cold rage returning with force. "Are you fucking kidding me?"

Cal shook his head. "We knew something like this might happen."

"The judges. He's bribed someone." I looked to Cal for confirmation, but it was Liam who nodded.

"More than likely. We could be back at square one."

"Can we get another judge?"

"Appeal?" Liam's lips pursed. "Perhaps. But that's in Selena's court. For us, it might mean—"

"They've just moved." I gripped the back of my chair, warping it out of shape. "We're not doing this again. And Jen needs some time out of the house."

"Unacceptable." Liam shifted from his patch of wall. "Get back into the cage fighting ring before it finishes up. There were two more fights scheduled, so you should be able to close the investigation off by then. Right?"

I stared. When Liam said *right*, there was a good chance no one else had managed to actually get what he was saying. Selena alone appeared to speak his language. The gears chugged in my head.

"You want me to have something fresh to pin onto Logan within a week." I ran my hands over my hair, slicking it back. "With a different judge."

"Keep it turning over faster than he can keep up." Liam nodded, typing on his phone as he wandered out the door.

I shook my head, looking to Cal. He laughed at me.

"What did you expect? It's Liam."

"Yeah, but you're used to him. Did he give you the investigation?"

Cal tapped a file on the table I hadn't noticed, Liam having consumed my available brainpower. My ex-partner kicked a chair out. I sat slowly, already flicking through the file, trying to find a new angle to approach it from.

Half an hour later, I looked up.

"Spit it out," Cal said, staring at the file in my hands. "You've been jittering like a rabid mongrel for the last ten minutes."

"Jen needs some time. Outside."

"You make it sound like a prison."

"To her, it is. Remember how Mila was for the weeks in your house?"

Cal snorted. "Yeah. She wasn't impressed."

"Jen hit that level months ago. She's only just holding her shit together."

"What does she want?"

"Time out. Apparently." I waved my hands in vague circles to demonstrate my utter lack of understanding. Jen wanted out of the house, but I had no idea what she wanted to actually *do*. It occurred to me to ask Micah. He was the only one of us with a hobby or a life outside of the unit.

"What the fuck does that mean?" Cal's forehead crinkled.

"I've got no idea."

We stared at each other, mulling over the intricacies of a woman's mind.

"Okay. I got time out for you."

Jen's ears perked up. She placed a finger to her lips, creeping down the hall and poked her head into Ashley's room. My knees jiggling, I dug into the plate of food she'd provided. Asian something or other, though I didn't remember buying her soy sauce. Maybe Mila had brought it with her.

I finished up as she returned, perching onto the couch with a small smile. "I don't want to get her hopes up if she overhears. You know, just in case."

"I get it." I swallowed a mouthful of food. "The boys will come out to give you a night off. I'll still have to go with you. No Mila for company, sorry. Cal's family is still a potential target for now. Possibly forever. They'll be on a tight rein, too." I grimaced.

She nodded. "Okay. So what does a day mean?" she asked neutrally.

"You could go um– shopping, get something done," I flapped my fingers at her face and hope that encompassed everything she needed.

Cal had drawn as many blanks as I had, but at least he shared his house with a female. I hadn't lived with a woman for over fifteen years.

"Something done?" she echoed, twisting her fingers in her lap.

My mouth dried. "Yeah. Or whatever you need."

She nodded, her short hair falling forward over her face. "Okay."

I was silent for a full minute before I couldn't stand it anymore, placing the plate on the coffee table.

"Jen, I lost a woman I loved because– well, for many reasons, and I was one of them. But mainly it was because when she said *it's okay* or *it's fine*, I took her at face value." I crooked my knuckle beneath her chin. "And this is one of those times I don't want to walk away from a hurting woman that I– that I care about." I cursed internally, pushing back on the need to wrap my arms around her.

You can't be close to her and do your job right.

Her eyes raised to meet mine blazing with a need that matched my own. I should have dropped my hand, but I didn't.

Jen slid from her perch on the arm of the sofa, landing on the pillow beside me with a soft plop. She leaned forward into my touch. My hand curved automatically, framing her throat gently. She fit perfectly into my hand, and I lost moments enjoying the sensation.

My mind whirled with images of her on her knees before me, beneath me on a bed, her head flung back. I blinked and realised she hadn't moved away. My fingers skimmed the sides of her throat, my palm coupled fully around it. I pressed my fingers into her skin gently. She stopped, her eyes widening. A flush began beneath my fingers.

I stared hard at her, my heart beginning to pound in my chest. I ran my fingers experimentally along her throat, down the softest, palest part. She arched, her eyes beginning to glaze, tilting her head back in response.

This time I swore aloud, pulling her roughly to me. My hand still around her neck, I pulled her close enough to taste her breath. Sweet, something floral from the tea she'd been drinking at night.

She didn't whimper, or move, or fight.

Jen stayed still in my grip, unmoving though it must have been uncomfortable as hell, leaning across us both.

"You are *not* just a lonely woman," I rasped against her mouth, my own desire flaring as she let me tilt her head back a little more, running the pad of my thumb between her soft lips. They parted, my thumb slipping between them. She licked it, a tentative touch that nearly undid me. I forced myself not to react, wanting to see what she'd do.

Her tongue flicked over the tip of my thumb, sliding across it. Her lips closed around my skin, and I was done.

I tore my hand from her lips, slamming my mouth over hers, damming the logic in my head screaming about my job. She softened in my arms, letting my tongue sweep into her mouth, responding to every kiss. Her hand curled up around my wrist. She tried to pull back, but I kept my hand steady — gentle, but firm around her neck. Her fingers stroked my wrist, then my cheek. She drew back again or tried to, and when I wouldn't relent, she nipped my lip. I pulled back just far enough to speak against her mouth.

"Cheeky wench."

"More of a brat, really."

"Damn, girl." I pulled her back to me, kissing her harder. Half because my dick had control of my blood flow, the other because I needed to be sure.

Keep telling yourself that, Black.

Squirming closer, she wrapped her hands around my neck, kissing me back, my hand still wrapped around her throat.

"I wanted time with you," she whispered, and I dropped my hand. Red stained her cheeks at the admission, the flush travelling downward. I traced it to the neckline of her shirt with my fingers.

"This isn't a good idea. I can't stay with you if we do this."

"Of course, you can."

"No, I can't." I ran a hand over my hair, tugging free of her hands. "I can't risk feelings for you, Jen, any more than I already do. I can't protect you if I'm thinking with my dick."

She tilted her head, her hair brushing over her cheeks. My hands itched to touch her again. I pressed them flat to my knees instead.

"I thought you said it wouldn't mean anything. Just a quick fuck." Her eyes flashed again.

"Did that not mean anything to you right now?" I snapped, standing.

"No," she whispered, the barest breath, only audible in the short space between us.

I paced before her then stopped as her insult ran through my head. I dropped over her, leaning forward with my arms braced either side of her head. I heard the sharp intake of breath, watched her hold it. Every movement gave me further evidence of her lie.

"Girl, when I fuck, there's nothing quick about it. And I'd want to take my time with you."

Having sufficiently tortured both of us, I grabbed my phone off the counter in the kitchen and walked out the door, leaving her in a dark house.

CHAPTER TEN

BLACK

I stood in Samson's seedy office, waiting for the short, sweaty man to decide if he was going to shoot me.

"Position's filled. And you missed a fight. So I don't need you anymore."

I stared at him with open dislike. It fit the profile; I was meant to be a cold-hearted, disdainful asshole. It wasn't difficult to pull off, because it wasn't a cover.

Cheers, to a stint on the job where I got to be myself.

I hated undercover work with a passion. Danny had a knack for it, getting what information he needed, but he also had the patience that I lacked. I had a life I needed to get back to, and guarding wasn't the young cop's strong suit.

The role reversal sat poorly on me.

"Sure, you don't. So, I'll leave you to it, then."

"Wait! I mean, we could use you back in the ring for the last two nights." Grease coated the slimy man's voice, adhering to my skin. It was like walking through a mist of recycled oil from a cheap, take-out joint.

"And what else?" I left my back to him and spoke over my shoulder. He seemed to be a man who would react to dramatics. I sighed under my breath, wishing I was back in the house, arguing with Jen about *not* fucking her.

Last night, I couldn't convince myself to go back into the house while she was still awake in the event I did just that.

I was not screwing my client.

I was not screwing with a minor in the house. Especially when that minor wasn't my child.

But she wanted a day — or a night — of freedom, and I wanted very badly to give her everything she wanted.

It was a terrible idea.

Everything else aside, Cal would shoot me himself. He adored Jen and would tear me a new one for fucking around with her. Liam, on the other hand, wouldn't give a damn, providing the job got done.

If I spent the night with her, I'd want more. She'd want more, and we'd be at an impasse. Not particularly a suitable arrangement for a guard and a woman under protective witness for the foreseeable future with no end in sight.

I was so lost in my concerns about her that I nearly missed what Samson was rambling about.

Distractions like Jen will get me killed.

I was more worried it would get *her* killed than me, but either way, it wasn't the outcome desired. The job wasn't getting done, and that *was* the point.

"I'll fight," I cut him off abruptly, rising from my stupor. "You've got someone for the other job?"

"Weedy little guy called Smitty," Samson laughed, spittle flying across the room. I sidestepped, ignoring the splat it made on the concrete floor. "Seen him in action. Left me a little present last time."

I swallowed my distaste, recalling the partial chopped up hand in the bin last time I'd been in Samson's office. Hell, if that was the guy they were using, then this was about to get a whole lot messier. What I still needed to find out was how Smason was connected to Logan. *If.*

"I'm bored with your fighters. What've you got that's bigger?"

It was all I could come up with on the fly. Maybe a private fight, with a smaller venue and more cash flowing, or a bigger set up that this mid-sized stuff that wasn't going to get a conviction.

Samson paused, beady eyes watching me. "Yeah, right. Get through these two, and we'll talk."

"You seriously don't have a better crowd I can do this week?" I raised an eyebrow.

Samson pursed his lips. "Mebbe. But first, I gotta get that little weasel onto his first big job, yeah? That snobby prick you wouldn't do."

Liam.

For fuck's sake. How many times would I screw this up with him? For him?

"I can still handle that one. What was it worth?"

"Win your fight. Then we'll talk."

I was in the cage for a grand total of nineteen seconds.

"Reckon he still has the hit on you," I said into the phone. I'd jogged back to Micah's where I'd left the bike. He was out, so I'd parked it on the street instead. I hadn't been happy about it, but my head wasn't in the right space, and it had cost me the set up for the night.

"Don't worry about me." Liam yawned. "I'll be fine."

"Be serious. I don't know who Smitty is," I grunted, "except that he's messy, and a total amateur. Unless you prefer me to do the job myself," I offered.

The worry about amateurs was that they often got lucky, blind dumb sort of lucky because they had no idea what they were doing. Unpredictability made them dangerous.

Liam huffed a snort. "Good luck to either of you. No, Black just wants a reason to shoot me. I'm going into the office. Yeah."

I waited while he finished talking to Selena. She seemed to live at his house most nights now, though I didn't think they were together, yet.

"You're going in? It's two in the morning."

"I get more done when there's no one around to interrupt me with useless meetings all day."

"Fair enough. I'll fill you in later, then."

"Going back to the house?"

"I'll let Danny off, but I'll need him back. Gotta see Dad."

There was a pause on the other end, then a roar. The line clicked as it connected to Liam's car. "It's fine. I'll sort someone for you."

I jogged the rest of the way to Micah's, the ride home blisteringly cold, but welcome. Danny met me at the door, plopping keys and remotes into my hand.

"You alright?" He frowned as I peered over his shoulder.

"Yeah. Jen still up?"

"Nah, she went to bed just after Ashley."

"What time was that?"

Danny raised an eyebrow. "Dunno. After her show finished."

"The cooking one?"

"Yeah."

"Right. I need you back, later this afternoon. Can you cope with that?"

I knew Liam said he'd cover it,, but I wanted to make sure the girls had someone decent. It irked me that Danny qualified — just — but he was a decent cop, and I trusted him to look out for them, even if only for a short period while I sorted family business.

"Not a problem." He went to hug me, but I put out a hand.

"We're not that close. Take your cuddles home to your woman. And get rid of the hair thing."

Danny grinned, slapping me on the back as he passed. I bared my teeth and locked up after him.

The house was dark as hell. I stood in the kitchen, listening. Danny clutch started his safari-looking Jeep halfway down the steep drive. He had some consideration. Relief washed over me that the girls would get some rest. I checked Ashley's room first. She snored softly. I smiled as I pulled her door almost closed and ducked my head into Jen's room.

A bump in the middle of her bed shifted.

"Theo?"

"Go to sleep, Jen," I said softly, beginning to back out of her room.

"I'll get up."

She rose, her hair fluffy in the dim light as she untangled herself from the sheet. She made it to the edge of the bed before I sighed. I pulled the door closed behind me and crossed the room to press her gently back down into the bed. I pulled the cover over her, my fingers lingering on hers.

She struggled up, bumping into me.

"Your night vision is shit," I murmured, steadying her.

"Apparently so. About last night—"

"Now isn't the time to talk about it." I sat on the bed beside her. Jen's legs coiled around my back as she scooted closer.

"I just wanted to say sorry. I should never have—"

I laughed softly. "That wasn't your fault, Jen. It was all on me." I traced her leg to her hip beneath the covers, squeezing her waist gently. "I need a shower. And I need some sleep."

"Okay," she whispered, and I knew it wasn't the same, pissed off *okay* of the night before. "If you need me, just wake me."

"You know I won't."

She made a soft sound. I caught her chin in my hand, leaning down to kiss her deeply. She tasted like chocolate and tea. Her arms wound around me as she arched, drawing me over her, and I groaned against her mouth.

"I shouldn't have started this." But I wanted to keep going. I wanted her bare before me, to find out who she was when everything else was stripped away.

"But you did."

"And I'm stopping," I groaned as her hands ran over my arms, finding every ridge and curve, tracing parts of me I hadn't known would make me so damn hard. "Fuck, girl. You're killing me."

I detached her gently to the tiny sounds of her protest and left her room without a *goodnight*. I made it as far as the end of the hall before I stopped, leaning my back against the wall. She'd felt too damn soft, tasted too good. I couldn't fall for this woman.

I couldn't.

You already have, asshole.

A smile curved the corners of my mouth into something that must have looked deadly, and I was glad Jen wasn't here to see it. The beginnings of a plan formed in my mind.

If that's what you want, Jen, then that's what I'll give you.

I left Danny minding two sleeping girls very early in the morning. I hadn't made it to see Dad the day before, and it was an overdue visit.

The drive was a short one through the city to the outskirts. My pocket crinkled with the little packet squashed into a too-small space.

The respite care home was set up as a small village, and I'd planned to move Dad into one before his condition grew too serious. It had escalated too fast, and he'd ended up in one of the rooms above the administration building.

I parked beside the main building that housed single rooms with a general space, swiping myself in. I waved to the nurses, trying to be polite as my humour faded. The lift pinged open. No one emerged, and I stood in the small space, trying not to listen to the happy music.

Too small. Too hot. Too happy.

I got out of the lift grumpier than usual, heading down the corridor straight to Dad's room. The handle turned under my hand. I frowned; it was supposed to remain locked for his safety. His tendency to wander had increased recently.

His room was empty. I grumped some more, tidying his things. Socks hung haphazardly out of the draws, his shirts in no better condition. I refolded them, noting the neatly made bed. Maybe he'd had a moment after the nurses had been in.

"He's in the common room." One of the orderlies spoke to my back. I recognised his thin, weedy voice from my last visit; it had grown no less irritating since then. I grunted in reply, and eventually, he closed the door and left me to tidy up in peace.

They should be doing this, not me.

Though that wasn't strictly fair. I slipped the packet under his pillow, straightening it. The room tidy, I swept my hands over my hair, squeezing my fist behind my head.

It was time to go see the old man.

The common room was full, in a sparse sort of way. Not one of the residents spoke to one another; they sat in their chairs, some pointing into the room, others like Dad's facing tall windows which overlooked the garden.

Weak sunlight fell on his knees. I grabbed a blanket from the excess stack beside an empty lounge, placing it over his knees as I sat down. His head turned, but his eyes didn't. Ruddy and red, he stared at something I couldn't see.

"Hey, Dad."

I twitched the blanket for no reason at all, tucking it down the sides of his chair, then decided it was too tight and loosened it again. His hand nearest mine trembled. I pressed my fingers over his paper-thin skin gently. After a moment, the tremoring settled. He shifted.

"Hope they've been treating you well. I tidied up your socks. And your shirts. Was there a mouse in there you'd tried to catch? I remember that one we couldn't find for days in the old house, chasing the stupid bugger about. Then something began to smell, and stunk us out so bad we pulled the house apart. Turned out the thing was nesting in Gran's chair, the one with the fuschia wings on the back? She loved it. You didn't. Bloody glad to have a reason to throw it away."

I grinned at the memory, even though he couldn't. So I remembered for us both.

"Has that guy been into your jelly beans again? I didn't see your jar in your room. I'll make sure they find it, get you another one. I brought some with me. They're stashed under your pillow. Is that why you tore the drawer apart? Looking for your jellies?" I shook my head, leaning on his chair. The orderly from before motioned to me. "I'll be back in a minute, Dad. This idiot wants to speak to me."

"You're a good boy, Peter. Always was a good boy." I started as Dad spoke, his hand patting mine.

He turned back to the window, and I was glad he didn't see the tears forming that threatened to fall. I squeezed my eyes shut, squeezing his hand carefully and crossed the room to where the orderly stood, watching.

"Peter. It's good you're coming in to see him. He misses you. Talks about you all the time. Now, the jelly beans. We had to take them away. Caused a fight with another patient. Maybe bring him something nice next time, alright?" He gave me a false, bright smile I was glad the residents would never recognise.

I thought of the jellies I'd slipped beneath Dad's pillow, and glared at the skinny fucker screwing with my Dad's remaining life. He lost his smarmy grin in a hurry.

"My name's not Peter."

My trailer had been trashed by at least one other occupant in my absence. The fighters loped out of the way fast when I walked through the parking lot. The trailers had been moved recently; no grass grew through the wheels or the blocks propped beneath the hitch at the front.

I unwound my knuckles as they scattered, peering inside. My fake life was scattered across the floor. Damn. I'd have to actually tidy, make it look like I cared about the place. Red leaned against the dented side of my trailer.

"Get out of here." I waved her away, stomping inside. Her being here could be a good or bad thing. Good, if there was something I could use in the case; bad if she just wanted to get laid by a sweaty fighter who smelled better than her boss' manky office.

Red tottered up the stairs, ducking into the small space and perched herself on the edge of my bed. "I wondered when you'd be back."

She pouted, wiggling her boobs at me. They swayed in their enclosure, a candy-pink dress a little longer than her usual one, though the fact it barely covered her breasts probably made up for it. Her obvious line was anything but sexy.

My hand clenched, still able to feel Jen's slim throat in my grip, the way she automatically arched into my touch without thought. Her need, unassuming and submissive. *That* was sexy as hell. Not this.

"Up. Out." I reached to remove her bodily from the trailer, but she held up her hands, a piece of paper sticking up between two fingers.

I didn't move to take it. "What's this?"

"What you're looking for." She didn't smile, pointing her talons in my direction. I sighed, tugging the slip free.

I read the address, *underground* listed as the level. "What the hell do I want this for?"

"So you have another place to fight. Maybe become part of their team."

I snorted. "I don't do teams." I held my arms out, encompassing the entirety of my caravan. "As you can see."

"Someone wants you to."

I stilled. "Who?"

"A man I know. Call the number, Black." She stood, raking her fingernails from my shoulder to my wrist. I kept my face blank, though it stung like hell and resisted the urge to see how far I could throw her across the bitumen outside my trailer.

"Sure." I stood stock-still, watching, waiting for her to get out of my space.

"Can I look after those for you?" She tapped my damaged fists, clenched, so they didn't strangle her.

"No, I have– enough to look after them here."

She nodded, her nails drifting to the waistband of my pants. "What about here?"

Get your fucking claws off me.

"Thanks. I'm good." I deported her outside, closing the door in her face. She huffed on the other side, marching off across the carpark, her spiked heels clicking an erratic staccato on the uneven ground.

I watched from a side window as she knocked on another trailer door, maybe twenty metres away. I shook my head.

Fucking unbelievable.

Flicking my phone into my hand, I switched off the lights, sending him a message. My phone vibrated in my hand a moment later.

"I need to get you out." There was an urgency to Liam's voice I couldn't ignore.

"What? I've spent all this time getting back in, getting you answers," I muttered, my hand over my mouth and the phone. This was a call I shouldn't have taken here, but ghosting Liam wasn't on my to-do list.

"When they connected me, they connected to *all* of me. But you're done. Out. Now."

"I'll get out when the job's done," I hissed down the line.

Liam sighed on the other end. "You remind me of someone."

"I used to be partner to that someone," I reminded him.

"Yeah. Well, if you won't come out, then I'll come and get you."

"I don't need a babysitter, Liam. And you can't do that. Not now."

"No, you need a partner. And while yours is off caring for his pregnant wife, you're stuck with me."

I grunted; there really was no arguing with the man.

"Fine, but you're the wife."

Liam laughed outright. I started; it was the first time I'd heard him do it.

"See you tomorrow, Black."

CHAPTER ELEVEN

JENNY

My feet bounced on the concrete, chilled air swirling around me as I stared down the empty driveway. Chad had left shortly before midnight. I'd finally caved to his demand to see me, guilt gripping my ego and giving it a good thrashing as he walked up the drive. I made him park around the back of the block, tracing his route on my phone.

His footsteps echoed too loudly up the steep concrete, and I wondered if I hadn't made a mistake in letting him come around during night hours. Or at all. His passage during daylight hours would have been lost in the constant roar of traffic.

My desire to see someone from my former life greatly diminished as he waddled up the drive, puffing and sweating by the time he reached the top. I knew I was breaking Theo's trust, and that killed me. Whatever was happening between us, he was right to demand that I listen to him. If not for my sake, then for my daughter's. He deserved better.

However I looked at it, it felt like cheating.

"Baby chick," my brother greeted me with a grin.

He stood the same height as me, dressed in the same faded jeans he always wore, but the leather jacket gleamed across his shoulders, reflecting the full moon. A thin scar on the side of his face warping his smile. I ran my fingers over it with a frown and pulled him into the house, locking everything tight behind us.

He gripped my hand tight for a second, then headed straight for the fridge.

"Don't they feed you in your new job?" I asked, his head buried between the bottom shelves.

"Sometimes. Sometimes not. No beer?"

I shook my head. "I don't drink often."

"What about your new man?"

I started. "What makes you think there's a man?"

I didn't say *mine*, as I doubted anyone could claim Theo, though a little niggle in my head reminded me I wanted him to claim *me*.

The grip on my heart lessened as Chad reappeared, clutching a bottle of lemonade and my leftovers for Theo. I bit my lip but said nothing. Nothing that would further incriminate myself when my conscience was already screaming that this was wrong. Apparently, I had taken to breaking all the rules.

The things that Wayde Logan did to your head, even from afar.

What had Theo called it? A total mindfuck. I snorted. Regret welled in my chest, but Chad was here now, and I had missed him.

Sort of.

I missed his ex-wife more — another thing to shake off.

I'm a terrible sister.

Chad eyed me, mutilating my leftovers with a fork. "So no man, eh. Right."

"What's that supposed to mean?" Frowning, I followed him into the living room. He took up the lounge, short legs stretched in front of him.

"Knew you wouldn't last long without Paul. You'd need someone to help pay for your brat."

I opened my mouth to argue and found I couldn't. Nothing I wanted to say could actually *be* said, so I stayed silent and let him come to his own assumptions.

The old adage of *an ass of you and me* bounced around my head. I just couldn't work out which was which.

"I'm glad you think so highly of me," I said finally, staring out the window, already wishing he would leave.

I can't talk to you about me, about Ashley, or any part of my mundane life. I've broken trust with the only man in my life who sees me.

Looking back at my brother, his rounded chest straining against a stained t-shirt visible beneath his unzipped jacket and knew I'd made a huge mistake.

"Always, baby chick."

"Don't call me that. Tell me about your job."

I zoned out while he rattled on, playing with my phone. The screen flicked every time I tapped it, the numbers ticking by. After twenty of the slowest minutes I'd ever experienced, I rose, stretching. Chad stared at me, suspiciously.

"Are you kicking me out?"

"Yeah. I need to sleep," I lied, attempting to look haggard. It wasn't a stretch.

Chad slapped my shoulder, leaving a stinging area that took up most of my back. "Waiting for that man, eh? I'm gone, I'm gone." He stumbled out my door, disappearing into the night faster than he'd arrived.

I closed the garage, spending the next hour guiltily eradicating any trace of my brother's presence in the house. I even went as far as spraying freshener in the lounge, then had to open the windows when I inhaled the lot.

Then I sat, my phone tumbling between my hands with the screen blacked out, and waited.

Theo's car pulled silently up the drive. I didn't know how he did it, but the motor never revved. If I hadn't been looking for him, I wouldn't have known he was in the house until he was standing next to me.

I hovered at the kitchen bench, rearranging junk mail. He stepped inside the house, closing the door behind him. It shut silently.

As though he wasn't really here at all.

Theo paused, his jacket hanging from his hand. Though I couldn't see the track of his gaze, I knew he watched me. My hands stilled, then dropped.

My omission of guilt.

I'd broken his trust. And lying had never been my thing. Nor revenge, or games. Even when I'd smelled another woman on Paul after his diagnosis, I hadn't tried to convince him to stop. I didn't live life with a death sentence hanging over my head; how could I judge someone when I didn't walk in his shoes?

"How'd your fight go?"

He snorted, placing his jacket on the benchtop. Moonlight slanted through the window, lighting on olive flesh, hard muscle defined beneath the curves of each sculpted area. "It was...short."

"Yeah?" I swallowed, trying not to perv. *Fail, Jen. Epic fail.* "So how come you're covered in bruises, then? And what happened here?" I moved around the island bench, tracing a long gash over his pecs that disappeared into his singlet. He smelled of sweat, but there was nothing stale about him. He just smelled like...him. Home.

"I let him come in close so I could get back here faster."

You didn't say come home.

Because it's not his home.

"I'm grateful." I pressed a hand to his side, pushing him out of my way. "Move. I need to get you an ice pack."

"Jen. I had a thought—"

"Move first. Think later." I pushed again, this time with both hands, but he didn't budge. I huffed, pressing both hands on his chest, looking up into his shadowed face.

His gaze dark, he held mine for a moment, his hands circling my wrists. My breath caught, I froze, but he pulled them away from his chest. I let the breath out softly.

"I'm sorry. Let's start again—"

He swung me in a semi-circle, still gripping my wrists, to pin me between him and the bench, the tops of his thighs pressed to mine. My breath left me in a whisper, or a whimper. His nostrils flared, his only visible reaction to mine.

"You wanted time, and I promised you I'd give you that. But you didn't like what I offered then, so I'm going to offer you something else. Once. Do you hear me?"

I nodded, my lips forming my agreement, but nothing came out. I hummed softly instead. He released my wrists, placing them back on his chest. I stayed frozen, torn between wanting to run from this predator of a man that he'd suddenly become, or stay. And become his victim.

His eyes hooded as he stared down at me, not an inch of him forgiving in any way. My stomach curled as he pressed the full length of his body against mine. His heart beat beneath my hands, steady, but maybe a little faster than normal for him.

Or maybe I imagined it.

Theo's head dipped until his mouth grazed mine, my lips tingling. I clutched at the desire to rise up on my toes, to press my mouth against his and taste him. To have him take my worries away for one perfect moment.

But this wasn't a moment for taking.

He spoke, looking straight into my eyes, his lips touching mine with every word. Tingles spread over my body until every nerve-ending raged with desire.

"One night. I'll give you one night, Jenny." My name tumbled from his lips into mine, coated in pure sin. "That's what you want, isn't it?"

I gave the barest hint of a nod, my lips just brushing his. My world narrowed to watching his mouth move.

"Yes," I whispered.

His lips curled in a snarl, or a growl. I couldn't tell when he was so close, *too close*, but either way, it was sexy as hell.

Theo's fingers drew a line from my waist idly along my spine until his hand cupped the back of my head. I leaned back into his touch, my eyes drifting closed. Safe and wanting at the same time. Everything about this man was so contradictory, made *me* so contradictory. His fingers pressed into the base of my skull, turning against tight muscles in slow circles.

"Answer me properly."

I opened my eyes. He leaned over me, looking directly into them. I swallowed, but I couldn't move, the prey beneath the wolf.

"Yes, Theo. I want you." My tongue tripped over the last word, heat flushing my cheeks, but I didn't look away from him.

I couldn't.

His gaze pinned me in place, the raw hunger reflected in them sending thrills of desire racing over me.

I wanted that hunger directed at me. In his eyes, in his touch. I wanted him to fuck me with it, tearing me free of this place where I was marking time.

My beautiful distraction.

"If we do this, it will be one night. Is that clear? Only one. I come back to the job the next day. You don't touch me, you don't kiss me."

"Unless it's to heal you. After the fights," I blurted, the sudden loss of something I hadn't had yet spurring my speech.

His lips curled again, but this time with the hint of a smile.

"If you like," he said off-hand, as though it were nothing to him.

Perhaps this is nothing to him.

My breath caught again, but I didn't believe it.

"Please," I whispered, unsure what I was agreed to, or was begging for.

"One night. It will be rough, and it will be filthy. I promise you, Jen." His lips traced the shape of mine. I inhaled, sucking his breath deep into me. His thumb brushed back and forth at the base of my skull. "Do you agree to that?"

I swallowed, barely able to think. My hands trembled. I clenched them over his heart, willing control of myself. I knew he saw my reaction; a harsh laugh brushed over my already flushed cheeks.

"Yes, I agree," I whispered.

Eyes hooded, he leaned into me, removing the fine barrier of air between us. His hands tangled in my hair, his fingers closing around my throat as his mouth crashed down on mine.

CHAPTER TWELVE

BLACK

Jen's mouth gave beneath mine, parting beneath the onslaught of my kiss. My rough handling of her was intentional; if she shied away from me now, what I had planned between us would never work.

Her curves fit perfectly to my body. I hardened past a painful point just at the feel of her, the anticipation of her moans beneath me encompassing me in infatuation.

This is a bad fucking idea.

I hid it from myself. Pretending I was giving in to her desires and not my own. The want, the *need* to have my hands curved around her naked skin. To hear her scream as she came while I was buried to the hilt inside her.

I couldn't focus, couldn't think about anything but her.

What was it about this woman that made me so damned possessive of her? The image of her telling Logan where to go even as he waved a gun in her face tented my pants. That she could drive that fear so deep down that she was able to stand before a psychotic fucking bastard, able to get up when he knocked her down and do it again.

This is a woman I can love.

I'd protected Mila for years after her trauma with the prick, but despite her will to keep moving each day, I'd never felt more than brotherly love for her. When Cal first came on the scene, I'd gotten riled. Especially when he started screwing with the layers of protection I had put around the girl, but I'd never wanted her. Not once.

Not like I wanted Jeny.

Her hands curled around my neck, her body arching into mine as I kissed her brutally, bruising her soft lips, demanding she open to me. I groaned at her eager response, curving my hand to the back of her neck, barely restraining the need to spin her around and hold her down with it while I fucked her over the bench.

This woman does bad things to me.

And I never wanted her to stop.

I broke the kiss with a groan, catching her chin when she leaned into me, seeking my mouth with her own. I curled my fingers around her throat in a loose but firm cage, preventing her from leaning closer. She mewled, straining against me, her pink lips swollen, their colour deepened from the way I'd fucked her mouth with my tongue. And she wanted more.

My smile threatened, but I held it back. This brave, sexy kitten of a woman hadn't been afraid of Wayde Logan. Why the hell would she fear me?

Did I want her to fear me?

Some small, sadistic part of me did.

I wanted to watch her backing across a room as I stalked her, to see my own want reflected in her. To feel her tremble beneath my hands, the small amount of uncertainty when I ordered her to strip.

"Good." I stepped back, my hand still around her throat while I retreated behind the wall I'd built between me and the rest of the world.

It wasn't there so no one could get in; it was there so I couldn't get *out*.

Jen froze, her eyes the only part of her alive, and I was drowning in them. I dropped my hand, letting her collect herself.

You're not touching her, so you don't fuck her right now.

But we weren't the only ones in the house.

Jen tilted her head back, closing her eyes. I watched in fascination as she wavered, breathing deeply. Like she was coming down from a high.

And the addiction was *me*.

Her eyes opened slowly. She stared at me with a dozy, heavy-lidded gaze, pushing herself away from the bench. I planted my feet as she approached, stopping just shy of touching me. Heat radiated from her small, curved form, the air changed between us. Her cheeks were thinner than before. Maybe a bit of playtime would be good for her, after all. I needed the justification in my head.

Her hands found the hem of my tee, tugging it upward.

"Not now, babe. You'll have to wait."

Her eyes narrowed. "I'm not that desperate for your attention, Theo."

Little liar.

"I told you to call me Black."

127

"When you kiss me with the intent to fuck me, *then* I'll call you that, but not before. You'll have to wait."

The sassy minx threw my own words back at me. I smothered a smile, knowing I'd made the right choices with her. She tugged the material of my shirt again.

"What are you doing?"

"I need to fix your back, or you're no good to me." She reached up and slapped my shoulder sharply.

I swallowed back another groan, this time for a different reason. Pain spiked across my shoulders, and I conceded she had a point. Shucking my shirt over my head and ignoring every nerve ending that screamed its protest, I straightened. Jen's eyes tracked over my torso, stopping at the waistband of my jeans.

Her small hands curled around the material, her fingers dipping just inside the material, brushing my skin. My dick twitched at the thought of her hands on me, and when she looked at me with glowing eyes, I knew she saw it.

"Sit down," she murmured, tugging at me by the edge of my jeans, walking backwards to the table. My hands closed into fists at my sides, my eyes holding hers. I watched her swallow and knew the wall I'd erected between us was thinner than I wanted it to be.

She pressed me into the chair she'd pulled out, ready. I sat, splaying my legs as I leaned forward, planting my elbows on my knees. Jen rattled about behind me, then the infernal balm was on my back. I grunted as she rubbed at a spot.

"This one's tight."

"Yeah." I twitched beneath her deft fingers. "How do you always find those ones?"

"There's a big red mark here where the other guy clocked you."

"Ahh. That will do it."

"Why did you let him in again?"

"Because I wanted to get home to you. Ahh fuck, woman. Careful."

"Sorry." Her voice was laced with unvoiced laughter.

"Minx." The corners of my mouth crooked up. I smoothed them before she could see me smile.

"It's good you wanted to come...home."

I twisted my neck, earning myself a light slap. I rubbed my stinging neck as a cold pack was slung over one shoulder.

"You should know that by now." My voice came out much lower than I intended. Jen's hands stilled.

After a moment she resumed her work, running her fingers over my muscles, digging in where she found a knot. All the tensions I held from work, the fights, whatever was between us dissipated. We fell into a comfortable silence as she worked.

My eyes closed from the bliss she offered, from too many sleepless hours. I blinked at the microwave clock, releasing I'd been dozing for the last few minutes. Reaching back, I caught her wrists loosely. Jen's movements halted.

"You should go to bed."

Her hands wound around mine, squeezing gently. "So should you."

I thought of her in my bed, waking next to me with those same dozy eyes. I couldn't think when she looked like that. I shoved the image aside; we could never be more than what I'd promised her. But before that happened, I had to tell her. I tugged at her fingers.

"Go sit on the sofa."

She frowned. I ran a hand over my hair, pushing it back. Meaningless words ran about in my head, but there were a few home truths we needed to talk about. I huffed out a humourless laugh, steeling myself for her pity and moved to the sofa.

Jen perched on the edge of the cushion, twisting to look back at me. Confusion clouded her eyes.

"Come back here."

I found her waist with my hands, tugging her back beside me. She shivered, pressing into the back of the sofa, her head tilted back as she looked up at me.

"I'm not sure what you—"

"I can't have a family," I said the words flatly. They hovered between us for a long moment while Jen mulled them over. She opened her mouth once, then closed it, waiting. I took a breath. "Nearly twenty years ago, I was married. We had a few years together, maybe a little longer than we've shared a roof."

I remembered Jen's comment about how long marriages lasted and realised I was one of those statistics.

"You've mentioned," she said softly. Her tone held no judgement. It wasn't in her.

I nodded. "What I didn't mention was that we conceived. Angela– it was all fine, and then one night she—" My throat closed, and I couldn't say anything else.

That night had lost me what little family I had. We might have stayed together for another year, but between us, everything had changed.

Jen's hand covered mine. I stared into her eyes, luminous even in the shadow.

"I can't say I understand that, but...I don't know if it helps, but I can't have a family either. No more than I have now." She gave a bitter laugh, her eyes never leaving me. "I'm the opposite. I– I can't conceive. At all. We tried, Paul and I. But when we found out I couldn't, he turned to other...avenues. Then he had a heart attack, out of nowhere. Completely fit man, and... I lost him." She gave a one-shouldered shrug, her eyes dropping to study her hands.

"Christ, Jen." And here I'd thought it was my sob story to tell.

My hands wound around hers, tracing her slim wrists. She nodded, still not looking at me. I kissed the top of her head, and she looked up in surprise.

"I'm sorry. I shouldn't have told you that," she whispered.

I cupped her cheek, stroking it with my thumb. Her eyes closed, she leaned into my touch. That she let a rough, broken man comfort her was more than I could bear. She looked so beautiful, all soft lines and love.

I leaned in to kiss her gently, already off the lounge by the time her eyes flew open, searching for me. She rose, unsteady. I slipped a hand around her waist, pulling her gently into me. Her arms wound around my shoulders, her body pressed to mine. Slowly, I pulled away, gathering her hands in mine to kiss her fingers.

"I'll lock up." I waited as her hands stilled in mine, her breath brushing my cheek as she rose on her to kiss me. My hands grew cold as she withdrew hers.

"Goodnight, Black."

I watched her shadow retreat along the hall. She disappeared into the gloom, and it wasn't until I'd stood and stretched that I realised which name she'd used.

I waited outside for Danny. Jen pottered in the house, banging things about louder than usual. The house's regular serenity had been broken by the proposal I'd voiced last night. I hadn't spoken to her, leaving the house before she got up, chicken shit that I was, drinking my protein shake in the shadows of the drive.

Traffic filled the street below, the city awakening after its never-ending night. It took me far too long to remember it was Friday. There would be a fight tonight, probably the one Red had suggested, and I'd know when to turn up about an hour ahead of time if the prior fights were anything to go by.

The less notice given to the fighters, the less time the cops had to find out the where and when of the fight. Unless, of course, we were already in there.

Danny turned sharply on to the drive, his feet pounding the concrete. I opened the garage door with the remote in my pocket, not saying a word. The big man followed me in.

"I'll be an hour. Two tops." I eyed him, draining my shake.

"I got you, man. Brought stickers for your girl."

I turned to say *she's not my girl* when his words caught up with me. Sheets of unicorn stickers covered his smooth hands. I sneered.

"Good to know you have to buy her loyalty."

"I'm not above a good bribe for a pretty girl." He grinned, wiggling his eyebrows.

Pretty boy is begging for a throwdown.

After I'd finished with these fights, I knew where to book my next stress relief.

"That's *my* pretty girl you're talking about," I growled. "Just keep them safe and have your fucking brain turned on."

Danny raised an eyebrow, his hand on the kitchen door. A light lit in his eyes, he slapped my back. "I got you, bro."

With a saucy wink, he disappeared into the house, leaving me seething and wishing I'd called Cal. Or Micah. Or Liam. I didn't have to worry about him — he'd settled into his relationship with Laura with an ease no one had expected. Anyone but that upstart of a shit. To be fair, I was sure he did have good qualities. Pity he chose not to use them around me.

It was good to drive again. If I wasn't on the clock, it would have been nice to have the time to just cruise for a few hours, leave everything else behind.

But Jen was counting on me. In more than one way. I headed into the office with the singular aim of pissing Liam off a little more.

The fire escape door refused to open; who locked an *emergency exit* for fuck's sake? I grumbled to myself, glad to be back in my regular element of *cranky asshole* as I waited for the elevator. Micah joined me, silently waiting. The bulky, younger man displayed more patience than I did as I tried the fire door again.

"Why won't this thing open?"

"Training Day."

"What the hell is training day?"

Micah's head turned a fraction of an inch as the elevator doors opened, shooing me inside.

"You're like a mother hen," I grumbled.

Micah gave me a bemused smile, rolling his shoulders and wrists. The giant of a man took up most of the elevator space. I leaned against the opposite wall.

"That's an interesting image." He stared at the doors as they closed in front of us. "Ally's learning to pick locks."

I turned to stare at him, incredulous. "She can't pick a lock?"

We were the cream of the task force units, and we'd hired someone who couldn't pick a fucking lock? The fire escape door was pretty basic; there was no way Cal would let her take on a case if she didn't own all the skills the rest of us had. It would likely put the rest of us in danger, not just her.

The team worked as a team because we had trust. Loyalty might be the biggest factor, but reliability came a close second. If we weren't there to defend each other in times of need, that placed each member in a potentially dangerous situation. That happened more than I liked to admit in recent times, and a weak link on the team didn't sit well with me.

Having one of us stuck in a stairwell in our own building didn't sit well.

"How long's she been at it?"

The elevator pinged as it hit our floor. "Since five."

"This morning?" I knew the time, but I checked my phone anyway. "That was two fucking hours ago. Did he get her up at dawn?"

"Nah. They trained all night."

"I don't want to know why."

My estimation of Ally's competence depleted with each passing moment. The elevator doors opened. Micah crossed the room in long strides, his gait unhurried despite his natural speed.

Danny better watch his ass with that one, or he'll have Cal's job ripped out from under him before he gets promoted into it.

I knew Cal was grooming Danny for his job; I just didn't like who he'd picked to do it.

The fire escape door was closed at the top of the stairs. My hand extended to grab the handle to check it before my brain caught up. I withdrew my hand, eyeing the door and the imagined person behind it, following Micah into the office.

My head down, I worked until Cal came in. The fire escape occasionally elicited thumps and curses. I frowned at my screen. "When is she going to give up?"

Cal sent me a tight smile, checking a stopwatch on Danny's desk. "She won't."

I shook my head. "Listen, Jen needs...time."

"We talked about that."

"Yeah, so, tomorrow night. Can you stay with Ashley?"

Cal lifted his head, his fingers pausing mid-type. "The whole night?" he asked with a raised eyebrow.

"Yeah." I scratched the side of my nose with my middle finger extended.

Cal's face pinked, his lips twitching. I glared at him. He just leaned back, folding his arms across his chest. "Anything you want to tell me?"

"Fuck off. You can't talk."

"That was a long time ago."

"Not that long. You're having a baby," I reminded him.

"Mmhh." With a straight face, Cal returned to his work. I glared at my screen a little longer, sorting through my files from the investigation and updating what I knew.

Finally, I finished up, running my hands over my hair, slicking it back.

The fire door swung open with force, banging the wall behind it. I winced, refusing to look. Ally tumbled through it in my peripherals, a slash of white amongst the reception area's beige.

"Did it!" she yelled, waving something that clinked.

I dragged my eyes from my screen to her, my mouth agape at the chain of randomly assorted locks dangling from her hand, a collection of handmade wire loops in the other. My gaze flicked to the door, covered with new locks, top to bottom, and back to her. Some even I didn't recognise.

Cal pressed the timer. "Three hours and small change. Nice work. You gonna get started on the bottom door now?"

"Do I get to pee first?"

"Yeah, as long as you make me coffee."

"Piss off. I'm not your receptionist any more, Cal."

"Yeah, you were a pretty shitty one," he laughed.

She grinned back, heading into the bathrooms. I stared after her.

Cal glanced over to me. "What, did you think it was only one lock?"

He returned to his work, a sly grin hinted at on his face. Behind me, Micah was silent. I had a feeling Ally would fit in just fine.

CHAPTER THIRTEEN

JENNY

I stood in the darkened kitchen, waiting. Cal and Theo talked quietly in the lounge, Cal's eyes occasionally flicking to me. My shoulders squared, I refused to back down. This was *my* choice; well, mine and Theo's. Certainly not Cal's. Who couldn't talk, because he'd done something very similar when he and Mila were watching Ashley only eighteen months ago.

Theo stepped back with his arms folded, staring at the ground. It wasn't his hangdog look; he listened to Cal as his ex-partner and best friend spoke to him, with the occasional nod. Cal's eyes flicked to me again; clearly, I was the topic of their conversation.

Or we were.

I couldn't tell if Cal was telling Theo to look after me or be wary of me. Since the showdown with Logan — I cringed at the dramatic word, but *clusterfuck* was about the only other word that sprang to mind for that particular life-altering event — I hadn't been as close to Cal. Or close to anyone else at all, really.

Except for Theo.

Ashley lay upside down across the lounge next to Mila, a unicorn dangling over her head. I'd already kissed her twice and going back for additional support seemed too obvious. I'd never been needy. She'd been over the moon with the thought of hanging out with Mila and Cal for the night, especially as Mila hadn't been around as often since she'd fallen pregnant.

It occurred to me that other kids her age would have had years of sleepovers, and the only friend my foster daughter had were the cops who were hunting her father.

A childhood could rarely get so screwed up, and she deserved so much more.

Theo finally looked up, holding Cal's gaze. They were of a height together; Theo stood maybe an inch shorter than Cal's six foot four inches. Cal clapped his shoulder, giving him a little shove. The stubbornness that was the man I'd fallen for didn't even budge. I smothered a soft snort. It became a small smile which remained on my face until that thought truly sank in.

I was in love with Theodore Black.

This is never going to work.

I blinked back the fear that mixed with adrenaline in a potent combination, heightening my senses in an instant. Theo crossed the room too fast, reaching to take the small, overnight bag dragging limply from my hand. My nerves stopped working. I stood there, staring at him. My brain ceased working as his brow dipped, his eyes darkening.

A warm hand wrapped around mine, his grip firm, but not constrictive.

"Sure you're okay?" he murmured in my ear, leaning past me to fidget with something on the bench that neither of us needed. "You tell me any time, and I'll bring you back. Or do something mundane." He grinned a little, knowing my answer.

I swallowed, bobbing my head as the warmth of him surrounded me.

This is a really bad idea, Jen.

That fight or flight instinct froze me, torn between wanting to run as far as I could from him, but have his arms wrapped around me at the same time. I pushed anything more away and tried to focus on him.

"I'm fine," I lied. "We're going?" I smiled too brightly. Theo watched me with storm-dark eyes that could see everything inside me, that had since the day he'd been assigned me as our protector.

My sentinel.

"See you when we get back," he called to Cal over his shoulder, not looking at him.

Puffs of glitter sprayed from the lounge room behind his back. I bit back an insane urge to giggle hysterically. Theo's eyes stayed on me the whole time. I gave him a tiny, very controlled and reserved nod. His lips twitched, but his tough facade never cracked as he led me out of the house.

What if it's not a facade? Have I got him wrong?

As soon as the door to the kitchen closed behind me, he pulled me into him. The garage was pitch black; he hadn't opened the door. All I could do was feel him around me. Theo's hand wound into my short hair, brushing small circles over the back of my neck. I shivered, taking the comfort he offered, pressing into him. At the same time, my traitorous stomach clenched and flip-flopped, resulting in a second burst of adrenaline until I was high on the stuff. On him.

"Are you okay, Jen?" He tipped my chin up, though I didn't know what he could see in the darkness, then pulled me back into his chest. "'Cause if this is freaking you out, I'll take you somewhere else. Whatever you need."

"How do you always know?" I whispered into his shirt, pressing my lips to a dip in his muscles just below his shoulder. "You can always tell."

"With you? Yes." His voice held a bemused note.

I nodded into his chest. "Okay. Let's do this."

His fingers turned circles over my cheek, cupping my face in a deeply familiar way. My eyes squeezed shut, I could have stayed like this with him forever. Just standing, being held by the man who'd supported me. I opened them as he pressed the remote, the light let in from the garage door as it rose, blinding me.

Theo's soft laugh surrounded me, drawing a shiver from the bottom of my spine to where his hand cupped my cheek. A hellishly sinful sound that should have been reserved for the bedroom. He opened the passenger door of his car for me. I slipped in, breathing in the spice and leather mix that was all Theodore Black.

The engine purred beneath us as he backed down the drive, fluking a break in the traffic. By the time the road met the river, he'd looked at me half a dozen times sideways, and my nerves were shot to hell.

"Spit it out, whatever it is." I clenched my hands between my knees, pressing my knuckles into the soft material of the black pants I'd chosen. Paired with a fitted, black knit top, it was my entire wardrobe apart from my regular jeans-and-tee daytime uniform.

His head cocked slightly to one side. "If you keep wriggling in that seat, I'm gonna start wondering what else you've packed."

My cheeks heated at his insinuation, but instead of being embarrassed, I laughed outright. "No, it's not that. Though, that could have been fun." My eyes slid sideways, noting the way he stared straight ahead, how his hands clenched the steering wheel. "I just miss driving."

It was his turn to look at me. "Really?"

I nodded. "Nearly two years. I wouldn't even have a licence anymore. Cal took my purse and changed everything after L– After that day."

"Right." Theo swerved into a sidestreet, pulling up sharply. I gripped my seatbelt.

"What are you doing?" I stared as he wrenched up the handbrake. He pulled the car out of gear and jumped out. Had I offended him already? The butterflies were back big time, but this time they were drowning in the sludge of my panic.

My door opened, Theo leaning over me to pop my seatbelt. "Out."

His hands caught my wrists, pulling me against him. His eyes glinted darkly, the stubble of his chin grazing my cheek. The butterflies rioted.

"You want to drive?"

I blinked, realisation washing over me. A wide smile made my cheeks instantly ache. "Hells, yes."

"That's my girl." Theo's fingers caught my hair, freezing me as he tugged on it, pulling my head back. His mouth hovered over mine, a breath apart. He released me, giving a little push.

Exhaling a slightly uneven breath, I walked around the front of the car, sliding into the open door. His seat was still warm. I hesitated over the seat adjustments.

"Do you mind if I—"

He waved, cutting me off. "Go ahead."

"And the mirror?"

"That too."

"Okay. Thank you." I still hesitated, my hands closing on the steering wheel; a familiar friend but one who had been absent for quite a while. And he'd parked me on the side of a hill.

"You okay?" Theo leaned his head back, eyes closed beneath dark glasses.

"It's been a long time," I confessed. "I'm not confident. Especially not in a car like this that I'd never have been able to afford in my life."

Theo's larger hand covered mine over the steering wheel. "Take it slow. Get a feel for it, but trust yourself. You've got this." I stared at the back of his hand, tanned, dark hairs gathered at his wrist, long, white scars covering his knuckles.

A person's story was in their hands, and Theo's had a hell of a one to tell.

I breathed in slowly, nodding and took stock quickly of all the gadgets in his Lexus. The clutch worked smoothly beneath my foot, and with a slight bunny hop, I drove for the first time in years.

The city's suburbs were as beautiful as ever, the darkening sky bringing to life a world of shadows and light, mixing together in a soft haze. Theo let me go where I wanted for a while, then began to give me directions.

After a while, I realised he was taking us in a wide arc to the other side of the city. We drove slowly along a suburban street that overlooked the city. At a gorgeous, old house, he directed me to stop.

"Dad's house," he said softly. "I haven't seen it in years."

I watched as he studied the place, something in his face filled with emotion that was so rare on this hard man. I reached out to squeeze his hand. His fingers curled around mine for a moment, then he shook himself, looking down at our joined hands with a small degree of surprise.

He snorted a laugh and directed me on, further around the suburban streets as the sun set, then into the city itself already lit with a bright nightlife that rarely stopped.

When we stopped at traffic lights, he pointed out a tall hotel that looked more like an executive resort in the city centre. His hand found my knee, squeezing as he tugged my legs apart, sliding his fingers up and down my thigh in a steady rhythm. My mouth dried, but I couldn't say the same for the rest of me.

"You should be driving. I'll crash your car," I whispered, trying for more volume but nothing worked.

Theo sent me an amused grin, squeezing my leg. He returned his hand to my knee, tracing patterns on the inside of it. Strangely, the motion relaxed me. I settled back in the driver's seat with a soft sigh, unclenching the steering wheel as the light turned green.

He pointed out the entry to the underground carpark, leaning over me to swipe a card he dropped in my lap. "Ours. But if you want to leave at any point, if you're not comfortable with me or don't feel safe. Anything at all. Just wave that card at me or say you want to use it, and we'll go home."

I thought about it as the gate slid sideways. "You mean like a safe word?"

Theo snorted. "Yeah. Something like that."

"Is that what tonight is going to be?" The words slipped out before I could fully think through what I was saying. A flush crept up my neck. Theo turned in his seat to observe me, his face falling into shadow, but it was unnerving all the same.

We were deep within the bowels of the building before he answered my question.

"If you want it to be."

Dim lights lit the parking area as I found the space matching the room number printed on the key. I parked his car carefully, desperate not to ruin the thing. My thighs protested as I scooted out of his car, so low to the ground. I closed the door just as carefully.

His hands squeezed my hips, holding me still as the heat of him pressed against my back, a wall of pure muscle. His lips grazed my neck, running along my spine from the scooped neckline of my top up to where my hair started.

My breath caught, I gripped the arm he wound around my waist, pulling me tight back against his body. Every inch of me throbbed with need as he pushed my hair aside, continuing his kisses around my neck to my ear, licking and nipping at the soft flesh there. I moaned softly, my legs jelly against his touch.

"You sure this is what you want, Jen?" he spoke softly into my ear, his lips brushing my skin.

If you keep touching me, I'm going to orgasm in a car park. Loudly.

I nodded, the barest movement, unwilling to break contact with him. "Yes, Theo. I want this. I want you." The last word came out on a breath; I wasn't sure if he would have heard me.

His arm tightened around my middle, hauling my back against him, his erection pressing against the cleft of my ass. Only the thin barrier of my pants and his jeans were between us.

It was nowhere near enough.

My body ached, his breath on my skin stirring reactions I'd never felt until he'd touched me. I had no illusions that this was an act of charity on his part.

"I told you what to call me," he growled in my ear.

"Yes, Black."

"Better."

He released me, my world spinning as he stepped away, grabbing my bag. My hands found the roof of his sedan, I gulped deep breaths to recover from whatever the hell he'd just done.

I chanced a look over my shoulder. He stood a few feet away, his face closed and hard. Determined.

If that was a taste of what he has planned, I am totally out of my depth.

He waited a few steps away, my overnight bag hanging from one hand. Swallowing my anticipation — mixed with no small amount of fear that the situation was already out of my control — I straightened my shirt, flicking hair out of my face. A quick breath and I was ready to face him, catching his eye with a cheeky grin.

If you think you can put me on the back foot, Black, I will match you, stroke for stroke.

His face never changed, but his eyes lit that tiny bit, and I knew I'd piqued his interest. The key would be keeping it, so whatever he wanted from tonight wouldn't be overwhelming. Well, for one of us.

He walked beside me, gesturing to a bank of elevators at the far side. My heart in my throat, I caught his hand.

Such a simple gesture, but the fear of rejection — to be more than a sex toy for the night, even though it was essentially what I'd begged him for — sat heavy in my stomach.

His fingers flexed, closing automatically around mine. Theo tugged me closer, drawing me to him, his thumb rubbing the sensitive skin inside my wrist. A shiver shimmied over my shoulders, as though his touch was already beneath my shirt.

Is it possible to be fully clothed but feel naked?

Apparently, next to a man like Theodore Black, I could.

His hand hovered at the small of my back while we waited for the elevator. Not quite touching, but there, all the same. My awareness of him heightened with every moment.

The elevator doors dinged, opening. I stepped inside, the doors closing behind Theo, but he didn't turn to face them; instead, he faced me. I retreated in the very small space until my back hit the rail behind me. He stalked the few steps between us, dominating the space, crowding against me.

His hands slapped the mirrored surface either side of my head, and he stared at me until I tilted my head back, giving him an invitation.

Then he dipped his head and kissed me.

CHAPTER FOURTEEN

BLACK

She tasted like cream and strawberries. Jen's mouth opened beneath mine, her tongue exploring despite the demands of my own. I wasn't gentle with her. They were long kisses, a compromise between my need to take everything from her and wanting to start slow, so I didn't scare her.

The taste of her was overwhelming; my palms pressed flat to the glass behind her, only my mouth contacting hers. Her hands clenched into my shirt, gripping it tight, her moans hardening me in an instant.

The elevator dinged. I dropped my hands, straightening my shirt and stepped back beside her. The doors opened, two couples entering the lift. The women had their heads in their phones, but both men stared at her. I snuck a brief, sideways look at Jen. Pink stained her cheeks, the flush travelling down to her decolletage, disappearing into the low neck of her fitted top.

I knew she'd dressed for me, but seeing the two men staring at her as she stared back, uncertain and flustered, was easily the highlight of my day. The taller of the two glanced from Jen to me, a smile on his face; the shorter took one look at me and turned around in a hurry. They got out a few floors up, leaving us alone in the lift.

I collected Jen's bag, watching the lights climb to our floor. Jen glanced my way a few times, but I didn't look at her. If I managed to keep her on the back foot, her experience would be unforgettable, a maelstrom of sensation and arousal she would remember forever.

I hoped it would be enough to tide her over for the nights I wouldn't be sharing her bed, until she had her life back, or had one created for her.

My teeth clenched at the thought. I hadn't realised neither Cal nor Danny had talked her through the witness protection process or discussed her expectations. Perhaps they'd expected me to do it, but it wasn't my forte. I was just the grunt protecting her.

Two fucking years and no one had explained to her what the hell was going on. The fury that was always ready to be unleashed inside me moved. I promised it we would give her everything she needed to make up for it.

The elevator stopped at our floor. Jen grabbed her bag before I could, wandering out into the corridor. I took the bag from her grip when she floundered on which way to turn, heading down the hall. The heavily-carpeted floor muffled our footsteps, but I knew she was still behind me.

Even without looking at her, I always seemed to know where this woman was.

She hesitated at the door when I opened it, motioning her through. Her eyes held mine for a long moment, indecision mixed with a measure of anticipation flitting across her beautiful face.

I took a step, and then a second. I let the door close quietly behind me, watching her venture into the suite, then flicked the additional lock hard. It snapped into place, effectively sealing us in together.

As predicted, Jen whirled, those soft lips parted in a small gasp. I wanted to cross the room, wrap myself around her and kiss her until she moaned, pliable, in my arms. Clenching my teeth on my tongue, I bit down, the pain a distraction that brought me back before I did just that, though the desire burned bright within me.

Not yet.

I crossed the room in slow, long steps, walking right by her. A soft breath was her only indication of relief — *or was it disappointment?* — at her reprieve. I placed her bag on the table, letting her take in the place. She walked deeper into our room, her eyes flitting from the full-sized kitchen to the open-planned lounge area with a dining table off to one side. A large, empty space stood between it, and the massive, king-sized, four-poster bed, complete with a black quilt. I'd requested that specifically.

Jen turned in a circle, hugging her elbows around herself. "Is this– is the unit paying for this?" I watched her thoughts run across her face, delight that turned to terror and embarrassment. She thought she was being selfish; I thought she was being human. But this one was *my* choice.

I smirked, leaning back on the table. "You mean, is Liam funding our dirty weekend?" The flush in her cheeks deepened, her eyes widening. I let it sit for a second, then put her out of her misery. "I paid, Jen. This is my gift to you for putting up with me for two and a half years."

"That's longer than most people are married," she whispered, staring at me. Her lips were still swollen from our make-out session in the lift.

I laughed, watched her shiver in the centre of the room, alone. Exposed and uncomfortable. I knew she felt it; the way she hugged her arms around herself, constantly turning though her feet never moved.

"True." I straightened, bringing her attention back to me.

I took one step closer, another. She never moved the entire time until I reached her. My hands settled on her waist, heavy. Her head tilted back, those lips parted, though they'd be more swollen than they were now, come tomorrow morning.

I pushed the thought out of my head, sliding my hand around her back and pulling her to me sharply. Catching her jaw, I angled her head the way I wanted it and lowered my mouth to hers. She whimpered before my lips made contact, a soft, sweet breath that completely undid me.

I pulled her up closer, sliding my hand over her round ass, kissing her deeply, slowly. My hand on her jaw controlled the kiss. I stroked the length of her throat with my thumb, pressing gently over her airway. She stilled, trying to draw back for a moment, but when I wouldn't let her, she leaned into me, her breath coming in soft pants.

Her hands slid up my shirt, teasing each button not quite free as she kissed me back. Jen's body arched to press her body the length of mine. Her arms wrapped behind my neck, rising up on her toes.

I crushed her against me, still kissing her slowly, deeply. Her moans did mad things to my brain. I wanted to take her to the bed and love her slowly for the night. For every night.

But I wasn't sure that's what this woman needed. What *I* needed from her.

Now who's being selfish, prick?

My heart pounded. I released her throat, my hands squeezing her, stroking over her body in a frenzy, completely at odds with the way I kissed her. Her curved body pressed against mine, her hips rubbing the front of my jeans, and soon she wasn't the only one moaning.

I broke the kiss with effort, drawing back carefully, wary of startling her. Her eyes still closed, Jen swayed in my arms, her hands sliding around my neck as her head fell back, the picture of bliss.

You are so fucking beautiful.

I was so far gone, I didn't know if I thought it or said it. Her eyes opened, and she stared at me dozily from beneath heavy lids.

Though my dick twitched within its confines, it was my heart that moved.

Fuck me if I haven't fallen in love with her.

I knew I would never forget this moment; it was easily the finest in my life to date. She moaned beneath my mouth, her tongue flicking out to meet mine.

"God, Theo," she whispered.

I grabbed the short ends of her hair, tugging hard. "Black. Tonight you call me Black, and nothing else." I tugged her hair harder when she didn't respond. My growl set off something inside her, her eyes snapping up to meet mine.

"Yes...Black." She gasped the words out. Her face flushed with colour, her small hands reaching back to wrap around my wrist where I gripped her hair, holding, but not trying to pull me away.

I dipped my head to kiss along her jaw, her neck, and across the front of her chest where her shirt dipped low. I licked across the tops of her breasts, her moans the music to the beginning of our dance.

"Good," I murmured, releasing her hair. I cupped her face, kissing her deeply. Her hands coiled around mine, but I stepped back. "Strip."

Jenny stayed stock still. Very slowly, her bottom lip sucked into her mouth, but her clear eyes were steady on mine, and I *knew* she knew what she was doing to me.

"I can't do that," she whispered.

"*Now*," I ordered.

Her hands played with the hem of her top, tugging at the bottom of the material. Tanned skin showed beneath. The hours outside the house had been good for her. She twisted the knitted material in her hands, began to lift it over her head. I stared at the lines of exposed, toned muscle where it met her soft curves. Contradictory and beautiful at once.

My hands clenched at my sides, but tonight was mine with her; there was no way in hell I would rush this.

Slowly, in a very controlled and ordered movement, she stilled and dropped her hands to her sides.

"No." The hint of a smile played at her lips.

I raised an eyebrow, wondering at her game. "No?"

"Mmhmm." She shook her head, her hips swaying a little.

I took my time running my eyes over her. Black, slim pants that tucked into a curved waist, breasts swelling against her stretchy top. Her lips were full in a smooth face, eyes dancing. Inwardly I grinned; the woman knew how to play,

and I fucking loved it. Loved her, too, though I wouldn't —
couldn't — tell her.

"Brat," I growled, my eyes flashing at her. "Come
here."

She shook her head, her eyes widening as I took a
step toward her. She backed up, one small step at a time, but
I knew she wasn't going anywhere.

"No," she breathed.

I smiled, letting the lust I had for her show, and
grabbed her arm, pulling her to me. "You agreed to what I
want tonight. Remember?" She nodded, her lips parted so I
could see the pink of her tongue. God, I wanted to kiss her,
to bury my cock in her mouth, feel her moaning around it.
"And tonight is what I want from you. If you want me to
fuck you, Jen, you do what I say. You come only for me, and
you obey every command, or I walk. Strip."

I released her arm, saw the moment in her eyes when
she made her choice.

Unspeaking, she peeled one garment from her body at
a time. Curves and strength merged in a perfect combination
of who she was. I held my hands still with no small degree of
resolve, though I desperately needed to feel her beneath
them.

The last item of clothing dropped to the floor until
she stood in a puddle of all-black cloth. She stepped out of
it, kicking her low heels across the room. Her shoulders
rolled back, she looked at me, completely open. Something
about her, completely bare, willing to play was far sexier
than all the fancy lingerie in the world.

"Th—" she caught herself, "Black?"

I made her wait a moment longer, then crooked my
finger at her.

Her steps were small, hesitant, and I could see her trying to work out what I was about. This time, I didn't make her wait.

I curled around her, tracing the lines of her body with my fingertips, running them along her spine, delighting when she shivered in response. My lips grazed her shoulders, her neck. With a soft sigh, she tipped her head back, giving me access to all of her.

I breathed hard through my nose, determined not to cave on my own intentions, and continued to kiss along her neck. Her arms rose, wrapping around my neck but I caught her wrists, lowering them gently to her sides. I brushed my thumbs beneath her breasts, drowning in her soft sighs, then walked to the table, around to the other side so I could see her without raising my head. I unholstered my gun, ejecting the clip, and placed it on the table.

My knives came next; each one taken from the custom-made sheath in my belt, laid out in a neat line beside my handgun. I kicked off my shoes and socks, unsheathing two more from around my ankles. Those and their sheaths went on the table too. My cuffs, I let sit in my open palm for a moment, then tossed them across the room in a long arc to land with a jangle on the bed. The silver glinted dully against the solid black cover, Jen's eyes tracking the moment.

She turned back to me with a soft laugh. "You're a walking arsenal. Do you wear these all the time?"

She padded across the hard floor, picking up one of my throwing knives without touching the blade. Completely nude and comfortable with herself, and me.

"Whenever I'm with you." I watched her very carefully test the point of the blade, laying it just as carefully onto the tabletop in its place. "This would scare most women."

"Is that why you did it? To threaten me?" She looked up with a serious face, but her eyes screamed mischief. I grinned back, unable to help myself.

"No. It's so I can grab them if anything happens."

For the first time, she stilled, the uncertainty of before creeping back into her eyes, but for a very different reason.

A real threat, not a playful one.

"Is that likely? Would he—" She broke off, holding my gaze. Watching me to see if I would lie to her.

"Here? No." I shook my head. "Out there? Maybe."

Jen nodded, accepting the truth with grace and ease. She left the weapons on the table, trailing her fingers lightly across the blades as she approached me. Her fingers toyed with the buckle of my belt, running over the thick leather.

I caught her hands, closing my fingers around her wrists and palms, lifting them to her chest and walked her backward to the bed. Her eyes held mine the short journey, though it seemed much longer, her chest rising a little faster with each step. When her knees hit the edge of the bed, they bent by reflex, but I held her up, dropping her hands back to my belt.

Unblinking, she worked the leather open, sliding her palms over my skin. I drew long, even breaths, controlling my growing need for her. She parted the denim, tracing the shape of me with light fingers, pressing up to kiss me. I pulled back, her pout testing my resolve not to devour her on the spot.

She pressed her hands against my waist, turning me, so my back was to the bed, and pushed. I sat back, watching her gaze flick over my shoulder, just the once before she dropped to her knees. She pulled my cock free, lapping at it with her tongue. I closed my eyes, enjoying the sensation of her mouth gliding over me and let her do what she had planned.

She rose off her knees, pressing kisses along my arms as she repositioned me where she wanted, one hand working my cock. It was a good distraction, even if I knew what she was doing.

Within a second she'd managed to line my arms beside, then behind myself. I tilted my head back, her fingers lightly tracing the shape of my cock, making it twitch against her hands, and let her play her game.

Cool metal snapped around my wrists, the cuffs jangling as she secured them. Her body moved over mine, straddling my legs, her soft skin teasing me with her nearness, yet unable to touch. She gave an experimental tug on the chain between my wrists, my eyes snapping open at the same time.

CHAPTER FIFTEEN

BLACK

Jen rose up on her knees, kissing me, pulling back then kissing me again. I growled, nipping her bottom lip into my mouth, biting a little harder than I normally would. She jerked back, her eyes flaring as she caught the depth of my gaze. My fury.

"I hope you're reevaluating that choice, Kitten." I leaned forward into her.

She gripped my shoulders to keep herself from toppling from my lap, her eyes wide. I relented after a moment, already twisting my wrists inside the metal casing without moving my shoulders.

I'd left my wrists turned, so the cuffs didn't close quite as tight, figuring Jen had no experience with them. One side had barely clicked. I wound my wrist about and managed to free it with ease. The second one held firm. I wiggled my fingers into my back pocket for the key, but the damn thing stuck.

Jen straddled me, brushing her drenched pussy over the tip of my cock, rocking her hips as she gave me a lap dance I'd never forget. Blood roared in my ears as I fought to maintain the control I'd promised us both.

I leaned forward, catching her mouth in a quick kiss, and a sharp grin. "I hope you have the keys for those so I can fuck you hard later."

Jen stilled, her hips lining up with me, sucking that bottom lip into her mouth. "Maybe I don't."

She began to lower herself onto me. I moved again, unsettling her balance, my lips brushing her ear. "If you keep going, I'll walk out and leave you here, completely unsatisfied."

Her breath caught, she rubbed her cheek against mine, her body curving around me, undulating, and I couldn't touch her. Every inch of me ached. I inhaled slowly.

"I thought you said no threats," she purred, arching and running her hands over her breasts.

I smiled, letting some of the darkness inside me show to her for the first time. "I'm not threatening you."

Her hands gripped my shoulders, squeezing in a reflex action. She dropped them to her thighs, reaching between us, then slithered to the floor in a single movement, engulfing my cock with wet lips.

I groaned, pushing my hips up. My cock slid into her mouth as she swallowed all of me. Straining against the remaining cuff, I finally managed to extract the key. Trying to work on it when the woman I dreamed about was on her knees before me, proved impossible. I bit my tongue, using the pain to bring me back from the edge. My breath slowed as she set a pace determined to test me.

The cold metal around my wrists warmed fast as I turned it, finding the place I needed to slip the key into. Her tongue glided over my cock as Jen slid her knees apart, bracing her hands on my thighs. Her nails grazed along the pale skin there, she pressed her lips to the top of my cock, sliding her mouth to the base.

My hands clenched into fists at my back, digging my nails into my skin as I willed myself not to come in her mouth. Jen's tongue swirled gently around the head of my cock as she turned those nails on my balls.

Tiny flicks and strokes in time with her quick sucks had me grunting despite my determination not to make a sound. My hips flexed, I swelled in her mouth.

I grunted again, though she hadn't earned that one, twisting the key in the warmed metal at my wrist. Her cheeky gaze met my half-smile, a silent promise of what she *would* earn, later on.

She'd asked me for one night together, but she had no idea how long tonight night could be.

Jen pulled her mouth back as she sucked, a tiny pop as her mouth came free of me. She rose, her cheeks stained a deep red. The flush covered the tops of her breasts, the nipples tight, erect buds. I groaned at her arousal, matching it with my own.

She stood, leaning in to kiss me. I let her, rotating one hand as I slid it free of the cuff and pocketed the key. Schooling my features into the slow burn anger she expected was a challenge when all I wanted to do was to slam her to the floor and fuck her senseless.

Jen stepped back with a small smile, her hips swaying in an invitation she thought I couldn't take.

Let her think she's got me here.

Her hands roamed over her body, her fingers disappearing between her legs for a moment, her head dropping back. Both hands freed, I slid the cuffs into my pocket after the key as her head came back. She didn't bring herself to orgasm, which surprised me, but she'd made me that promise, and apparently, it was one she meant to keep.

Stepping into me, she ran her hand coated with her own juices over me, sliding gently up and down the length of my cock. Her arousal covered us both. I kept my face still, boring my glare into her. She flicked her thumb over the top of my cock. It twitched in her hand, though I managed to keep my hips still, my breath even. Just.

Jen turned on her toes, presenting her back to me. She pressed that cute, round ass against me, bobbing it up and down, my cock sliding between her cheeks. A tiny drop of precum glistened in the slit at the top of my cock. It was a delicious sensation. I let myself enjoy it for a moment, shaking my hands quickly out and waited for her to slide up again.

When she reached the apex of rhythm, I grabbed her hips tight, pulling her back, so the tip of my cock pressed against her pussy.

She squeaked, bucking a little, but I held her firmly where I wanted her. Her hands covered mine. I laughed.

"Did you think that was going to hold me, girl?"

Her answering shudder as I rubbed her over the tip of my cock was all I needed. She was drenched, coating me easily. I slid only the tip of my cock into her, her muscles fluttering around me in her eagerness, but I wasn't letting her off that easily.

She wiggled, trying to slide down onto me but I pushed her forward, rising from the bed. She whirled, her chest heaving as she stared up at me.

"Theo, I—" she started to back across the room.

I didn't move except to crook my finger at her. She bit her lip, her eyes widening with the sweetest mix of uncertainty and desire. One foot stepped in front of the other, but I shook my head.

"On your knees."

She blinked, assessing the distance between us, and I relished the moment she realised I meant for her to crawl halfway across the room.

"I can't—"

"You put yourself over there," I said firmly, "and you started this game, Kitten. Knees."

She nodded, still biting her lip, and very slowly sank to the floor. She hesitated a moment, and I wondered if I would have to give her additional instructions, but she placed her hands in front of her knees, arching her back a little as she looked up at me, crawling toward me across the hard floor.

She reached me, stopping only just before her lips touched my legs, still looking up at me. Her breath kissed my balls. I exhaled slowly. I'd never had to exercise this much control with a woman in my life.

I held out my hand, and she nestled her cheek into it, kissing my palm.

"I'm sorry." She whispered.

I nodded, curling my fingers under her chin to draw her up, so her lips touched my cock. "Clean," I murmured. "But without your hands, this time."

Her lips opened, resuming their rhythm from before. I cupped my hand against the back of her neck, pulling her up the slightest bit onto her toes as she knelt before, just into the realm of uncomfortable. Her eyes closed as she tasted herself on me, hesitant at first, then a little faster.

I eased her back, smiling at her moan when I motioned for her to rise. She shook out her knees silently, attempting to stand still as I looked at her. I leaned forward. A small tremor ran over her when my lips touched her ear.

"Get a chair from the table and put it in the middle of the room."

She stepped back, her eyes on me as she did what I asked and stood by it. I took the time to zip my jeans up, but let the belt hang loose. She looked back to me, her brow furrowed, but she hadn't worked out what I had planned. Yet.

She went to sit, but I caught her arm, stopping her, and sat myself. Jen smiled, placing her hands on my shoulders, lifting one knee to my hip. I let her think she had control, kissing her slowly. She moaned, opening her lips to swirl her tongue against mine, settling against me.

I drew back, brushing my mouth over hers, and guided her hand to my belt. "Pull."

Her eyes snapped open, flaring with alarm as she tried to back away, but my hands wrapped around her upper thighs, preventing her from moving off me. "Trust me," I murmured against her mouth, kissing her again.

Her hands fumbled, the job all the harder as I kissed her deeply, her body moving unconsciously against mine. Finally, the leather snapped free. She froze, burrowing against my shoulder, her eyes squeezed shut as she held it out to me.

"Theo, please, I can't—"

"Drop it."

Her eyes flung open, relief relaxing her face.

"My God, you scared the shit out of me." She slapped my shoulder, smiling.

I let my gaze harden again. "Good."

Sliding one forearm in front of her legs, I flipped her. She squeaked as I lowered her across my lap, her head hanging down to the ground. Her fingertips brushed the hardwood floor. Her toes didn't. I pressed a hand to the small of her back. She shifted, but couldn't really move.

I ran my hand over her rump, tracing the curves with my fingertips. She shivered.

"Theo— Black," she corrected herself, "I said I was sorry."

"Yes, you did."

I lifted one hand, letting it fall quickly. She gave a muffled squeak, cutting herself off.

Good girl.

A pale pink hand print outlined where I'd smacked her. I did the same to the other side, but this time there was no squeak. I experimented, making that beautiful ass she'd teased me with pink. Her body shuddered over and over again. I stroked my hand over her sensitive skin, lightening the blows to faint taps, and slid my fingers between her legs.

She whimpered, arching as I discovered what she liked so much. My fingers coated with her slick fluids, I ran them gently from her pussy to her clit, tapping lightly against her nether lips with my full hand, alternating from side to side, then a little harder.

Jen moaned, bucking against my legs. Each time I slid my fingers over her clit, I parted them slightly, widening the spread of my touch. Shudders tore over her body, her legs trembling, straining as her orgasm built.

Almost there.

"Come, Kitten." The taps came harder.

Circling her clit between my fingers at the top of each stroke, faster until her pleasure broke over her in a wave of moans, her entire pussy pulsing against my hand. Her cries filled the room. Shudders wracked her legs, her thighs quivering as I stroked my fingers over her until her body became boneless over my legs.

I drew her up, wrapping my arms around her and lifted her, carrying her to the king-sized bed. She sank into the pillows, blinking at me with lazy eyes. A light sheen of sweat covered her entire body. I took a moment to rid myself of my clothes and slid in next to her.

"You okay, Kitten?" I murmured against her hair. "We can stop if this is too much for you."

She curled into me, winding her arms around my neck. Her perfect body pressed to mine as she kissed me, straining to be closer to me.

"I asked you for this," she whispered, her voice catching as my hands ran gently over the skin I'd reddened, "please, I need you."

I caught her chin, looking deep into her eyes. My brow furrowed. "Was that the first time you've been spanked in play?"

Her eyes widened, her lip slipping between her lips. I kissed her, tugging it free with my tongue.

"Yes, but– never like that. Ever." She shivered, winding herself closer into me.

"You've never come from it before."

She shook her head. "No."

"But you're shocked you enjoyed the pain?" I guessed, my cock hardening against her stomach as she wriggled the tiniest bit.

"Yes."

I nodded. "Okay."

"Okay—" She yelped as my hand came down firmly over her ass, covering the sound of my flesh on hers. She wriggled wildly as I held her in place.

"Can you do that again?" I asked softly against her mouth, letting my hand fall again.

"Do what?" She whimpered, wrapping her leg around my hip on her side, shimmying to give me access to every inch of her, her lips touching the ink on my chest.

Her breaths came fast, heating the skin there as she mewled against me.

"Come for me again." I slapped her ass twice in quick succession.

Her body, her eyes widening as she rubbed herself against me, slicking both of us with her need. I let the next one hit her pussy. She whimpered, the shiver starting again. My cock sprung free between us. I spanked her once more, and that was all it took.

Her hands gripped my arms tight, wrapping around me, her eyes holding mine as her mouth opening in a silent scream. I caught beneath her thigh, sliding her very slowly the length of me as her orgasm rolled over her. Her muscles clenched around my cock as she pressed down, impaling herself on me. I exhaled sharply, willing myself to hold off my own pleasure as she came around me.

The scent of her intoxicated me. I could barely think as she came down from her high. She sighed her last moan, her head sinking onto my shoulder. I gave her a moment then shifted, meaning to roll her onto her back, but her eyes flew open as my hips flexed, pushing a little deeper inside her.

"Black," she gasped, her voice raw from her moans. Her silky walls fluttered around me again. I nudged her head back, kissing her, flexing deeper inside her. She moaned again, moving with me, sweat pooling in the crevasses between our bodies.

"Christ, Kitten, you're going to kill me," I groaned against her mouth, rocking her gently.

Her walls fluttered again as she moved in time with me, aftershocks of pleasure that grew to something more. Her leg slid around my ribs as I deepened my thrusts inside her, our bodies winding together, every inch of skin pressed together.

Her hips undulating, she clenched tight around me, a deep moan rocking my insides. I slipped an arm beneath her knee, plunging into her hard, fucking her fast, knowing I couldn't hold myself back but wanting to make the last orgasm I gave her to be the strongest.

To remember.

My own need building, I gripped her hips hard, slamming into her as she came around me. One orgasm rolled into another, each wave crested together. I held back as long as I could, then I let her carry me with her, drowning in the feel of her as she screamed my name.

CHAPTER SIXTEEN

JENNY

I woke in the giant bed, tangled in pristine sheets. My body sank deep in the black sheets, sated in a way I knew I'd likely never experience again. Even my mind was clear, for the first time since our time together had begun.

Bright morning light fell across the bed. Sunlight warmed my skin as I stretched, every muscle straining. Between my legs was tender, and my ass still stung from his hand. I smiled with my eyes closed, remembering everything Theo had done last night — what we'd done together. That he'd given me his time when women would fall at his feet whenever he wanted, set something aglow in my chest.

I relived the feel of his hardened body against mine, teasing each other until we fell into oblivion together. Tracing my fingers over the ink on his chest afterwards, though I could barely lift my head from his shoulders. His arms closed around me like a vice, my body revelling against his, free despite the control he levered. Stretching my arms across the bed, I found his side of the bed cool. The single divider between the living area and the kitchen blocked my view of him, though scents of something — *was that bacon?* — drew me from the bed.

A pile of black material lay heaped at the foot of the bed. I picked up the item on top. Slinky, and full of his own brand of male spice, the shirt wasn't mine, but I put it on anyway.

Black stood with his back to me when I emerged from the bedroom. Shirtless, his jeans sat on his hips. A deep line ran the length of his spine, muscle flaring away from it, sculpted into something that was both art and sexy as hell.

"Hey," I murmured, pausing at the edge of the island bench that formed the kitchen. "Can I help?"

Theo turned, his face closed. His slate grey eyes swirled with a storm of emotion he refused to let come out to play. My uncertainty returned full force, rocking me physically. I clutched the edge of the stone bench, a barrier and a crutch.

"It smells really good," I said too brightly and winced.

His expression never changed. Only his eyes gave any hint of the turmoil within him. I took a hesitant step into the kitchen, swallowing as his eyes tracked me, holding to my face. He might have been stone for all the reaction he gave me, nothing of the man who had given me hours of his time, who had trusted me with a hidden side of him.

"Are you going to say anything?" I asked softly as I reached him, not bothering to disguise the plea in my voice. My hands dropped to his belt, just resting there, as they had last night. I might have woken wanting — hoping — to play again this morning, but now, nothing could be further from my mind. I just wanted *my* Theo back. My knuckles brushed the carved muscles of his abdomen. "Theo?"

His hands rose slowly, curling around my wrists with the lightest touch, dropping them back to my sides. He took a step back, his nostrils flaring, his eyes steady as they ran the length of my body and back to my face, his expression dispassionate.

"Why don't you get dressed? We should head back soon," he said. The words soft, an utter contradiction to the coldness of his face. I took a step back, too.

Run, Jen.

The same voice that had told me to run the day I stepped in front of Theo, between him and Logan. For my daughter. This was no less important, not to me. I knew last night had been sex and a whole hell of a lot of fun. But he had carefully planned out our time together, which meant on some level, he cared. How deeply, I couldn't tell, because the stone golem in the kitchen refused to say more than ten words.

That fast, I fired back up.

"After everything, that's what you give me? That's it?"

He folded his arms, massive muscles popping everywhere. That did nothing to soothe my temper, my frustration rising in notches. He followed my graze with a smirk.

"I promised you one night, girl. And that's what we had. One hell of a fucking good ride together. But I have to protect you and your daughter. I can't have you as a distraction." His eyes roamed over me, his raking gaze hungry, giving him away.

I dared take a step toward him again. He watched me with the coiled grace of a great cat. I just didn't know if he planned to launch at me, or away from me.

"I'm always going to be a distraction to you," I said softly, my temper settling in an instant as I read his desire. Theo's gaze returned to my face, bearing the brunt of his cold rage.

"Then I'll find someone else to protect you."

Unfolding his arms, he turned back to the stove. My heart in my throat, I swallowed past it with difficulty.

"Don't." The word tore from my lips before I could stop it. His head turned in my direction, though he didn't look at me. "Please don't change out for someone else. I'll— back off you. Ashley would be devastated."

So would I.

I swallowed that back, too. He nodded.

"I promise. But get changed. Into your own clothes, Jen." A hint of his old humour crept into his words.

I closed my eyes as I turned to obey his command without thinking and fled into the bedroom — anything to keep him in our lives.

We ate in silence, packed in silence, and I waited for him to sort our check out before he escorted me to his car. I hesitated at my door, remembering the way he'd kissed me yesterday, where I stood now. But now, I had a very different man with me. He opened the door for me while I brooded, not even realising he was behind me. I nodded, my energy sinking, sapped away by the emotional turmoil within me.

His hand grazed my lower back. "Get in, Jen. I'll take you home." His voice was low, full of gravel. I looked over my shoulder to find him right behind me, close enough that his breath caressed my cheek. I wanted to lean back into him, to tip my head back on his shoulder and let him kiss me however he damned well pleased.

Hell, I would have let him do anything he wanted to me right there to be back in his arms, to recover the incredible man I knew hid behind his hard exterior.

"Thank you," I whispered. "For everything you've done."

I ducked my head, sliding into the passenger seat, the desire to drive, to have freedom in any form gone.

The drive back was quiet. He played music at a low level, quiet enough to talk over, but I didn't speak, and I didn't listen. The city passed me in a blur until we returned to the house. I walked straight in, not bothering to grab my bag, knowing Theo would get it for me. It might have been a little princess-y, but I was more than a little pissy right now, and the mood suited me.

And we're back to being selfish as hell.

I brushed past Cal, ignoring his questions and headed straight for the unicorns scattered about the living room floor.

Ashley looked up at me, a big grin on her heart-shaped face as her thin arms wrapped around me.

"Mum! I missed you. The unicorns are having a day out." she chattered, looking over her shoulder as Theo entered the kitchen, already snarking at Cal. She waved, turning back to me. "It's salon day. I'm so glad you're back. See, this one has green hoof polish, but this one wants her horn to have more sparkle."

I held back a snort. Barely. "They look like they're having a lot of fun."

"They are." Ashley looked at me. "They went out this morning, and some things might have happened to them, but they came back together, and that's what's important. They're together, and that makes them a family."

Speechless, I let her press a lurid orange pony into my

hands. "This one isn't a unicorn at all, but he feels left out. He wants a horn, but I don't think he really needs one, do you? He just needs to be himself, and everyone will love him because he's fabulous. Don't you think?" She dangled a makeshift horn that might have once been part of a toilet roll in front of my eyes.

"I don't think we need that extra decoration at all," I said firmly, nodding as she discarded it and handed me a pony comb instead. "I think he's perfect just the way he is, and he doesn't need to be anything he's not."

A mug of coffee hovered in front of me. I took it, grateful, lifting my eyes to meet Theo's, knowing he would have heard every word of my short speech. His charcoal eyes held mine, a spark passing between us.

"Thank you," I whispered.

The corners of his mouth quirked. "Any time, Jen."

I settled back at the unicorn salon and let glitter erase my worries while Theo watched the outside world at my back.

CHAPTER SEVENTEEN

BLACK

I'd nearly towed Jen straight back to the bedroom when she arrived in the kitchen wearing nothing but my slinky black under armour shirt. She wore nothing beneath it, the material clinging to where it filled out with her soft curves. Every step she took made the shirt ride a little higher as she approached me, my balls fit to burst. Curves I knew well, had mapped them in my brain in the hours I'd spent worshipping her last night.

And then I'd broken her heart.

One night.

I knew it was a bad deal when I made it. With a woman like her — the perfect mix of sass and submission, a woman capable of trusting herself and her heart with me — who couldn't fall in love with her? I had to be honest with myself; I'd given her my heart a hell of a long time ago.

No woman needed the baggage of my life weighing her down.

She'd managed not to run back to the bedroom when I told her to get dressed and was proud of her for not continuing her hissy fit. I could call it fighting for what she wanted, but it didn't suit the grumpy asshole I was fast becoming.

Jen had left my shirt on the bed, still warm from nestling close to her skin.

Which was where I should have been all morning, tasting every inch of her, cradling that soft, gorgeous body against mine while I made her moan again.

And having to wear the thing when it smelled like her strawberries-and-cream flavour was a whole new level of torture. She sat silently throughout the ride back to the house, not seeming to listen to the radio, although the lyrics of Lady Antebellum's *Need You Now* would have told her what I couldn't.

My mind whirled, torn between the scent of her and the need to crush her against me and knowing my job to look after Jen and her daughter came before my personal feelings. The corner of my black heart I'd allowed to feel closed over, a hard barrier between it and anyone who got close to me.

I relieved Cal, his hand gripping my shoulder too tight as he looked between Jen and me.

"If you've fucking hurt her, I'll—"

"I thought I sensed a threat in the offing." I turned to face him coolly, though he stood a good head taller than me at six-foot-four inches. But I knew my ex-partner too well, and at fifteen years my junior, I'd done almost everything he'd only just begun to experience. "You'll do what, kid?

Don't fucking second guess something you'll never know anything about."

I held the door open to the garage. With a quick look at Jen, already ensconced in a unicorn game with Ashley on the living room floor, Cal left. I knew I'd hear more about the whole situation the next time he had a sleepless night and needed someone to snark at.

What a pack of whiny bitches we are.

I watched Jen play with Ashley on the floor, making her a cup of coffee. I added milk and sugar the way I knew she liked and kept my own black. I didn't drink the stuff often, but this morning I needed something that would burn away the emotions I'd let loose.

I placed it in her hands, fighting the urge to sink to my knees, apologise for being a complete asshole to her this morning, and beg her to let me love her the way I wanted.

But none of that would get the job done.

The moment emotion came into our work, attention spans suffered, earning us nothing but chaos and mistakes. With an opponent like Wayde Logan — even temporarily imprisoned — any distraction could be fatal.

My girls deserved the best I could give.

I watched them play from my post at the window. When the room grew too dark for even dayglo unicorns, Ashley and Jen curled on the sofa together beneath a thin blanket. I secured the house a third time and headed outside to the targets.

My knife points flew cleanly into the board, each throw harder than the last. Collect, return, repeat.

Over and over, until my shoulder ached.

Then I switched sides.

The blade edges had blunted by the time I slipped back into the house. Jen lay on the sofa alone, rising groggily when she noticed me and flicked off the TV.

"Are you okay?" she rasped, her voice thick with sleep.

She looked sexy as hell with her short, mussed hair framing her oval face. All I wanted was to take her to bed and curl my body around hers as a barrier from everything in the world that wanted to hurt her. Then I could sleep, knowing she was safe.

Instead, I became a cold man with a closed heart.

Only a soulless black heart — hard and unforgiving.

I'd spent years behind the mask, and it had kept a lot of people alive, including the unit and Mila.

Nothing could persuade me that needed to change; what I wanted never came into it. I pressed a hand to her shoulder until she sank back onto the sofa, looking up at me with a small frown.

"Go to sleep, Jen," I murmured, collecting a thicker rug from the end of the couch. "Unless you want to go back to your room."

"Where will you be?" she whispered.

"Right here, cleaning my knives. It'll be quieter in your room. Or Ashley's."

"I'll stay." She resettled on the lounge, closing her eyes.

I stood over her for a long moment, fighting every urge to curl myself around her. Finally, my feet took me back to the kitchen where I'd laid out my knives. She'd wanted to be near me, so I leaned on the wall at the end of the living room, looking over her as I honed each knife to a wicked edge.

The quiet night hours calmed me, stopped the chatter and white noise the rest of the world ignored during daylight hours, but bordered on overwhelming to me. I turned over the conversation I'd overheard between Jen and Ashley earlier, thinking of the little girl's words. Jen might be worried about her daughter's social aspect, but the kid was growing up fast.

She was surrounded by a dubious collection of role models for a nine-year-old girl, but her life experiences were nothing like anything other kids her age would deal with, and her life experience to date was far from normal. We'd always indulged her in her creative and colourful pursuits, letting her lighten our lives while trying to give her everything she couldn't have in the best ways we could.

While we hunted her father, and he, in return, hunted us.

And her.

How fucked up could a kid's life get? She should be at the beach, beginning to flirt with boys, or going to the movies with her friends. Playing weekend sport, not listening to us strategise our way around her father's criminal pursuits. Hell, we hadn't even thought to have her intelligence tested.

Logan's mind easily passed into the genius level. Would his daughter have inherited the same tendencies? I almost made a mental note to suggest testing to Cal in the morning. Liam would know someone who would do it very quietly, but before the thought formed fully, I'd discarded the idea.

Ashley's IQ didn't matter; it would have little bearing on her life. What she needed was love and family. For the second time in my life, I wanted to run. But this girl had no one else, and her mother took the brunt of it all on her bare shoulders. At least with me around, meagre support that I was, she didn't have to bear it alone.

This time, I had to stay.

Every knife sharp and weighted in my hand, I slid them back into their sheaths, recalling Jen's reaction — or not so reaction — to their presence on the table. She'd stood there naked, comfortable in her own skin as she studied weapons I'd flung at men with an intent to kill.

Another part of her that was strong as hell and made me love her all the more for it.

I checked her, telling myself it was part of the job, tugging the blanket around her back. My own eyes heavy and dry, I sank onto the floor with my back against the couch, close enough to feel her breath on the back of my neck. Stretching my arm across her thigh, I tilted my head back, letting her breath caress my cheek as I closed my eyes for just a few seconds.

Just for a second, my hands wound around the woman I loved but could never have, while she slept.

I opened my eyes, knowing something was wrong. My ass ached from being planted on the floor for too long, my shoulder frozen in a backward twist. But neither of those things were what bothered me.

I turned my head slightly, not looking behind me. I already knew what I'd find. Who I'd find there.

Her fingers stroked the back of my neck as I struggled not to groan against her touch. Instead, I sat dead upright, the stick up my ass nailing me to the floor.

"You need to stop doing that," I ground out between clenched teeth.

Her fingers stilled on the nape of my neck. "Sorry, Black."

My jaw ached within moments of waking as my dick rose to the way her mouth formed my name. The name I'd asked her to use only when we played.

"It's fine."

In no fucking world is this fine.

I shifted, wiggling my toes to wake muscles before I fell over myself trying to get off the floor.

"Wait. Please," she begged, her hand pressing briefly over my arm, withdrawn in an instant as though she'd been burned. "I need—"

She broke off, but what she needed came through clearly in her voice. I nodded, settling back as I stroked her denim-clad leg that had escaped the blanket, winding my hand around her calf. She sighed behind me, her breath shuddering against my skin. I closed my eyes, resting back against her.

Why should she be the only one who takes pleasure from this?

By the time the sun rose fully, my ass was completely numb, and my legs refused to work. I groaned, standing. Or attempting to stand.

"This was a really bad idea." I twisted, looking down at Jen still curled beneath the blanket I'd covered her with. She stared back with wide eyes that reminded me just *how* bad an idea this whole thing had been.

The woman had lodged into my heart, and I refused to let her loose.

I hobbled across the room, shaking out my feet. Jenny snorted behind me.

"I'm glad you find me amusing."

"Your backside wiggles so well."

"What I'm here for. To impress you girls." I held out an arm and Ashley ran into it, from down the hall, wrapping her arms around my waist.

"I missed you yesterday. I thought maybe you wouldn't come back." She buried her head in my side.

I locked eyes with Jen over her daughter's tousled head, remembering our conversation the morning before. "Morning pumpkin." I detached her arms from my waist, flicking the coffee machine on for Jen and squatted down to her level. "You know I'm never gonna leave you, right? You or your Mum." I threw the remark out there, hoping Jen heard and understood.

Ashley's eyes filled with tears. She threw her arms around my shoulders. "Everyone else leaves. Always. I never get to have a proper family."

My heart ached for the traumatised nine-year-old. I pulled her into my arms, looking at Jen over the top of her head. She sat upright on the bed, her lips pressed together. Worry swarmed in her face.

I rose, putting Ashley back on the ground. She looked up at me with trusting eyes, her lip still trembling. Collecting coffee cups, I gave her a small smile and a promise.

"I'll never leave you, Ash. Or your Mum."

Ashley smiled brilliantly, flouncing back to her room with the tenacity of an almost ten-year-old. I only wished adults had the same resilience to life. The mugs weighed heavy in my palms. I put them down, turning my back to Jen so she wouldn't have to read the lie in my eyes of a promise I had no way to ever keep, regardless of how much I wanted it.

My routine resumed, the majority of my hours spent minding the girls, occasionally heading into the office to annoy Cal and pick fights with Danny. Nothing much changed, except that I had become hyper-aware of Jen wherever she was in the house. If her body brushed by mine, the urge to seize her and kiss her senseless grew until I grumbled something, pushing by her and took my arousal out on the targets set up in the yard.

I tugged the last blade free with a decent amount of effort; the thing had embedded to the hilt. I either needed a harder target or to ask Liam to put me back into the fights Red had suggested.

Darkness fell over the house as I flicked the floodlight off, my shoulders rolling back. The lock clicked beneath my hand. Jen's sweet scent permeated the room, over the damned tiger balm that coated everything else, but not her.

I sat silently in the chair she'd pulled out, clenching my jaw. My teeth ground at her first touch, my restraint already tested. My hands balled into fists as she massaged the overworked muscles along my shoulders, running her fingers over the front, digging deep into the tissue. Her arms were close enough that if I turned my head, I could have kissed her skin, had the taste of her on my tongue.

Instead, I savoured the memory of her, and planned pleasures and punishments I'd never perform on her.

Everyone has their dark little kink.

Jenny is mine.

CHAPTER EIGHTEEN

JENNY

"I can't go back. I need to be here," Theo spoke softly into his phone, pacing the grassed area of the backyard. He'd left the lights off as he wore a strip of grass bare. I eavesdropped shamelessly from inside the house, though the few times he stared into the darkened glass, I knew he suspected I loitered, waiting for him.

"No, Cal gave me the details. I'm not swapping out with anyone else. The girls need regularity, Liam. Oh, fuck off." He hung up on Cal's boss, slapping the phone against his thigh. His silhouette was the only solid object in the constantly-moving shadows.

Quietly, I stepped outside, letting the door close softly at my back. Theo prowled the grass. I dropped my eyes to my hands, studying the fine lines I knew decorated their backs even though I couldn't see them.

"Did you hear everything?" Theo's voice came from my back — very close to my back. Heat radiated from him. I wondered if I stepped back into him, would his arms fold around me, turn me in his arms to—

I snapped the fantasy off before it could reach its completion. That would only ever be a fantasy. He'd made that clear enough. I knew we had his heart, Ashley and I, but I couldn't seek refuge in his body.

But we had him here with us, where he fought to stay. That was enough.

It had to be enough.

"Yep."

I shrugged. I didn't see any point in hiding from a man whose job was to know everything, anyway.

"The promise I made to Ash—"

"You're trying to keep it," I spoke to the sink, not daring to face him. At least we had him in the house with us. If he gave in to what I wanted, would he leave? Desperation bubbled in my throat. "I get it."

His hands grasped mine, something hard and warm that cooled quickly pressed into them.

"What's this?" I stared at his knives in my hand, keeping my fingers away from the edges he regularly sharpened.

"You need to be able to defend yourself if I'm not around." He said the words so casually, but I remembered vividly what it felt like to have him incapacitated, unable to be between me and whatever new threat jumped out at us.

I nodded, silent as Theo pressed the small knife into my hand, showing me how to grip it, how to throw and where to aim. Cold night air hand sunk bone-deep into my skin by the time I'd got the hang of it, barely.

"Practice any time." He helped pry my stiff fingers open. I nodded again, my head whirling with the information pounded into it.

"Thank you," I whispered, clenching and unclenching my hand. Circulation returned. I inhaled an icy breath, shivering. I stepped into the house after him, pausing by the kitchen bench, my mind blank for a second.

"Jen." The air around me moved. I froze, feeling his presence with every inch of my skin. "I have to work. I can't protect you if—" He broke off, cursing softly.

The presence behind me moved closer, compressing the thin layer of air between us. His lips ghosted along my neck, my head tipping back as a moan tore from my lips in a whisper.

"Black," I whimpered, my waist tingling as his palms slipped over the air over my hips.

"You can't call me that, Jen," he groaned, his body curving around mine. His lips barely brushing my jaw, lingering at the corner of my mouth.

Then he was gone. Cold night air seeped into the places only his ghost had touched, leaving me in a ragged mess of desire and heartache, clutching the kitchen bench.

"I'm going into the office. Mila will be here...well, now." Theo peered out the window as he packed a satchel bag, stuffing his laptop and a sheaf of notes into it. I frowned.

"When do you have time to do those?"

He grimaced at his laptop bag, not looking at me. "When you're asleep."

He didn't see my raised eyebrows, but I made sure he felt my glare. I put my hands on my hips for emphasis. "You're going to crash if you don't get more sleep. Do you sleep?"

He cocked his head. "Occasionally."

"It's not enough."

"No."

I squinted. "Are you agreeing with me?"

"If you keep doing that, you'll get wrinkles."

"'Cause I'm such an old woman?"

"Well..." He let the word hang between us. I solved it by punching his shoulder. "Ow." He rubbed the area. "That really hurt, Jen. Maybe you shouldn't be fixing me."

He eyed my curled fists with no little apprehension.

I scoffed. "Are you being serious? This is you. Badass and all." I flapped at him to indicate pretty much everything about him.

"I think there's only one true badass here." He rubbed his shoulder, rolling it.

"Are you still on that?" I groaned. "I'd never be able to do it a second time. Doing something twice is where real courage comes in. The first time, you have no real idea what you're doing until it's over. What the consequences are, or could have been."

"And the adrenaline wears off." Theo watched me with a steady gaze. I held still beneath his study, letting him see whatever it was he felt he needed to look into. "I think you give yourself far less credit than what you're worth." His voice dropped a notch, a shiver working up my spine as his gaze darkened. I tried not to show it but suspected I failed horrendously.

So much for badass.

I snorted. Theo looked at me with a speculative glint. "Jen—"

Mila's car turned up the drive, the engine of Cal's truck roaring. Theo swore. "She'll never fit that in the damned garage."

"Cal's just thinking about keeping her and the baby safe."

Theo only gave his usual grunt, opening the garage for Mila. She flew into his arms, disappearing into the safe haven his bulk offered. I smiled. He'd been her refuge for so, so long.

Now, he was ours.

Theo caught my eye, jerking his head to the kitchen door.

"Lock me out?" he asked lightly. I frowned, padding across to him while Mila went on a unicorn tour.

"What is it?" I stopped inside his space, tipping my head back to look up at him. He didn't back away, his face closed. Light flickered in his glance, the only hint of what bothered him. It disappeared from his glance in an instant. "You know I'd never not lock the door."

"Call me if anything changes. Any worry, anything at all. I'm not comfortable with this, but there's no one else, and I won't have some random rookie looking after you. Any of you."

I nodded. "I can understand that. Thank you for looking out for us."

"It's the job." His mouth quirked humorlessly at one corner. I tried to read him, but I couldn't as he closed me out. Again.

"But that's not all," I said, still frowning. "What aren't you saying?"

"I feel—" he hesitated, running both hands over his hair, smoothing it back over his head. "It's nothing. Just a feeling."

Rough-edged and hardened, his determination and loyalty broke me. I wanted to show him his worth, but I also knew he'd never let me.

"You had that feeling last time," I reminded him, following him to the kitchen door. Behind me, the unicorn tour continued. Thank god for Ashley.

"Yeah, and it got me a lump on my head and you—"

"I was safe, because of you."

"No." He shook his head, a dark glint in his eye. "You were safe because of *her*." He nodded to Mila, something akin to pride in his voice. I smiled at my feet, wishing I had that same place in his heart. "Hey."

I looked up, blinking. Theo's thumb brushed my cheek. "We'll be fine." I gave him a gentle push, flustered.

"Mmm. Call, message and I'll be straight here. I'll only be an hour. Maybe two, if Liam is his usual self."

I grinned. "You just can't take it that he's more a man than you," I teased.

Theo's arm whipped around my waist, pulling me into him. I gasped, my palms flat on his chest, but his heartbeat maintained its usual, steady rhythm. Mine, on the other hand, ran the Melbourne Cup.

"Can you still say that after the time we've spent together?" His chin grazed my cheek, his touch leaving a searing path in its wake.

"No, Black," I whispered, my eyes wide. Adrenaline rushed through my veins.

"Good girl." He released me and stepped back, his eyes never leaving my face as he nodded to the door. "Lock it."

I closed the door after him with trembling hands.

For a man who refused to touch me, he did a terrible job of holding to his promise. I passed Mila her cup of coffee, gone slightly cold, and pretended to be a domestic goddess. Or just domestic. But *playing house* had never been my strength.

Mila's small but growing presence replaced Theo's hard one. The shadow he cast over us as a darkening barrier between us and Logan's many eyes lightening as it left us. He drove away almost human, while Mila sat with me. Not a protector, but a confidant.

A friend.

I had a distinct shortage of those who didn't also draw an income from the job of protecting Ashley and me, and I welcomed the chance to talk to a real human being. Theodore Black did not count as a real human.

More a robot with a heart.

A very sexy robot with a heart.

Mila returned from the hall, straightening her dress, immediately accosted by Ashley.

"Gentle!" I called, finishing up two cups of decaf I'd asked Theo to buy on his last grocery stop in an effort to be healthier. One more measure of control. "Baby. Remember?"

Mila waved my concerns away. "I'm always there." She rolled her eyes, jerking her thumb over her shoulder in the direction of the bathroom.

I sipped the coffee, disgusted with it as Ashley spoke to the barely-there bump of Mila's tummy, keeping up a running commentary as she towed Mila about the house. "He's a grumpy man, but he's loyal to a fault." Mila took her coffee with a quiet *thank you*. "Grumpy, though."

"You said that already." I grinned, thinking of the many nights he'd barely spoken to me, though comfort came from his company alone.

"But it's true."

"Oh, totally."

Mila stared over the lip of her mug, her eyes unfocused. "When they took me to the station after the bank robbery, the first one, Cal...well. He nearly lost his job. I knew nothing about him, then. While his boss was reorganising his career, before Liam stepped in, Teddy sorted therapy and a new identity for me. Everything I needed to become me."

I tilted my head on the side. "He is your rock."

"My God, yes. In so many ways. He helped me pick out hair dye. That was...I had blonde hair. Platinum blonde." Mila smiled, tugging at her dark brown hair. "I've never seen a man so interested in which base colour I needed to make the brown work without turning me green." She grinned at the memory.

I hid behind my own mug. "He's certainly something else," I agreed dryly.

"Let him help you, Jen. If you need something, tell him. Don't ask," she held up one hand with a laugh, "don't give him the chance to say no or change it to what he thinks will work best. You know your situation better than anyone. Let him do his job."

"Just the job, huh."

"It's always more than a job with him. With all of them." Mila's cheeks pinked. I grinned.

"Cal broke all the rules for you."

Mila held my eyes unashamedly. "Teddy will do the same for you."

I held her eyes for a moment. "I know."

One hour became two, sliding into the next as seamlessly as my life drifted away, taking Ashley's with it on a detour that kept us from actually living. My thumb rubbed over the cool surface of my phone, but the only messages coming through were from my brother. Ignoring him, I elected to wallow in self-pity for the duration. I collected the cup from the arm of Mila's chair, making sure she was comfortable.

Tiny snores came from her. I shushed Ashley as she pranced about the room, gesturing for her to read. Her face fell when she saw Mila asleep, but I shooed her back to her room, unable to face the convoluted explanation of what pregnancy did to a woman.

Not that I'd ever know.

I had Ashley, and now we had Theo for whatever period we were graced with. A light purr raised my head. I half-turned to the kitchen door before I registered that Theo had returned.

"You took a while." I flicked the door handle as it turned beneath my hand, stepping back to let him in. Theo walked into the house, slinging his laptop satchel to the floor in a none-too-gentle drop. I winced. "Maybe be careful with that?"

"What? Oh." He stopped in the middle of the kitchen, running a hand over his tired face.

I waited as he stared at me blankly. Nothing appeared to be forthcoming. I frowned.

"Mila's asleep. Maybe you should get some rest, too," I prompted.

Theo leaned back against the kitchen bench, sliding both hands over his dark hair, to slick it back. I stepped forward.

"Yeah, you're probably right."

My eyebrows rose. "Did you just agree with me?"

"Yep."

I studied him. "Have you been fighting?"

"Danny offered up."

"Uh-huh." I looked at the shadow around his jaw. Red marks peeked out from beneath the neckline of his shirt. I pulled it back, surprised when he offered no resistance, then swore at the swelling around his shoulder. I grabbed an ice pack from the freezer, tossing it at him. "Use that, or you won't be able to throw. How does he look?"

Theo grinned, rubbing his jaw. I tracked the movement with my eyes, mesmerised. "Worse than he expected."

"Good fight, then?" I strived for a casual tone. Theo's eyes narrowed.

Do you miss it? The fighting?

I couldn't ask, and he didn't answer. My unasked question hovered between us as he yanked his black tee over his head. I wondered if it was the same one I'd worn as a bare expanse of chest and ripped abs presented before me, and my brain jammed.

Bare, except for the ink covering almost every square inch of skin, so artistically done, the wings and scales appeared to move with his every breath.

My eyes traced the curves and hollows where he'd spent hours developing the muscles. Not a gym junkie like the other boys, Theo's muscle came from bare-handed fighting and hard work alone.

Sweat beaded his skin in a fine sheen that settled between the muscles.

"Jen, catch."

I blinked, coming back to reality in just enough time to catch the ice pack that came flying at my face. Theo grinned, brushing by me on his way through the kitchen to Ashley sprinting from her room. I saw the outcome before it could happen, but I tried to stop it anyway.

"Wait, shhh, Mila's—"

"TEDDY!" Ashley's scream could have woken the houses either side of us. Good thing we weren't meant to be hidden.

My snark rose out of its sexy-man stupor as Mila raised her head, smiling at Theo. He dipped to kiss her cheek. Her arms wound around his neck in a long hug, my stomach curling and flopping with a decent measure of despair.

"—asleep," I finished quietly, watching Theo, Ashley, and Mila chat, their arms around each other. Very quietly, I let myself out into the bright, sunny yard, looking for the only type of warmth I would get.

CHAPTER NINETEEN

BLACK

The knife thudded into the solid wall behind me. No cage, this time. Just an open square with walls closing in the small square on two sides and a limited number of onlookers seated close to the edge at the others. A closed fight, with an exclusive breed of spectators in an undisclosed location.

Undisclosed, because it sat beneath the city, in the basement of a building I didn't get to see. The fighters didn't talk to each other; the organisers barely spoke to anyone.

Tyler Durden, eat your heart out.

The next knife flew my way. I moved, but his aim was off, to be fair.

Here, Theodore Black didn't exist. I wasn't my job; not a cop or a protector. I was nothing more than a moving target with his back to a wall and a row of spectators I tried desperately not to hit with my return throw.

They might have paid good money for the experience.

My limited exposure to the very wealthy, especially criminal-organised-type wealthy, had taught me they'd do anything for a buzz. Maybe I should start aiming at them instead.

I flicked my wrist, tugging the two short knives free of the board, keeping my eye on my opponent, in case he had more blades than I'd initially assessed. I didn't want to find a third embedded in my back.

The blades came free. I focussed on him, then on the woman seated behind him slightly to his left. The knives left my hands, and I spread them wide as he crumpled. I'd aimed for his shoulders. Well above any critical centre of mass and high enough that if I managed to mistime it, I wouldn't clean up anyone sitting in the small crowd.

My palms empty, I wiggled my fingers at her.

Look, magic.

She tittered, though her eyes stayed hard as glass, and just as transparent.

The ref stepped back in, giving his spiel. A pair of medics helped the injured fighter onto a makeshift stretcher where they'd doctor him in a corner behind a screen. Doctoring meaning they would dope him and send him on his way with enough cash to keep him from gabbing on about the fights, though we all knew better.

Threats hung inherent in the limited ambience of the quick set up that would be raking Red and her partner in thousands for each fight. The medics hefted the stretcher, but I halted them silently.

"Alright if I take these?" I muttered quietly, my hands on the handles of his blades. He glared at me from his prostrate position, baring teeth. The medic gave me a resigned nod I took as permission and ripped the blades free, ignoring the extra work I made for them as blood dripped to the floor around my boots.

The men seated around the square murmured with appreciation. These people liked a little showmanship, and if that's what it took to worm my way deeper into their closed circle, then I'd push boundaries to do it.

Sometimes, it felt a little *too* good.

A little too easy.

I wiped the blades on my pants, glad I'd worn black cargos with a little stretch in the material. Although technically it was a bare-knuckle fight with blades, if the need arose to defend myself with my legs, I didn't want to be hindered by my fashion choices.

The bookie nodded to me, sliding cash to one side of his small table. I sneered slightly at the wad but pocketed it anyway. Liam would have to work out how to file this one. Not my problem.

The crowd shifted as I walked across the dimly lit floor. A click of heels told me what to expect next. I sighed, rolling my shoulders. This would be a different sort of battle.

"Nice work. I liked your last touch."

I glanced at Red sideways without turning my head. "I didn't peg you as bloodthirsty."

"You haven't pegged me at all, honey." She laughed, the sound anything but musical. I winced as it bounced around us in the enclosed space.

Think of Jen. My clean, no-bullshit girl who'd put this fake bimbo out to pasture any day.

Thinking of Jen got me through everything. Rather than a distraction, she had become my focus. My zen. I snuffed out a snort with the back of my sweaty hand. Laura's inspirational line was contagious. How fucking wonderful.

Soon I'd be like Man-Bun Boy, getting my ass handed to me in a meditation zone.

Not going to happen.

Danny fought well, but he hadn't been prepared for the few new tricks I'd added to my arsenal. My learn-on-the-job experience. Neither had he been prepared for my speed or that I could take his blows.

It had been a while since I'd fought the younger man. The first few rounds we'd felt each other's styles out, but after a while, I'd gotten bored, and planted him firmly on his ass.

The tough prick had bounced right back, three fucking times.

My knuckles were actually swollen by the time I put him down for good, leaving him in the ring beneath our offices. Cal could fix his little protege up when he whined about having his ass handed to him.

I'd moved well past the point of caring. With the bullshit cases we were working to tie Logan up with a pretty little gift bow for the courts, I looked forward to the day Liam closed the case — the day I'd hand in my resignation.

A life of retirement beckoned, and I had nothing to fill it with.

"I don't mind a rough man. In bed or out of it." Red shimmied in her dress while she managed to walk in her stupid high stilettos.

"Are you fucking done flirting?" I yawned. She looked a little put-out and a lot pissed. I grinned, not bothering to hide it. "What do you want?"

"Smitty wants to talk jobs. He says you could be helpful." She looked me up and down, the predatory look in her eye revolting me.

"Your boy who left the hand on Samson's desk?" My lip curled, remembering the mess. She nodded. "Fuck. That was foul. Bloody traces of shit everywhere. I don't work with anyone that unprofessional."

"Really? Then you can tell him yourself." She called the elevator, taking us up two flights. The doors opened to a dingy row of offices just above the street level. Fluorescent tubes flickered above beige and dull green corridors, the doors scarred hardwood.

"Jesus. It looks like the eighties never left."

"Mmhmm." Red picked a door, turning the handle. She paused, checking my belt.

"What the fuck are you doing?"

"Did you take the extra blades? You might need them," she whispered. I frowned at the odd note in her voice, a harsh laugh bubbling up.

"Fuck me, Red. Is that concern?"

She smirked. "Only so you don't lose your pretty face. One of the joys of the job."

I raised an eyebrow, shoving my disgust further beneath the surface and followed her into the outdated office.

A blonde man with a barrel chest sat behind a cluttered desk. Perhaps he'd been talking to Samson. A brown suit jacket covered his yellow shirt, its buttons straining. The shirt bore some food stains — I hoped they were food stains — his tie at least as old as his office.

Someone's been shopping in the discount bins.

For a job that didn't require a suit, it surprised me that he bothered. My eyes narrowed, studying his pudgy face. He didn't get up but gestured for me to sit in the chair opposite his desk. I didn't, and Red slipped out the door, squeezing my arm, her glossy talons digging in.

Smitty watched her go, lighting a cigarette. I held back a cough, wishing I could take several steps backward.

"Fucking her?"

I raised an eyebrow, biting back a string of choice curses. "No."

"Good thing. Hear she's not clean, eh?" The short, fat man laughed. Though he wasn't as big as Samson, he wasn't too far off his weight, either. A few more months in that chair and they could be twins.

"You wanted to talk jobs?" I folded my arms, trying not to obviously stretch my shoulders, the muscles already gone cold, and wished I'd brought a jacket.

Jen would have her work cut out for her. A twinge of guilt sucked my breath away for a moment. It wasn't fair of me to keep coming back to her and demanding she fixed the issues I'd essentially inflicted on myself.

A warm shower would do just as well, but her hands on my skin were soothing. My eyes snapped back to Smitty, who appeared to have been talking for some time.

"He doesn't want us to split the jobs up, and obviously, I take the lion's share of the money, for setting up the jobs, but—"

"Who are the jobs?" I cut in, annoyed that I'd let my thoughts wander.

Smitty paused, unable to hide his dislike that I interrupted him.

"Small businessmen. Dealers who might be skimming off the top, pretty much anyone who doesn't do their job." He leaned back, disappearing behind a small cloud of smoke.

"It comes with the job description," I tried not to breathe, ignoring the irony of our stunted conversation.

Smoke hung just below the ceiling. If the sprinkler system went off, it would be an improvement.

He peered at me, one eye twitching at the corner. "Yeah, yeah. Some targets are coming up. Maybe a little something different first up. You okay with a bit of variation in your work, Theodore?"

"Black."

"What?"

"Black. My name." Memories of the last time I'd asked someone to call me that washed over me in a wave of strawberries and cream. I took a deep breath in and promptly choked on second-hand smoke.

"Yeah, yeah. Sorry, man. Wait, I'll open a window." He turned, wedging his hand beneath a window so opaque I'd taken it as part of the wall, but nothing moved. Not bothering to get up, he wiggled it a bit more, then gave up.

I rolled my eyes, my mouth open to ask about the job for the third time tonight when a photo skittered across the desk at me.

I didn't pick it up, scared I would tear the thing into confetti then rip his throat out for good measure. Swallowing back the dark fury that brewed inside me, boiling to the surface fast, I tapped the familiar face in the photo.

"This isn't what I do." I folded my arms again, letting my dead smile come out to play.

Only I wasn't playing anymore.

"Oh, no, not a hit, not a hit! I wouldn't ask you to do that on your first one. Just bring her in. Boss wants her."

"Which boss?" I snapped, but I already knew. I had what Liam wanted, and now it was time to get some answers, but Smitty only reclined in his flimsy chair while I stared at a photo of a tousled blonde head, Ashley's sweet face staring up at me.

CHAPTER TWENTY

JENNY

My phone was ripped from my grasp. I whirled, a cry lodged in my throat. Theo glared at me, holding it out. "Thumbprint. Or I'll break into it anyway."

I raised an eyebrow, determined to keep my cool in the face of his storm. "You only had to ask."

The screen opened at my touch. Theo plucked it from my fingers when I craned over his hand. A unicorn cake flashed on the screen, the last thing I'd looked at.

"What's this?" Theo frowned.

"Ashley's ten tomorrow. I wanted to get icing. She– she didn't get a cake last year." My words caught in my throat.

Theo's jaw clenched. "I'll get something tomorrow," he said through his teeth, flicking through my folders.

"What are you looking for?"

"Your messages."

"Oh." *Oh.*

Oh, fuck.

I tried not to fidget as he scrolled through, his brow furrowed. He placed the screen face-up on the table, carefully laid without a sound. Theo, holding back. Inhaling, I wondered if I could weather the storm of him when it broke over me.

"Who?"

I pressed my lips together.

"My brother."

"Mmm." Theo folded massive arms over his chest. I couldn't work out if he was drawing a barrier between us or trying to be intimidating. "Your real brother?"

My nose twitched at his scepticism. "Yes, Theo. My real brother. Look him up. All my family info is in my files. You know that."

A pause. Then—

"Are you fucking him?"

I raised my eyebrows higher, concerned I'd lose them into my hairline. "He's blood, Theo. What the fuck is wrong with you? That line you crossed? It's receding behind you. At speed." I shook my head while he rolled his eyes, still staring at me. "I messaged him before we– um."

I stopped, unsure of what to call it. A night of passion seemed cliche and overly dramatic.

"Before we fucked. Get on with it."

His eyes were hard, and I told myself this wasn't anything I hadn't seen from him before. My cheeks ached with my fake smile.

"Before we fucked. Thank you. That's so much simpler."

"I thought so." His eyes glinted. I stared into them for a long moment, trying to work out if he was seriously pissed at me. "Jen?" he prompted.

"I was lonely– not that kind of lonely. That was just sort of a 'you and me' type thing. But," I continued hurriedly under his hard look, "I missed my family. Having friends. Life."

"You have us for friends." He hadn't moved an inch. I swallowed.

"Yes, but...I'm always at odds with you. Selena comes here to torture me with the threat of testimony, and Mila is exhausted, and she still comes to see me here. Not me going to her place, to help look after her, or go shopping for the baby, or– or—"

Tears stung my eyes.

I blinked them back as my breath caught, but I knew Theo saw them. His arms loosened, wrapping around me to draw me to his chest, his lips pressed into my hair. The warmth of his breath tumbled down over me. I sank further into him.

"It's okay, Jen." His voice turned hard, and though I believed him, I knew there was something more.

"I had a mid-incarceration life crisis." I grinned into his chest. His arms pulled tighter around me.

"Yeah." He didn't try to contradict me; we both understood the reality of the situation.

"What's going on?" I covered the quiver in my voice, burying myself in the scent of him.

"I got asked to kidnap someone."

"At least it's not a hitman job," I joked, looking up but his face closed, his eyes dark and fathomless. I got dizzy just staring into them. "Um. Who is it?" I asked, drawing myself back to reality with effort.

A small piece of paper slid into my hand. I curled my fingers gently around the glossy photo where it stuck to my hand, afraid to look. I didn't need to.

I knew.

I placed the picture of my daughter on top of my phone, the screen black.

It had been taken at the old house. I recognised the fence palings behind her, the second day we'd been there, I'd taken her outside until Theo herded us back in.

Reality hit me. Two days in a new house and Logan knew where we were, even from a prison cell.

I stared up at Theo, still within the ring of his arm, iron bands that protected me in so many ways. I arched back to look up at him properly, letting my understanding sink into my gaze. He gave a short nod at my acceptance.

"Who?" I whispered.

His eyes stayed firm on mine as he answered me.

"You got a picture of your brother, Kitten?"

Oh, fuck. Fuckity fuck.

The tears warred with the low blood pressure, but they were ultimately overruled. My knees failed, Theo holding me up against him. I didn't fight; I had nothing left.

Logan had stripped me of every haven but this.

Theo's strong hands kneaded my back, and I wondered if he knew he was doing it.

"In my phone," I managed to get out. He nodded, lifting me off my feet and walked the few steps to the couch, depositing me there. He returned for my phone and pressed it into my hands, opening his laptop on my knees.

"Show me." The command in his voice was unmistakable, and I had no desire, no reason to push against his hard limits now. Not with Ashley's safety on the line.

This was all for her.

This was all about her.

And he would take her away from me.

I wished that Logan had remained a faceless enemy, an image in a file that had never seemed real. Until the day he took us, *all of us*, and showed us the real threat.

I couldn't reason with him. I couldn't negotiate or appeal to him. He had no heart.

So I did the only thing I could. I stood between him and the man who always had my back. Between him and his daughter.

I wondered for the millionth time if I would be able to do it again.

If I would *have* to do it again.

Photos of my brother appeared on the screen. There were older ones of him in a family album, first with his then-wife, later, alone. His face grew a little broader, his appearance grew more unkempt. A squint came into his eyes, pinching them at the corners, pulling his features into a mean, shifty expression.

"I'm sorry," I whispered, my head dropping. Theo shifted beside me, his arm slipping across my back, tugging me toward him. I leaned into his shoulder. His laptop showed the same pictures, and some newer ones I didn't recognise. "What are these?"

"Mugshots. Surveillance. These ones at the fight ring. They call him Smitty." He changed to a new window, a file opening. I stared at my own face on my licence. Jenny Smith. "I should have fucking known."

He returned to Chad's file, his picture staring at us, an ugly smile stretching his face. I noted a sliver of Liam's face in the crowd behind him. "Did you take these?"

"Yeah." Theo squeezed me against him. I snuggled closer, desperate for the contact he offered, his solid presence soothing. My thoughts skittered around. "He knew a man was living here with me," I said without thinking.

Very slowly, Theo put his laptop down. He turned to me, cold fury writhing beneath the surface of his face. His arms came up, the one around my shoulders sliding up to hold my neck still in tight fingers, the other catching my jaw as he angled my face towards his, staring down at me.

"When?"

"Months ago," I whispered. "Maybe two, three weeks after we moved in?" I couldn't think straight. I had no idea when Chad had been here.

"Months." His eyes closed, but he didn't let me go. I didn't move, though every inch of my wanted to run. I'd screwed up on him, and now I had to help him fix it.

"We move?"

"You'll have to." Though his face was right there in front of me, his voice became distant as he worked through all the options.

I saw the moment his attention returned to me. A shiver ran over me, spiking with jolts of electricity everywhere he touched my skin, none of it pleasant. His hands loosed, then dropped away, but somehow, the absence of him was worse.

"Jen— I'll fix this. But I can't trust you. Not any more."

He rose, dropping my phone back onto my lap, heading out the back as he raised his own phone to his ear.

I sat, stunned.

Until it occurred to me that he'd said *you'll* be moving, not *we*.

I waited outside the back door, it's cool surface a stark reminder at my back of the corner I'd put myself in — the threat to my daughter. Theo paced the yard as he talked, occasionally swearing. My feet grew numb, the light fading with the day. I put Ashley to bed and returned.

Finally, he ended the call, slipping the phone back into his pocket. He stood with his back to me, his shoulders slightly curved in his familiar position. I didn't need to see the front of him to know his arms were crossed over his chest.

"Come over, Jen. I know you're there."

My feet pressed into the dewy grass, the night's chill sinking deep into my skin. I stopped within arm's reach of his. Theo's face blended with the shadow, his eyes glinting inside the cloud of darkness surrounding him.

The effect was far more intimidating than anything he'd tried to do earlier.

"I didn't think you'd want to speak to me again. Will they take her?"

A phantom smile curved the small section of his mouth I could see. He stepped out of the shadow, his hands grazing my arms. I shivered. He frowned. "Christ, Jen, you're icy. Let's get inside."

"No. Not yet. Say...whatever it is you're going to say to me."

"You really want to know?"

I laughed, a brittle sound. "She's what it's all about."

He studied me, crooking a knuckle beneath my chin, tipping my head back. I held his dark stare. But it didn't emanate his fury any more.

"We haven't been fair to you. Too many of your transitions were rushed, and you've never had the process fully explained to you. We should have prepared you better. Both of you." He nodded to round off his speech while I gaped at him.

A laugh bubbled in my chest, and I fought it down with effort. He looked so serious, and I didn't want to ruin his moment.

"Been talking with Liam, have you?" A giggle escaped, and I clapped my hand over my mouth. It didn't stop. I bent over at the waist, my elbows propped on my thighs. Finally, the giggles subsided. I straightened, wiping tears from the corner of my eyes.

Theo stood with his arms predictably crossed, though he stared at me with a bemused smile. "Are you done?"

I laughed again, my stomach aching. "Not nearly. That was just so cute."

One dark eyebrow arched. A single line of silver shot through it. "I don't do cute."

I snorted. "Maybe, but you managed that pretty well." I stopped, smiling, but it slipped from my face as I thought about what we needed to overcome. "Any chance you'll forgive me for endangering her?"

"Your brother has been on our radar. We should have watched him closer. Our fault," he leaned toward me, "not yours."

I swallowed. "I should have spoken to you."

"You tried."

"I should have told you I needed to see my family."

"Will you stop apologising if I kiss you?"

I froze.

"What?"

Theo's arms unfolded, his hands cupping my cheeks. "You're so cold." He leaned down, speaking against my mouth. "I know why you lied to me."

"I didn't—"

"It was close enough." His lips pressed over mine before I could argue with him further, drawing me into him.

Theo's kiss was deep and slow. His hand cupped the back of my head as he showed me how much he'd forgiven me. I'd broken trust with this man who valued loyalty above all else, and yet, he still wanted me. His tongue stroked mine, his fingers kneading the back of my neck, tilting my head back a little further. His deep kisses became harder, more demanding. I pressed up on my toes, leaning into his chest. His heart thumped at its usual steady pace.

"Don't you ever get out of breath?" I asked against his mouth, swaying in his arms as the ground moved beneath me.

"Don't you ever get lost in the moment?" he grumped back.

I grinned against his mouth, nipping his lip. His hands squeezed my hips, the memory of his body pounding against mine, wave after wave of pleasure overwhelming me, and my own breath quickened. Theo's eyes narrowed.

"Sometimes," I whispered, not looking at him.

"Was it too much? What we did." His hands were back on my face, his thumbs stroking along my neck.

"No." I shook my head vehemently.

"Would you do it again?"

I blinked, remembering the question I'd asked myself earlier, my answer dying in my throat. His hands fell away.

"No, that's not what I—"

Theo's jaw clenched, a muscle ticking in his cheek. "You should have told me. I would have stopped," he said through his teeth, his hard gaze sweeping over me.

With a shake of his head, he dropped his hands. His back filled my vision as he strode away, the back door closing silently after him.

Chase him. Explain.

But I knew I wouldn't. Chasing him never occurred to me. He hadn't been prepared to listen, had jumped to the wrong conclusion, and who could blame him after what I'd done?

I stood alone in the dark night, too numb to feel anything other than his disappointment.

CHAPTER TWENTY-ONE

JENNY

Unicorn glitter floated around me. Ashley hummed to herself as she made toast and eggs for us both, ostensibly under my direction, but she was more than capable of doing the tasks with minimal supervision.

A takeaway coffee arrived in front of me. I blinked at it, then up at Theo. "Where did you get this?"

"I got it for you." Cal hugged me from behind while I stared at Theo, reaching back to give Cal a quick squeeze. Theo tracked his ex-partner's arms around me with a contained energy. I gave it a moment, then extracted myself from Cal's embrace.

"Thank you. I really appreciate it." My lips twitched as I stared up at my protector. Nothing in his face moved, but his presence thrummed with heightened intensity.

"Then you'll appreciate this," Cal said from behind me. I took a sip of my coffee, groaning as the flavour exploded over my tastebuds.

"Oh, that's good. What will I appreciate?" I looked over my shoulder at him. A jangle brought me back to Theo. "Those aren't your car keys." I frowned. Cal snorted behind me, and I shot him a dirty look.

"No. They're for the bike." Ashley passed him on the way to the table, her arms were laden with plates. He stayed quiet until she left the room. "I thought we might get her some decorations, something to make a cake with. I didn't think she'd like a bought one."

"I don't think she'd care either way. Are you serious?" I looked between the boys, trusting the slow rise of Theo's mouth as it curled into a grin.

"*After* breakfast." He nodded to where Ashley set the table.

Cal prodded me in the back. I looked over my shoulder at him. "Thank you."

His smile rose at one side. "Anything for her."

I gripped Theo's waist, torn between exhilarated and terrified. I grinned inside the helmet as we whizzed along the road, faster than acceptable. He shifted, tapping my hands. I loosened my grip just slightly, my fingers still hooked into his stomach. The city became a flood of colour and movement.

Theo pulled up at the party supply store. I tugged the helmet over my head with his help.

"Your first time?" His eyes sparkled at me as he hung the helmet over the back of the bike.

"How could you tell?" I said dryly.

"I'll bear the marks for life." He grinned, throwing an arm around my shoulders as we walked, drawing me close to his side. I looked up with no small amount of surprise.

"This is new?"

"What, you think I'm a hardass all the time?"

"Pretty much."

"A high opinion. I'm flattered."

I laughed, lacing my fingers through his. Half an hour later he'd stuffed a collection of decorations and balloons into his backpack, sliding it over my shoulders. I shook my head at the domesticity of it all; us out together, shopping for my daughter's birthday.

Like we were a normal family, a normal couple.

I tightened the backpack's straps on my shoulders, straddling the bike behind Theo. My arms slid around him, and he squeezed my wrists.

"Not quite so tight this time, alright?" His helmet muffled his voice. I squeezed back, wiggling into him. His hand clasped mine a moment longer, then the bike came alive beneath us and the city streamed by in a blur.

The moment we turned up the drive, I knew something was wrong. The open garage door glared at us. Theo revved the bike to the top of the drive, not walking it up silently like he'd done so many nights after his fights and I knew he'd had the same thought.

Cal and Micah's trucks sat at the top of the drive, a silver coup that looked hellishly expensive parked across the drive behind them.

I pulled my helmet off as soon as Theo stopped the bike. He turned to help me off.

"Liam," his voice came out rough and terse, answering the question I knew I couldn't ask.

Theo caught my helmet as I dumped it into his arms carelessly, sprinting past the cars to the internal door. It opened easily, Micah pulling the door open on the other side. I barely glanced at him and ignored Liam altogether, heading straight for Cal.

"What's going on?" Black asked from the garage door, closing it behind him. I bit my lip, staring at Cal, who looked at me once and with a small shake of his head, studied the floor.

"Where is she?" I finally got to ask my own question. Black walked around us, his hand lingering lightly on my back. I felt more than one pair of eyes on us.

I didn't care. But I knew she was already gone.

"Where?" I spun on my heel to attack Liam, knowing Cal would give me nothing. I'd seen him close up too many times over the years when I'd asked about his investigation to bother prodding him. Micah, I didn't know at all, the enormous young cop taking up most of the kitchen. Or the house in general. But Liam had the answers I needed.

A tiny doubt began to grow in the back of my mind. I stored it for later when I knew I'd likely have tears to share.

"She's not here. She's gone."

"Gone." The first time anyone had actually said it. I blinked. "Gone. Wait, is that why you're here? Is she– I thought– Did Logan—" Panic bubbled to my lips, overflowing in a babble of half-formed thoughts. I twisted between Cal, looking forlorn, and Theo behind me. His stance was the same as always, leaning against the wall, but a muscle ticked in his cheek, his jaw clenched tight. His eyes blazed — not the closed face he used when he wanted to keep me from prying — but a cold rage, edging on fury.

Pointed at Cal. "Where is my daughter?" I whispered softly in a voice that wouldn't work properly, but it still filled the room with its vehemence. "Where did you take her, Liam?" I asked again, softly this time, and I saw the reaction in his eyes. I wouldn't back down, and both of us knew it.

"Safe." He bent his head, his thumb moving over his phone, then nodded to Cal. "I'll see you soon."

Without another word, he left, the engine of his car barely making any noise over the roar between my ears. Micah shrugged. There weren't any answers there. Which meant I had to poke the clam. Hard.

I stepped away from Cal, my head whirling. It gave both of us a reprieve before I went back into battle with him.

A moment's grace before I accepted my entire world had gone to hell.

Theo leaned against the window, half-turned to watch Liam's car disappear and half watching what was going on in the house. His chin moved an infinitesimal amount. I exhaled, a grey shape on the floor catching my eye. Sliding the backpack I still wore from my shoulders, I crouched down.

Ashley's stuffed dugong sat on the floor, its fur worn on one side. I collected it, realising it was too quiet in the house for so many people as I assessed the thing on whether its stuffing would burst out at me if I squeezed it too hard.

I turned in a slow circle, ready to address the elephant in the room — or not in the room — clutching the stuffed animal.

Cal's lips thinned, and he breathed out. Slowly. Control. That's all Cal had been, ever since I'd known him when I'd first adopted my daughter.

"Liam organised her transport to a safe house with a dedicated team." He held up a hand to forestall my questions. Heat radiated against my back. I knew without looking that it was Theo. "He's wanted her away for some time. From us, from anyone traceable to Logan. And we're all connected to him. She'll go into a witness program, possibly interstate. She's...safe."

Liam's word bounced back at me. I blinked through Cal's polite and well-executed speech. The passionate man who'd kept Ashley supplied with chocolate for nearly seven years had transformed into a stoic robot in my living room. I wanted to rant at him, to slap the sorrow from his face.

His private pity party. But this was *my* fucking daughter. I refused to lose her.

"Are you shitting me? You guys, *you*, all of you, protect her, protect *us* more than anyone else because you *care!* What sort of a dedicated team would she need but you? Us!" I shrieked the last word, not realising until it ripped from my throat, leaving me gasping in its wake.

Not realising I had raised my hand to actually attack Cal, until Theo's gripped my wrist, halting me midair. His other arm wound around my waist, drawing me back against him, his arm a band of iron at my waist. I panted slightly in his arms, tugging my wrist free.

"Not yours to take," he murmured in my ear, holding me tighter to him. "I'll do that later. And my slap will be a hell of a lot harder than yours." His voice raised as he addressed Cal, "I'll save that for those who deserve it."

"It's her birthday," I spat from my refuge within Theo's embrace. "Please make sure she enjoys it." I nudged the backpack with the bag of party things Theo had paid for across the floor.

Cal nodded, resignation written across the slope of his shoulders. Without uttering a single word, without offering any sentiment or reassurance whatsoever, he collected the bag, closing the door quietly behind him. I stood in the middle of the room, Theo's arms around me, clutching a tatty, stuffed dugong.

I am alone. I have no real family, and my daughter is gone.

Gone.

I'd known this day might come, but not like this. Not without saying goodbye, or knowing where Liam had hidden her. Not without hugging her.

The tears brewed and fell in a whitewash of anguish and heartbreak. I screamed, bent at the waist with the force of my desperation, my grief, hanging over Theo's arm where he held me up. Rage and fear flooded me. I turned in his arms, hammering his shoulders, his chest with my hands curled into fists.

Theo wrapped his arms around me tight, letting me rail at him, not uttering a word until I sank into him, my energy depleted. His hand curled into my hair, pressing my face to his chest until the tears began to slow. My eyes ached, the sun had set, and we stood in a dark room, his arms still tight around me, not having released me once through my ordeal. His mouth pressed to the top of my head, he pulled me even closer.

"You're not alone." He kissed the top of my head again. His chin scraped over my cheek as he nudged my head back, kissing my cheeks, the tracks of my tears. One hand loosened on my neck as I stared up at him, the pad of his thumb gently wiping my tears away.

I closed my eyes, my head heavy, sinking to his chest. His knuckle crooked under my chin. Peering at him through swollen, sore eyes, my body went limp in his arms. A shuddering breath left my chest, taking all feeling and emotion with it, leaving me numb.

"You'll never be alone. I promise you. Jen, I've never seen you cry. Well," he grinned, "Maybe that time Logan tied you to a bomb."

"I wasn't crying for me," I said softly into his hand, leaning my cheek against it. "I couldn't see Ashley. And you were mouthing off at him. I thought he would kill you," I whispered.

"Takes more than that, girl."

"Don't you ever feel fear? Desperation?" I asked, searching his eyes for an answer that would heal the Ashley-shaped hole in my heart.

His head canted slightly. "Sometimes. Not often. Most I remember feeling is when I woke up with him standing over you, ranting you weren't a fit mother for his child. Spitting insults that flowed over you. When he hit you, I was ready to fucking kill him."

His arms tightened around me, hardening to steel. A measure of comfort and exhaustion warred, but eventually, I just nodded to his words without really listening.

Theo stopped talking, scooping me into his arms and walked us to the sofa. He sat in one corner, swinging his legs up, curling me up on his lap. Our legs and arms tangled as he pressed my head to his chest.

"Will I see her again?" I raised my head. His hand pressed between my shoulder blades. Theo looked at me, honestly, and I saw a determination there, but also uncertainty. "You don't know."

"I don't know."

"What can I do?"

Theo didn't answer for a long moment, his hands stilled. Finally, he released a breath that hissed between tightly clenched teeth. "Right now? Nothing."

"Thank you for not lying to me."

"I won't bullshit you, Jen. You're worth more than that."

One hand cradled my cheek as tears began to fall again. He leaned into me. Kissing me gently, salt mingled between our mouths. He pressed his forehead to mine. I drew in shuddering breaths, clutching to him as my lifeline.

"We don't have to stay here any more, do we? I mean, he's not going to care about me, only..."

"Yeah. Worry about it in the morning. I got you tonight. Every night." He pressed me back to his chest, his legs and arms engulfing me in a cocoon of protection. "Cry all you like, Jen."

CHAPTER TWENTY-TWO

BLACK

She shifted in my arms, waking slowly. She'd cried herself into exhaustion, sinking into my arms with snuffles and hiccups even when she slept. The tiny noises of her desperation, her fear of *not knowing*, broke my heart.

Hours remained until the sun rose. I used the quiet hours of the night, letting my brain tick over everything coming our way, and what had already happened. Where we would go from here with so many changes. It was one of the reasons I rarely slept; those quiet hours were as good a reprieve as actual slumber.

I continued to stroke Jen's hair, noting the small flexes in her hands, the sinuous way she shifted, boneless in her sleep. Slowly, she raised her head, gazing at me through dozy eyes.

"You're so beautiful." I swept the hair back from her face, curling the blonde strands behind one ear. The curve of her cheek filled my hand perfectly, her skin pale, though I knew it tanned well, despite the night filling the room.

She huffed, a small smile curling her lips. I traced over them with my thumb, then leaned forward to kiss her. She pressed against me, her lips opening at my touch, but I wasn't demanding or brutal like the last time I'd kissed her.

My mouth had ached for her soft skin pressed against me since the night we'd spent in each other's arms, the memory of her taste haunting me every time she came near me. I kissed her sweetly, and when I drew back, her eyes were glazed with tears again.

"What are these for?" I murmured, brushing her damp lashes with my finger.

"Happy. Tired. Lost," she whispered back, her hands sliding around my neck. "I didn't think I'd– that you'd ever want to kiss me again."

"Miss that?"

"Hell yes."

I laughed, holding her tight to me, tracing her face with my gaze. I sobered as she wriggled. "What I said before is true. If you want it."

Her brow dipped, her eyes searching mine. "I'm not alone?"

"Never. But, you might not want to be with me either."

"I've lived with you for over two years, Theo." She propped herself up on my chest. My hands dropped to her hips as I waited for her to tell me she wanted far away from me. Her eyes held mine, staring deep into them until I stood bare before her. "If I couldn't live with you, you'd know that. But I don't know—"

"If this can work," I finished for her with a sigh, closing my eyes.

I should have never let her get close. Too close.

"No."

"Okay. I'll get you set up somewhere. There are plenty of places you can go to, and Danny's great with the logistics side of things." I dropped my hands to the sofa, its surface rough after the soft contours of her body.

"Theo. You're grandstanding. Or wallowing." Jen peered at me, her lips pursed. But her eyes were dancing, though tears still glazed her cheeks.

"What?"

"I want to stay with you. But I have to get Ashley back."

I flushed, looking down. How quick had I jumped to that conclusion? I nodded. "We'll get your girl. But we'll have to wait for Liam. He's organised this, and he won't tell Cal. We need to wait him out."

She huffed at me. "I'm not very patient."

I laughed outright while she slapped lightly at my chest. "That's a conservative statement. You sure you can live with a heathen like me?" The joke died on my lips. I watched her eyes as they widened, then hooded, and I couldn't read her.

Is this how she feels with me?

Jen sucked her bottom lip into her mouth. I watched, mesmerised, as it slowly popped free from between her teeth. "Yes. If you're offering, that is. Maybe, make some sort of a home with you."

My chest exploding, I crooked a knuckle beneath her chin, lifting her head again.

"Say that again," my voice came out hoarse. She leaned forward, kissing me gently.

"I want to stay with you," she whispered the words, smiling against my lips.

I crushed her to my chest, kissing her deeply. She mewled against my mouth, tiny, low noises that brought memories to life. Memories of her mouth on me, her screaming as she came in my arms, the taste of her seared on my tongue.

With a groan, I flipped her beneath me, bracing myself on my forearms to peel her shirt off without breaking the kiss. Her hands tugged at my clothes, her warm fingers sliding along my stomach to my chest.

Reaching over my head, I shucked my tee off. Her eyes left my face to track down my body. I watched her, my eyes hooded as she stretched beneath me, running her hands down the planes of my torso, over the ink that attempted to cover a multitude of scars.

She looked up at me with wide eyes.

"Should we be doing this when—" She broke off, sucking her bottom lip into her mouth again.

This time I didn't hold back the urge to lean down and suck that lip into my mouth, tugging gently at it with my teeth. She moaned when I let it go, swollen now. I tracked my tongue across it.

"We can't change anything right now. Liam won't appreciate us racing after her and putting everyone in potential danger."

"So we have to wait?"

"Yeah." Impressed with my own line of reasoning, I bent to hover my mouth over hers. "Any more distractions?"

"Just you," she whispered, her lips brushing mine as she spoke.

I hovered above her a moment longer, then gathered her in my arms and kissed her until the strawberries and cream taste of her lips surrounded me. She wriggled beneath me, hitting all the right places. I groaned, gripping her hip tight to still her movement.

"Take it easy, Kitten. We've got a lot of time to waste."

Jen dropped her head back onto my arm, squirming in an s-shaped movement. I watched the way her body undulated, sliding against my skin to where my legs trapped her beneath my weight.

"Kitten?" she asked softly, her eyes wide.

"I thought you said you didn't want that." I settled my full weight on her. She groaned, and I made to push up, but her arms wrapped around me tightly.

"Don't you dare move. You asked me if I could do it again, and all I could think of was standing in front of Logan, between you, and I– I froze." Her eyes closed, the admission coming out fast in one long breath.

Like she'd purged it from her body, her mind.

Our time together hadn't been overwhelming to her at all.

She could handle my type of distraction.

Gathering her wrists in one hand, I lifted them over her head, pressing them firmly but gently into the arm of the sofa. Her eyes tracked my movement, then returned to my face. She swallowed, but said absolutely nothing, though her eyes told another story.

Anticipation. Desire. Need.

I released her wrists, and her eyes widened.

"Don't move."

I slid down her body, sliding her bra strap off her shoulder to expose the plump mound of soft flesh, brushing my lips and stubble over the sensitive skin. My mouth tracing the curve of her breast, I slid the other strap down, uncovering the other side, but didn't touch it. Just left her exposed. The cool air would heighten her senses, although the only person here to see her body was me.

My teeth took the nipple of the breast I worked into my mouth, holding it delicately. The implied threat that I could hurt her vying against her trust that I wouldn't, had her gasping with anticipation in soft breaths.

My tongue flicked over the tight bud, hardening with my attentions. I lightly stroked and rolled her other nipple, tugging it gently to make it equally tight. Her hands played with my hair, stroking my neck as she enjoyed the attention, her breaths coming a little faster. The nipple hardened quickly under my fingers.

I flicked my tongue again, nipping it and releasing at the same time as I pinched the other.

Her hips bucked, a cry tearing from her mouth. She writhed beneath me, but there was nowhere for her to go; my weight pinned her jean-clad legs to the sofa, my hips pressed hard against hers. The only thing her movements were doing was turning me hard. Fast.

"Theo," she whimpered, her hands on my shoulders urging me up. "I can't handle– that." She finished her moan in a whisper, as I gazed hard at her.

"Black." The word came out deeper, rougher than I intended, but she responded to it, whispering my name back at me.

"*Black.*"

I gripped her wrists tighter, pinning them over her head.

"I told you not to move," I growled, nipping the soft, tender flesh inside her arms. She tugged inside my grip, but there was no way I was giving her freedoms right now.

My mouth crushed hers, demanding her response as I kissed her, my hand wrapping around her jaw. I released her mouth after a moment, working my way down her throat in a series of brutal kisses that would leave marks the next day. I released her wrists, curling my hand beneath her neck to angle her head the way I wanted it.

Her hands wound in my hair, her nails scratching my shoulders as they travelled my back, hunting for purchase. I nipped around her nipples, slashing my tongue across them. She whined, pulling me back when I continued lower along her body, yanking her jeans off and disposing of my own.

"Knees." I grabbed her wrist, yanking her to me. She collapsed against my chest, sliding lower along my body until her knees hit the floor. Her mouth trailed my skin in a series of wet kisses until she trailed those same kisses the length of my cock. Her knees spread slightly, she took me in her mouth, tearing a groan from my throat. Jen raised her hands over her head, fully extended, and crossed her wrists against my stomach. My fingers wound around her hands, holding them together as she licked and sucked every inch of my cock.

I let her take me as close to the edge, bringing my orgasm close before I lifted her up by the wrists, bending to scoop her over my shoulder. She yelped, earning a smack on her gorgeous behind as I marched us down the hall.

"Where are we going?" she whimpered, gripping my back hard. I smacked her again and again, each time she made a sound. By the fourth smack, I realised she'd done it on purpose and made the next one harder. Her whimper became a moan. I stopped in the doorway, giving her something to grab on to. I smacked her again, then ran my fingers along her exposed slit, coating their tips in her need.

"Fucking hell, Kitten, you're dripping."

"Sorry, Black."

You are fucking not sorry.

I smacked her again, stroking my fingers along her, and repeated the process with her draped over my shoulder.

Smack, stroke, smack, stroke.

I made a quick rhythm out of it, bringing her close to orgasm twice, her toes straining, and brought her back, twice. Then I set her on her feet.

"Bed."

I released her arm. She sent me a confused look, wavering. I kept my grin back, knowing that when she came after edging it would be magnificent and I wanted to be deep inside her when she did.

Her inner thighs glistened with her arousal as she tottered to the bed, collapsing against it.

I closed my fist around my dick, pumping it twice, though I didn't need it. Jen gave me everything I wanted. I gripped her hips, lining myself up with her swollen pussy, rubbing the head of my cock through her juices. She moaned, propping herself up on her elbows though her head dropped down between them, panting.

I traced her spine the length of her back with my other hand, earning a shiver that coursed over her entire body. Her arched back rose and fell as I touched her. Her pussy clenched against the tip of my cock. I slipped two fingers between us to lazily circle her clit, tugging the tiny nub until it swelled beneath my fingers. A few flicks there and she cried out, her orgasm so close. I removed my fingers from her clit. Watching as she turned to me, red-faced and panting.

"Breathe, Kitten," I commanded her. Her brows drawn, she did, inhaling slow, long breaths. Her colour evened, she nodded. "Better?"

"Yeah."

"Good. Let's do it again."

Her shocked look almost tipped me past the brink, but I held back, wanting her to experience the most powerful orgasm she'd probably ever have.

I pressed the head of my cock inside her, feeling the delicious tug as her swollen lips closed around me. Her walls constantly fluttered as I brought her to the brink and back, over and over again.

Her clenches on my cock were almost too much, and soon she wasn't the only one breathing hard between rounds. Her face a soft pink, her body covered in sweat. It pooled along her back, tiny rivulets running down her sides. Her legs were beaded with a heavy sheen, my own body hot as I brought her back one last time.

I waited till her breathing slowed, and she nodded, then put my fingers onto her clit again.

"Black—" she moaned, but that was all I let her get out before I slammed into her, pounding her body with the energy I'd reserved for her. Her body clenched tight, she arched off the bed, her knuckles white where she tore at the sheets.

Her pussy clenched on me as I drove into her, her orgasm starting. I bit my own tongue for the distraction pain offered, anything to forestall my own pleasure until she'd had hers.

Jen screamed, her hips bucking wildly against mine, her legs thrashing where I pinned her to the bed. Her body jerking, she screamed between pants, her walls clenching me tight. I released every inch of my control, pounding her in rapid movements as I came, gripping her tight as she took me with her. We collapsed together, our hearts beating a staccato to their own music.

CHAPTER TWENTY-THREE

JENNY

Huge arms wrapped around me, pressing me to a solid chest speckled with dark hair. I rubbed my cheek against him, his hands stroking my hair as the sun rose on our naked bodies. I couldn't care less if all the city saw us.

I woke in his bed, in his arms. Every dream, every fantasy of him true, except one.

We weren't a family.

Ashley was gone.

The thought stole my peace. It flitted away, out of my grasp as I pushed off his chest, the phoenix inked there aflame beneath the morning light. Two hands gripped my hips solidly, and I couldn't move.

"You okay, Kitten?" Theo watched me with bright eyes. I wiggled, trying to shake him off me. "Whoa, girl. You're not going anywhere just yet."

"Let me up, Theo."

"So you can pace the room, get yourself worked up, and call Liam and abuse him?" He watched me with knowing eyes and a half-smile. I snarled, but his last words gave me pause, my eyes shifting to his phone.

He moved it further aside. "Uh-uh. So, cuddle?"

I snorted. "You don't do cuddles."

"On the contrary. I'm an excellent cuddler." He pulled me into him, rolling onto his side and tucking me back against his enormous body. "See?"

"I'm going to disappear," I grumbled as his arm wrapped around my waist, pulling me back against him.

His chest rumbled — a deep, heavy sound that reverberated through my body. His warmth soaked into my skin, into my bones. I scooted back a little closer.

"You right there, Kitten?" he murmured somewhere about my head. I nodded.

"I feel safe."

"That's how this works. Sleep, girl."

His arm snug around my waist, his breathing slowed, not fooling me for one moment that he slept at any point. Neither did I, but at least when I closed my eyes, the comfort of his strength and care overwhelmed any visions of disaster.

The horror of potentially having lost my daughter hung over me, the situation completely out of my control, but in Theo's arms, it became a little more distant, a little more bearable.

The thought of having a normal life, with a normal man was a fun fantasy that filled the too-early hours of the morning. I snorted at the thought of Theo as a normal man.

"You'll never be normal." I yawned against his arm wrapped around my chest. "Shouldn't we get up?"

"Still flattering me." His arms tightened around me. "Rest. For now."

I blinked into his skin, his sweat melding with tears that never got to fall from my cheeks, listening to his unsaid words swim about in the morning mush of my brain.

After all, what else is there for you to do?

Bacon and eggs on a bagel slid across the breakfast bar. I propped my elbows on the hard surface, staring into my undrunk coffee. The plate nudged between my elbows. I stared at it, too. Theo gave it a hard shove, pushing it between my arms and a fork clattered onto the plate.

"Eat, Jen." His voice held a warning note, but it bypassed me. I looked up at him, then back to my coffee.

"Can I do anything?"

Theo snorted. "Yeah. You can fucking eat. What is this, your third day without a meal? And the weeks before that, barely snacking."

I shrugged. I hadn't been counting. "What's the point?"

Silence permeated the kitchen, filling the stale air in rooms I hadn't left in too long. The plate disappeared. I resumed studying the internal diameter of my mug.

"What's the point?" Theo's hands folded around my upper arms, pulling me around to face him. I blinked. "The point is, you need to eat or you'll make yourself sick. Eat. At least, so you have energy when you see your daughter again."

I lifted my eyes to meet his, wishing I could fall into their depths and be drunk on him again; the perfect distraction. "Is she coming back? Do I get to see her?"

A drop of hope hung in the air between us.

Theo's eyes only reflected my own desperation, a void inside me that couldn't be filled by anyone but her. He shook his head, more of a violent jerk than any normal movement. My head went back down, the drop of hope missing me by a mile before it shattered silently on the kitchen floor.

"Eat, Jen." Theo's hands squeezed my arms in a gentle massage. "You need to look after yourself. Or let me. Dammit."

I frowned as his hands dropped from my arms, patting at his pockets. He answered the phone, turning away from me. The back door banged before he'd said a word, and I already knew what he would say when he came back in.

He didn't keep me waiting, and I was grateful for it. The door banged again, his quick strides and furrowed brow the only confirmation I needed. His lips moved in quick patterns. I traced them with my finger. His hand clamped around my wrist, jolting me out of my reprieve.

"Jen. Have you heard anything I've said?" Theo frowned, his hold firm but gentle as he stared at me assessingly. I got the impression my sanity may be on the line, but at this point, what did his opinion of me matter?

"You're going. Back to the thing." I waved vaguely, flapping my hand in his grip. He released it, still frowning. "Work stuff. You'll be back, blah blah."

His eyebrows twitched, giving him the look of an overgrown hawk. "Did you just blah me?"

"Uh-huh." I nodded, my coffee slopping over the edge of my cup onto my fingers. I ignored it, patting his eyebrows. He brushed my hand away, liberating my coffee cup from my hold.

"Are you okay?" he asked in a soft voice. That dramatic one reserved for mental patients you don't want to rouse or the dying relative you don't want to piss off in case they write you out of their will.

I held back a giggle and that fast, it became rage instead. Looked like I sat squarely in the former camp.

"Am I okay?" I asked brightly, moving for the first time. Theo straightened, his arms crossing his chest in that all too familiar barrier pose.

The *I'm-working-and-she's-getting-emotional-again* pose.

Well, fuck that.

"Yeah." Even his voice came out guarded.

I sighed, shaking my head in mock disappointment.

"You boys think you're all so smart, and know so much about Logan, but at the end of the day, you're on the back foot at every turn, and it pisses you off. Right? But the bottom line is that you're all predictable. Everything you do is predictable. He's in fucking jail, and you *still* can't beat him!" Theo opened his mouth, but I held up a hand, forestalling him. "And then you have the gall to ask if I'm okay? Theo, he took my daughter. The one *he* abandoned, and you took her away! All of you! I didn't see you raising a hand to stop Cal. Or Liam. You didn't even ask where she IS!"

My shriek rose to a yell at the end of my tirade, every inch of vitriol Logan had poured into my life vomiting back out onto the man who had invested years of his protecting us. But there was no *us* anymore; we were just two people held together by the memory of a little girl I might never see again.

Might never find out what her new name would become, might never be able to hug, or tell her I loved her, and I'd wasted one of the precious nights I'd had left with her, knowing this could all go to shit at any time with the man in front of me for what? Sex?

My body and brain ached. The feeling eluded my heart that had become a shrivelled seed rattling somewhere about in a big, empty chest cavity it was supposed to live inside.

Theo's arms dropped to his sides. He leaned forward as though he would take a step in my direction, halting when I glared at him.

"I'm going in to ask Liam those questions now," he said quietly, his tone absent of the anger and derision that had laced mine. My ego and importance shrank by the minute. I didn't deserve his rage. "I'll be back when I'm done."

He held my stare for a long moment, completely unrattled. Cold. His hands clenched once at his sides as he nodded, swiping the bike key from the bench.

The garage door slid closed quietly behind him.

I stood, tears running down my cheeks, wishing I hadn't screamed at the only ally I had, who I'd blamed for my own shortcomings, though part of me reminded me I'd been right about some of it. A lot of it.

But they had worked hard on the Logan case, and his daughter — *our daughter* — sat in the centre of it. The thought sickened me. I clutched my stomach, bumping the mug on the counter. It wobbled as I stumbled blindly toward the hall and somewhere in my foggy brain, I registered it smashing behind me.

Something nipped my foot, but I ignored it, following the path worn into the carpet that led to the bedrooms.

Ashley's bed hadn't been made, her unicorn compendium half open on the floor. She'd been rushed from the house without choosing her toys, under what I hoped was an adequate guard, knowing neither Liam nor Cal would tell me if something happened to her.

Black would.

Somewhere in that empty cavity, the remains of my heart lurched. Theo would tell me. He'd try to get her back, first talking, then fighting it out with Liam, then doing whatever he had to, to help me find her.

He'd break all the rules for us, and I'd pushed him away.

Just because he hadn't shown anger didn't mean he didn't feel it. Under all that badass, he really was a giant marshmallow. Mila had tried to tell me, had tried to show me through her own experience with him, but I hadn't listened. It had taken too many hours sitting with him, working through as much of his night — what little he could tell me of his work — to discover the man beneath the heavy armour he coated himself with against the world.

And I'd pushed him away.

Tears streamed down my face, though I doubted they'd stopped at any point since my rant. I hadn't noticed, lost in my own head, wallowing as I clutched her soaking pillow. I slapped my tears away, angry at myself for giving in to the emotions. Being numb had kept me going for so long, but the feelings were overflowing now that I had let them free.

I needed to apologise. I needed to beg for forgiveness. I needed to ask my friend to come back because both of us needed that hug right now. I tapped my pocket, but my phone didn't fill the small space — I'd left it in the kitchen. I snorted, the tears slowing, then stopping. I rubbed my swollen, tired eyes, and pushed up, determined to call Theo and beg for that hug. He'd come back. He would come back? Then it would be okay.

If he came back.

I swallowed the doubt alongside a decent dose of salt and a disgusting glob of phlegm and swivelled around. My foot stung as it touched the carpet. I frowned at the blood smeared where I'd stepped, pulling my foot onto my lap. A fine sliver of china poked out from my heel. I picked at the shard, extracting it from my foot. It bled more than it should for a small cut. Pinching the thing between my fingers, so I didn't leave it lying in Ashley's room, I rose tentatively, leaving my heel up.

Shaking my head at my own stupidity, I tottered to the door, thinking of the mess in the kitchen I needed to clean up. Preferably *before* Theo came back and saw how widespread my breakdown had been. Though he'd worn the brunt of it, earlier. The rooms had come into shadow, and I wondered how long I'd wallowed in my own misery on Ashley's bed.

Hours of days I'd mourned the loss of slipped away from me now, a day at a time, and I barely noticed their passing.

I thought about the mess in the kitchen with a sigh. I hoped the coffee hadn't spilt all over my phone, and I closed my eyes at the thought I couldn't call Theo, though I'd never used his number.

Maybe today, I would.

A warmth hit me as I stood there with my eyes closed, a smile creeping across my face.

You came back.

Cigarette smoke and stale sweat wafted over me, coating me in a greasy stench.

That's not Theo.

But the smell of him was too familiar. Something ingrained into me from our days still living together as a family, from my childhood.

I opened my eyes.

"Get out of my house, Chad."

CHAPTER TWENTY-FOUR

BLACK

Liam observed me through heavy-lidded eyes, his phone slipped into his pocket for once. I had his full attention, but nothing I could do would change his mind. Cal's face was a quandary. Torn somewhere between a frown and pain, he'd become little mini-me of his mentor. A perfect Liam replica with no feeling.

And Jen called me hard. I snorted, folding my arms over my chest.

"She'll be alright, Black. She's got the free time to do whatever she likes now." Liam gave the hint of a smile before it disappeared. I was used to this face; it came out to play when he refused to budge. But we were still on even par for the course. "With the girl gone, she can probably live on her own. She'll be of little interest to Logan at this point."

I stared, transferring my astonishment to Cal, who winced and studied the floor. A new habit. Cowardice didn't suit him. I said the words in my head, not yet ready to fuck up our friendship. But if he continued this way, that day would come soon.

"Are you fucking kidding? That *girl*," I spat Liam's word back at him, "is her daughter. For seven years. The entire reason for her life being turned upside down."

"And now she can have it back." Liam nodded, the benevolent uncle giving the world's worst gift. "I'll fix up her accounts and give her a new identity. She'll be fine."

She's not fine. We'll be lucky if she's not fucking suicidal.

The thought clenched my gut hard. I battened down the urge to tear from the building and back to Jen, but I had to get these two idiots around to my way of thinking. Which was a hell of a lot harder than I'd expected it to be.

"She's not fine," I growled through gritted teeth. "She's far bloody from it. Ask your girl what it would be like to have a child taken away from her. Ask her." I wheeled on Cal. He had the grace to look abashed. I snorted.

"It's not her child." Liam had his phone out, flicking through a screen only he could see.

The urge to slap it from his hands buffeted me, but striking a senior officer would only lose me my job, and I needed the task force's resources to protect Jen.

Otherwise, I wouldn't have given a fuck.

"You're a heartless prick."

"I've been told." Liam paused, looking up. "You wanted off this duty before. Do you still want that? I need you back on the fighting ring. You did well there." He said it in the same tone you'd invite someone for a picnic at the lake.

I was beginning to get an inkling of how Jen had felt all this time, and my respect for the woman grew another notch for what she'd endured. Time to make good on some of those promises I'd flung around.

"If you don't think she still needs protection from Logan, you're kidding yourself. She's his daughter's foster mother. Regardless of where you put *Ashley*," I put emphasis on her name, and Cal winced, but Liam remained impassive, "that won't change. You know Logan will kill her one day."

Cal's wince turned to the same hard face Liam frequently boasted. "We know that, Black."

"Yeah? Sounds like you need a harsh reminder."

"You're good at the house, right?" Liam wandered to the door, the picture of the vague, immersed businessman but the asshole was anything but. "Want back in the cage?"

Nerves jumped under my skin, energy writhing within me, desperate for release.

"Yeah. I'll go back to the cage."

If nothing else, I could find her fucking brother and put my fist in his face.

The new fighting ring held more people than I'd expected after the last fight. Extra rows of seats were laid out the back. Samson had pulled the last one down; it's flimsy cover story as a legal fighting ring having held to the last, though even I had to admit it had been a poor set up.

I paused mid-step to examine that.

My head had been so far up my own ass with Jen and the infighting with Liam and Cal that I'd never stopped to assess whether Samson's set up hadn't been something more. I cursed, firing off a quick text to Liam. My phone buzzed less than a second later, his reply lined speedily beneath my own.

Me: Check local cops. No one called this thing in though it had been up for months.

Liam: Thanks. Will check.

Liam: You'll have no backup tonight.

Me: I'm good.

Not having Liam at my back didn't bother me, but I hadn't told Jen when I'd be back, and that part *did* bother me. I opened a new message to her, staring at her photo, the tiny pinprick that it was. I should have hugged her before I left, have told her she wasn't alone. That she had a place with me.

That I loved her.

I hadn't done any of those things. Instead, I'd been the same asshole Cal and Liam had and walked out without another word.

The ref called my name from the ring — not over the loudspeaker like last time, but a simple yell across the internal space beneath the building. I blacked the screen, shoving my phone across the small table used for the fighter's personal things.

Most of us skulked in the corners, as far from each other as possible. It was difficult to hurt someone you'd just befriended. Well, for some. But it had never been something I'd been in the habit of doing, and I wasn't about to start now.

A meaty hand thunked down beside mine. His fist glinted dully, brass knuckles raised across both fists. I looked up at the fighter I didn't recognise, and up.

His equally-meaty face split into a brainless grin, but his tiny eyes squinted at me, piggy and mean-looking.

Without taking my eyes off him, I held out a hand silently to the attendant. When it stayed empty, I flicked my fingers, then finally looked away from the fighter as he moved off, lumbering slightly.

Gotta be fast, stay outside his reach, or get inside it and get out.

A different feeling clenched in my gut, one that told me tonight may not go the way I'd planned.

I wished I'd sent that message to Jen.

"Where's mine?" I asked, glaring at the attendant who stepped back with open hands. Beside him, the bookie coughed. My mouth sprang shut with a snap, rattling teeth that might not be in my head at the end of the night. "Fine."

I reached for my ankle knives, but the ref tapped my arm lightly, stepping back with wary eyes when I swung around on him.

"No weapons," he said quietly, but he may as well have yelled it, for all the sound in the converted car park.

Every spectator sat silent, watching us. Perhaps this made as good entertainment for the rich pricks.

"Fine," I grated, rolling my shoulders. I'd engaged in an illegal fight, and nobody forced me to be here. It wasn't like I had a union rep to complain to, though Liam would have a sore ear by the time I'd finished gnawing it off.

The ref held out his hand in the same manner I had a moment ago, his fingers flicking up in rapid movements.

With a sigh I held back, I pressed four blades into his palm. He raised his eyebrows with his hand still extended. I folded my arms over my chest, glaring at him. There was no way in hell I'd enter the ring unarmed against that tough-looking bastard.

The ref held my gaze, jerking his nod quickly and folded the knives into a bundle. The blades shrieked against each other as he clattered them carelessly onto the small table. I winced, glaring at his back as he took his position. If I survived this fight, I would be having words with the man before I left.

If I survived.

My eyes swept the crowd, but the absence of my support crew hit me hard. This time, I fought alone. I pushed Jen's face, her feel, her smell from my senses, sinking deep to the place I had to go to walk out of this fight.

Last time.

I stepped into the ring, the light chatter that had sprung up dying an instant death as I circled the behemoth of a man.

He took a few, long and slow swings at me, warming his arms up. I could jump into him quickly, risk everything to end the fight fast. But risking mistiming it with no understanding of his reflexes sat poorly on me; I hated going in blind. My alternative was that I could wait him out, wear him down until he dropped and batter him on the ground until he couldn't get up.

Probably the more sensible option.

Jen's face drifted across my vision. I shook my head. I needed to be clear on this, and I wasn't in the right headspace. My opponent lumbered a swing again, and I saw an opening. Leaping in, I attacked his throat, his eyes. The big man stumbled back.

I narrowly missed his arms closing around me. I'd opened a cut beneath his eye that bled, but it wouldn't obscure his vision for some time. I cursed myself for the rushed hit. That quick entry wouldn't be allowed again. I'd wasted the opportunity and my initial burst of energy.

Breathing deeply, I settled my heart rate, shaking off excess, jittery energy and set into a prowl around him. It was a crowd-pleaser; regardless of whether I won or lost, they wanted to see drama, and the constant, regular movement kept my muscles warm.

He came in closer, and I let him, ducking beneath his long swings to deliver a series of punches to his gut, then bounced back, around him. I got in a kick to his kidneys before he turned, faster than I expected, and clipped my temple with his knuckle jewellery.

Lights flashed in my vision. I closed them, taking a breath and ducked, hoping I predicted his movement right. I opened my eyes, shaking off the blood that streamed into it — what I'd been trying to do to him earlier.

I collected his chin with my fist in a textbook uppercut. He swung again, tottering back, then lumbered forward as my own vision began to spiral. I swiped at my eyes with my forearm, not wanting the slippery blood on my fists; every punch I landed had to count. I set up for a final tornado kick, but somehow I underestimated his last haymaker and spun right into it, the concrete collecting us both as we went down.

Lights dimmed around me, the room sinking as black as my heart, and I hoped the big fucker would stay down.

CHAPTER TWENTY-FIVE

JENNY

My brother stared at me, menace warring with hatred in a mix that suited him all too well. "But it's not your house at all, is it, sister?"

"Get *out*," the words spat from between my teeth and I knew Chad had no idea how lucky he was that that's *all* that came out. I wanted to punch him. But if I started down that road, I might not stop. "You lost me my daughter."

Red, swollen eyes turned flint-hard as my brother attempted to stare down at me from the same height. "She's not yours, barren bitch."

He tossed the comment out so idle, so uncaring, my world dropped out from beneath me. *This* was who I'd broken Theo's trust to see? My last family. My stomach flopped heavily on itself, taking my lung capacity with it.

I gaped, in shock. He knew about all the years Paul and I had tried; knew the times I'd cried when Paul had come home late from work, but it hadn't been work that ate his hours away from me. Chad knew because I'd cried to him. I hadn't had anyone else. He'd smoked and patted me on the head like a belligerent puppy come to atone.

"I know you have something to do with...with..." My throat sucked together, and I couldn't get a breath out, let alone a word.

"With what?" Chad sneered, pulling a mostly-dead cigarette from behind his ear and lighting it. I said nothing, hoping the smoke alarms would go off in his face.

"With Ashley." I bit my lip, wishing I hadn't said her name. Like I wished harm on her in doing it. "Why would you be involved in anything that hurts your family?"

I shook my head, looking at him; the rumpled, cheap suit, stained material, uneven growth on his chin. I knew Chad cared little about himself and less about anyone else.

"Pays well," Chad grunted through a cloud of smoke. He threw the used butt on the ground, rubbing its carcass into the worn carpet. Glitter sizzled around it.

"Money." Well, I could have guessed that. Still, disappointment flooded me, removing any pity for my last remaining family member.

You have Ashley. She's not gone.

And I'd do anything to keep her that way, even if it meant losing her. She had to have a life, and I was clearly doing a bang-up job on my end.

"He turned up one day, a guy with these dead eyes, and offered me a job. More money than I'll ever fucking need. Apparently, he's in jail now, but the money's still good. Fuck him."

Chad lit another cigarette while ice lanced through my stomach.

"Put it out," I snapped by reflex. He rolled his eyes at me. "Chad, the man. What's his name?"

"Logan. Like the fucking Wolverine." He laughed, turning away to take a long drag.

My throat closed, sucking air from my lungs. I swallowed back the bile that rose in its place. "And the job?"

My brother turned to me with glinting eyes that mirrored only one person's I had seen before. A shiver started in my lungs that somehow connected to my stomach. I bent at the waist, retching. Chad grabbed my arm as I heaved up bile, acid burning my throat. He jerked me along the hall, still bent at the waist, my head banging against the walls. I stuck out my arms to protect myself, then I was in an open space.

My senses came back to me in the kitchen.

You got as far as the kitchen without defending yourself. Wake the fuck up!

My brain screaming at me in what sounded suspiciously like Theo's voice, I clawed at my brother's hand, my fingers slipping in his clammy grip. My mouth opened to yell as I hit him at the same time.

Those dopey, bloodshot eyes and pudgy face spun on me faster than I expected, a wicked-looking blade in his hand ending with a curved point. It touched my skin, deceptively smooth and cool, and every inch of me stilled, a survival instinct snapping in. The tip dug into my arm, sliding too easily beneath my skin, the threat implicit.

I winced against it, refusing to give him any satisfaction, but the pressure increased, a thin drop of blood rolling to where his hand gripped my wrist. In the end, I yanked back, a muffled yelp launching from my clenched jaw.

Chad didn't release me, pausing as the blade moved away from my skin. Another person might have taken this for a reprieve, but I knew my brother; I'd been on the end of his violent fights as a child.

He swung my arm wide in an arc. I tripped over my feet, and by the time I'd caught my balance, he swung me again. My feet moved without permission, my cheek slamming into the side of the refrigerator.

I groaned, my tortured skin pressed to the cool metal surface. I puffed short breaths as my world slowed, halting, but he turned me again, pressing my back to the hard surface behind me and punched me in the stomach.

I crumpled to the floor, a wilted wail dying in my throat as I gasped for breath. Eying the tiles as they crept closer, I hoped they would be as cool as the fridge. He laughed above me, kicking at my ribs.

"Fuck off, Chad," I wheezed, strained breaths sucking in and puffing out too fast to be of much use. My groans echoed between my ears.

"Your man doesn't do you hard enough?" He sneered, staring down at me, a sickening version of excitement brightening his eyes. He kicked me again.

Nausea claimed me. I rolled, drawing my knees over my stomach for protection, but he'd only ever had one big go in him, even as a kid. He got bored after that, and couldn't be bothered continuing.

The first flush swelled his face, coated it in a fine sheen of sweat, though it wasn't hot, warning me that tonight could be different.

He made a lewd gesture with his fist and tongue, my bleary eyes barely making it out. I refused to answer him, pressing my fingers lightly into my cheek to see if anything had broken. Everything hurt, and after a minute, I stopped trying to assess myself and focused on trying to stand instead, though nothing cooperated the way it should.

My brother hoisted me to my feet. I stumbled, crying out involuntarily when I crashed into the pantry door.

"Stupid slut," my brother grumbled, the connecting door to the garage clicking open.

I tore my arm from his grasp, turning in a disoriented semi-circle, still hunched and ended up facing the wrong direction. This time his boot came up. I backed away quickly, but the toe still caught my shoulder.

Suddenly staring at the ceiling which swam in bright star shapes above my head, I lay on my back, gulping breaths, barely able to move. Chad's shadow covered me as he muttered away to himself, gripping my arm to yank me back up.

I swayed, disoriented, my stomach and mouth arguing over precedence and the moment I was distracted, a soft cloth covered my eyes. A familiar, but unwelcome scent, clinging to my skin the same way it had lingered the last time Ashley's father had manhandled me. Hit me. When he had intended to kill me.

Nearly killed Theo, too.

My stomach revolted, winning the battle, and this time I threw up properly. I vomited the remains of food I didn't know I'd eaten. The splatter not quite hitting the kitchen tiles, and I smiled. Chad cursed, slapping me with a damp hand he wiped on the back of my shirt, but I was inordinately pleased with my unintentional collateral damage.

The cloth bounded around my head blinded me, stars flashing on the inside of it. The world swayed with me, and then we were moving again. Barely able to keep upright, I lurched as he dragged me from the house, instinct holding back the last remains of far too little food that day. I needed all the energy I could muster to fight whatever was coming. Pity; I would have liked to cover him in vomit. It was the absolute least my weakling brother deserved.

He spun me, a cloud of smoke paired with stale breath hitting my skin. I slammed into the side of Theo's car, my head contacting the roof with an actual ding. That struck me as funny as the stars returned, streaming across the backs of my eyelids, then darkness filled my vision. I hung in the air, suspended, then rolled onto a rough surface.

Rust, blood, and something that would remain unidentified sucked up my nose. Twisting my head, I tried to get away from it, the space too constricted for me to move much. For the first time in many years, I wished I had longer hair to form a barrier between me and the rest of the world.

Which grew smaller as I compressed into a too-small space. Rubber shrieked, alternating with an engine in its death throes revving in my ears. Gasses filtered into the boot with me, my head warning me not to breath as the sister in me rolled virtual eyes at the thought of my brother typically owning a rust bucket of a car.

My head swam with every turn, too many to keep track, and nausea warred in my gut. While I had no hesitation spewing bile on my brother, I wasn't keen to do it in the boot of his rusty bucket of a car, and all over myself.

My personal battle lasted an eon, and just as I thought I'd lost, the car stopped. I coughed, squinting as the boot opened. Hands grabbed at me. I pressed my forearms to my head, barely able to keep my eyes open. My mind split open with the brightness, the world disappearing.

What the hell was wrong with me? Maybe he'd given me a concussion when he'd thrown me around the house.

I was a moth to a nightlight, and the glare outside my tiny compartment encompassed me as my feet hit the ground, skating across the surface. I leaned against Chad's sweat-stained suit jacket, hoping I rumpled it, though further damage to his unkempt appearance was unlikely. My mind flitted between where he'd moved me to and what had already happened, replaying the events over in my head in a random and out-of-sequence order.

A door clanged, and I found the floor with my face again, crumbs and more unidentifiable substances adhering to my skin. Even if I bathed in sulphur, I knew the smells would be in my mind forever.

However long *forever* would be.

The pain receded faster this time. The industrial carpet cooled my swollen cheeks. I let the sensation sink into my overheated skin. My stomach stopped lurching, but the urge to sleep remained. Staying awake became a chore. The office darkened, and I lay there, alone. I tried to sit, pushing my arms beneath my body, but the weight slammed me back to the floor, and the world swam once more.

What's the point if you've lost her?

I ignored the sassy little voice, no longer anything like Theo's, it became more like my own, snarking at me, mirroring the self-derision I buried daily.

I haven't lost her. And if I have, I need to make sure she's safe.

Though how in the hell I was going to make that last bit come true, I had no idea. First thing, I had to get off the carpet. Then wash.

Priorities.

Which worked just fine, until Theo tumbled onto the floor in front of me in absolute silence.

I stared at the lump, waiting for a breath, a laugh, some snide, badass comment he usually came out with. Anything at all that told me I wasn't looking at the back of a dead body.

Clammy hands closed around my upper arms, dragging me across the carpet before I could call out. I found the doorway with my head, and by the time I collapsed to the equally-filthy carpet of the room, shadows closed in the edges of my vision. I had enough awareness to peer through slitted eyes at Theo's still form, my mouth dry, and whispered a plea for him to rise before the darkness found me a second time. I tumbled into its unwelcome depths again, this time utterly alone.

Warm drops flicked onto my face. I flinched at their warmth then tasted its salt. Groans followed my assessment close to me, and the next drops that hit my lips weren't sweat.

A solid mass knocked into mine. I curled in reflex, uncurling just as fast as Theo's scent wrapped around me. My hands patted his skin before my eyes tugged open, reluctantly giving up their dark haven to the dim light of my brother's office.

If *office* was the correct term.

I didn't bother with him, my attention was taken up by the great lump of the man I loved slumped in a heap on the floor next to me. My hands traced his muscles, the familiar shape of him. It seemed an age since I'd touched him last, though it had only been this morning.

"That tickles," his chest rumbled, vibrating against me, his forehead pressed to the floor. Blood pooled around him, glugging into his hair. I used the corner of my shirt to try to stem the flow, but he batted me away.

"Are you okay?" I whispered, knowing it was a stupid question.

He wouldn't tell me if he was injured anyway, thought it looked like a forgone conclusion, and he certainly wouldn't say anything of the kind in front of a threat. I asked, anyway. Theo laughed into the carpet, bracing on his forearms with a groan, his back arching. Muscles and bones popped along his spine. I stared, hoping he wouldn't come apart on me, my eyes tracing the lines of the musculature beneath his black tee regardless.

He pushed back, only to receive a boot in the throat from my brother I didn't have time to protect him from. I launched to my feet, the room swaying around me precariously. Chad leered at me.

Large hands gripped Black's arms, the man hovering over us so massive, he made Theo look small. Heavy belts attached to a sheath wrapped around his arms behind his back. Even with the belts cinched tight to restrain his forearms, the case seemed a little loose. I looked up at the mountain of muscle working on Theo speculatively.

He gave a final tug on the black creation, Theo's shoulders rolled back. Swelling on that same shoulder I'd spent hours working on — his throwing arm — began to swell. A small thing, but it annoyed me past all else. I lashed out at the giant of a man securing him, clearly nowhere in my right mind as the giant could have killed me with a few fingers.

A hand planted in my chest pushed me back into my brother. He held me while I flailed, digging his filthy nails into my skin.

I watched, useless, as the big man that made *my* big man look small punched him again and again. The room's movement around me made me seasick, and I screamed myself hoarse. I collapsed to my knees, retching, but I had nothing left to throw up.

Theo groaned, casting a sideways glance at me, his uninjured eyebrow lifting. I caught his eye, nodding. He lumbered to his feet, but it didn't last long. One knee hit the ground, then the other, his quads trembling visibly through his black pants covered with a darker fluid. I hoped the blood belonged to someone else.

His head bowed, Theo flexed his shoulders, but no trick would going to remove the belted sheath fixed around his arms.

"Think I wouldn't be able to take you from him? You're pathetic," Chad sneered, pacing around us in a circle. I stared at him, hyper-aware of Theo in my peripherals.

Chad tottered his way about; for a nugget of a man, and one I was sadly related to, he had no centre of gravity. Instead of appearing as a predator, he looked more like a clown performing warmup laps at the circus, with a big knife. A drop of scarlet painted the tip; he hadn't even bothered to clean it off from threatening his sister.

"You're pathetic," I spat back at him, rising on my own knees to shuffle closer to Theo. My arms wrapped around his shoulders, refusing to budge when he nudged me back. "No more."

I shook my head at him and stared up at the big man, holding his gaze with a hard one of my own, and hoped I'd copied Theo's. I'd seen it aimed at me more than I liked, after all. My voice stayed firm and unwavering; another fluke. I had little hope that it would accomplish what I wanted.

To my surprise, his dull gaze turned speculative as he looked over the pair of us. His chin jerked as he stepped back. I risked taking my eyes off him to watch my brother, trying to work out how in the hell we were getting out of here alive. I struggled to stand, planting my feet in a wide, protective stance between our aggressors and the man I loved.

Again.

The big man stopped his retreat against the wall. Chad glared back at me, my own disdain reflected in his face topped with a solid measure of hatred. He stepped toward us.

I turned my back to Theo's front, raising my hands. "*No*."

I couldn't work out which one of us he wanted to hurt more.

"Bitch," he bit off the ends of his words.

"I think you take the award for that one," I said quietly, watching him pace. Theo huffed behind me, the floor shaking with his laughter.

Chad circled, drawing off from the place I defended Theo. The room swirled slowly around me. I gripped the floor with my toes, willing myself not to topple, or this might all be over. My brother thumped Theo with his boot, but he didn't so much as wobble. The big man appeared to be content to stand back and observe, for now.

I grinned. Chad glared at me, his red-rimmed eyes bulging a little. I swallowed back my repulsion at being related to such a pitiful excuse of a human.

Doubt crossed over me — should I be giving him some sort of leeway because he was my brother? My back straightened as he left Theo alone and stomped toward me, waving the knife.

"Jen. Move," Theo said quietly behind me.

I knew he meant to take whatever was coming, but I'd promised myself this wouldn't happen again to us, and if it *did*, that I wouldn't back down.

My brother was looking at a woman who had nothing left to lose and everything to give. No matter the outcome, he wouldn't win this from me, and that gave me power.

It turned my fear into something else altogether.

Theo shifted behind me, and I knew the moment his attention snapped to Chad and the blade in his hand. Their rhythm became a dance, one I knew well, even though I couldn't see Theo. He was just *there*, as always.

Chad stopped walking and faced me. I couldn't shield Theo as much as I wanted, but for right now, it would have to do. I didn't want to draw my brother's attention.

My foot skimmed back into Theo's shin. The material around my ankle pulled back —covertly, I hoped — exposing the ankle holster Theo had made up for me. He grunted, shifting his leg against my foot. My hands squeezed into fists at my side as I floundered for ideas. Chad came at me, the knife pointed at me in a classic stab gesture straight from Hollywood, and my muscles froze.

I promised I wouldn't run. I promised.

Light flashed in the sides of my vision, panic setting in at my refusal to dive out of the way of the madman coming at me. I couldn't knife fight; I'd end up dead on the manky floor of my brother's office. Theo nudged my leg. I took a long breath in through my nose as I sank back in what I hoped looked like a fighter's crouch.

The flashing in my vision settled along with my pulse as I held my ground, my fingers slipping back for the knife at my ankle.

I'd set myself up to kill my brother, or at the very least, maim him heavily, when Theo's scornful laugh, coated with derision filled the room.

"You're not going to stab her with that."

CHAPTER TWENTY-SIX

BLACK

Chad's mouth dropped open comically. "I'm not?"

"He's not?" Jen asked, twisting to turn her back on her brother for a moment to stare at me. I could have told her it was a stupid fucking idea.

Chad grabbed for her hair. I swung around on my knees, knocking Jen aside to headbutt the insolent prick, my knees digging into the threadbare carpet. He fell back with a cry, clutching his face. The big man in the shadows of the room did nothing. I glared at Jen's brother from my half-crouch, then sank back to my knees.

"No." I shifted to face her, my legs shaking beneath my weight. I bit back a curse, and let them fill my head instead. I nodded to the giant asshole who'd put the belts on my arms. "But he will."

Jen looked between us, her eyes holding mine for a split second before she stood, brushing her clothes off. "Well, that was fun," she spoke to the room.

I frowned; I had no idea what she expected to achieve, but at this point, her game was a dangerous one. Chad still curled on the ground, his knife in his grip.

"Stay down," I growled at him. The small man looked around the room with wide eyes and started to rise. I thought about sweeping a foot out to knock him back on his ass, but Jen held a palm out behind her.

"Take those off him." She stood in front of the big man, nodding back at me. Her arms hung loosely at her sides. I sighed, still eyeing Chad, waiting for him to do something else stupid. Smitty. Whoever this bottom feeder wanted to call himself.

The bands on my arms loosened. I looked back in surprise. The giant gave me a dopey grin, backing off. I didn't want to admit I had no idea what was going on, but if it worked for my woman and saved our combined asses, I was good to go with it. I rolled my shoulders, knots popping in them, covering her brother's pathetic protests.

Jen nodded at the big man as he turned to leave. I called him back, but when he turned, his eyes gleamed in a silent challenge. I frowned, then jerked my head. "Who set this shit up?"

The giant looked from me, then to Jen and his gaze softened.

What the actual fuck?

"For you." He lifted a shoulder that matched his bulk, a card floating to the floor at Jen's feet and lumbered out the door. Chad twitched beside me. I leaned over to punch him without looking at him and swiped the blade away with my palm.

"Pity. I wanted to watch you throw under pressure. See if I taught you right."

Jen spun on her heel, a grin lighting her face, her fingers held up, an inch of empty space between them. "So close. But, glad that's not a choice I had to make."

He's her brother, asshole.

But he's a sweaty little prick, I argued silently with myself.

"Understandable." I shrugged.

Jenny caught my eye, still grinning. Her smile inverted as she stared over my shoulder. "What do we do now?"

"We? Nothing. You sit, I'll call it in."

"Seriously?" Jenny's eyebrows rose.

I sighed, sore and worn out. Plus, I wanted to hold her, make sure the bravado wasn't just that, and my words came out terse. "Yes. Let me fix this up—"

Jen laughed at me. I stopped talking.

"No, I meant I'm not sitting anywhere in this disgusting place." Her hand ran down the side of her face, which bore some red marks and swelling. My teeth clenched so hard I thought I might actually break one.

I nodded, grabbing my phone off the cluttered desk at the back of the small room where it lay with my collection of knives. I shoved each one into their holsters as I tossed a message back to Cal. A message vibrated back before I'd put the last into my ankle sheath.

Slipping my phone into my pocket, I turned my back to the desk, folding my arms over my chest. Jen stared down at her brother, her jaw grinding back and forth. I took the chance to examine her bruises, the way she could barely stand up straight. She'd self destruct if I didn't distract her, and it would stop me from killing him for touching her that way.

"What the hell happened? With the big guy." I jerked my chin at the door, my attention divided between monitoring it and Chad simpering on the floor.

"Oh." Jenny's cheeks flushed, the stain spreading down her neck. I followed it with my eyes then dragged them back to her face. There would be time for that later. Maybe. If she hadn't had enough of me altogether by then. "Um, I thought the arm-binder thing might have been...his? It was big enough to fit you, after all," she clarified. "A little loose at the top when he put it on you as well. And he's sort of a giant. So, I wondered if he might be like me. Submissive. I decided to take the gamble." She swallowed, her cheeks flaring a bright pink.

I watched the change with interest as my mind slowly processed what she meant. "That would never have occurred to me, Kitten. And you did a fantastic job of giving orders. So does that mean you want to switch play later on?" The corner of my mouth curled, thinking back on the way she'd handcuffed me. How she'd danced. But Jen shook her head.

"Oh! No. I just— I guess I knew that was what he needed." Her tongue shot between her lips, dampening her bottom lip, snapping away just as fast. I tracked its progress, returning my attention to her words with pure determination alone. My head cleared.

"You read him." I watched as she stilled. "Didn't you? While the rest of us were battling it out with fists and insults, you were watching. You read me as well?"

"Could you have this conversation somewhere else?" sniped Chad. I kicked out at him, ignoring his pathetic mewl when his ribs creaked beneath my foot.

"Can you?" I repeated to Jen.

She nodded mutely.

Her reactions to every situation together in the last two years — hell, more than two years — hit me square in the face.

Every time she'd waited up, dealt with my grumpy ass not speaking, just being with me. Every silent conversation which conveyed more than words could have done.

I loved this woman more than anything in the world.

The revelations of the last hour rocked my foundations.

Jen stood still, watching me with cautious eyes. "Is that okay?" she asked softly. I barked a laugh. Coming from a woman who'd just talked a giant down with a grand total of four words, her statement seemed ridiculous. But it was just *her*. Jen did what she needed to survive when all she wanted was a partner to get through the day with.

I'd done a daily shit job of the last part and left her in survival mode for far too long.

"Liam should hire you as our negotiator. I'm sorry you had to be the one to stand up to him."

"Are you kidding?" She stared at me, her mouth hanging open as her hands flapped at my face, which had to be battered-looking after the beating I'd taken.

I shrugged, pasting a bored look over my throbbing face. "Job perk."

She snorted, pressing a hand to her own swollen face. "A perk." Laughter bubbled out of her, but I didn't return it.

"He did this?" I jerked my head backward.

"Yes," she whispered her admission. I turned to face her brother. Jen wobbled on her feet again. I frowned.

"Little shit," I said idly, trying not to wince from the pain drumming in the back of my head. Chad skittered backward under my glare. "You know how many people he's maimed in this new *job*? Shitty cuts, unprofessional as well.

269

Is it polite to kick him?" I asked Jen. She stared at her brother.

"You didn't ask last time."

"I'm asking now."

He sneered back at her, and it took everything I had not to wipe the smirk off his face. Yet.

My resolve would only last as long as she stayed in the room.

"Do whatever you like." She held her ground as she had before, stared the little fucker down. *Family*. She'd called him when I hadn't filled the gaping space in her life, lying to myself that she'd been just a job. No longer.

He'd wanted to take her daughter, not for money, but for the chance to hurt someone who loved him because she wasn't alone, and he was. Then he'd taken her instead and hurt her. The little recap opened the cold fury smouldering low in my chest.

I nodded, smiling at her brother and cracking my knuckles.

"Don't you let him near me!" Chad yelled from the floor, crawling across the carpet to cling to her ankles.

Her expression one of disgust, she tugged her legs out of his grasp. He cowered at her feet. I watched him carefully. The thing about slimy bastards is that they often had an ace up his sleeve.

"What?" I asked as Jen looked up at me. "That was my nicest smile."

She snorted, shaking her head. Blonde hair flicked from side to side, her diamond studs sparkling in the hazy light.

I have to get her some sort of financial independence.

She needed it. Badly. This woman couldn't syphon money or love or favours. She wanted to work hard, to earn her way, and if I had *my* way, then she'd get to play hard, too.

And if she wanted to earn that, it would be fine by me.

Her hair swished around the curve of her neck as she looked up at me. "Put him in the cell with Logan."

My lips twitched. I tried to hold my grin back, but it wasn't happening. I looked at the little shitbag. He shook his head, oily blonde hair, a manky mirror of her own, flicking across his face.

"You can't do that! He'll– he'll—"

Yeah, you're fucked, asshole.

Smirking, I sucked in his panic. Jen swayed again. I slipped an arm around her, stepping her sideways to make room for the familiar bulk of a man who stepped into the room.

"You're enjoying this far too much." Cal reached between us, grabbing Chad Smith by the arm and removed him bodily from the room, passing him off to Micah.

The sleazy blonde mess disappeared into the poorly-lit corridor. My arms tightened around Jen, relieved when she sank into my embrace. Holding her to me, her gentle curves fitted to my bulk, and both of us covered in grime, I wished I could keep her there forever.

Cal caught my eye, giving me the tiniest shake of his head. I sighed, kissing the top of her head and inhaling deeply. "You alright, Kitten?" I asked softly as Cal retreated.

I appreciated the gesture. The time.

Jen snuggled, pressing her lips to my sweat-soaked shirt. "*Will* you put him in with Logan? Not that I have a right to ask." Her brow dipped as she tried to hide the concern in her eyes.

I laughed, the sound grating out of my throat. "Hell, no. He'd wind up dead within a day. Unless you want that?" I offered, in case I'd mistaken her intent. "It won't take much to convince Liam." Though he might be useful if we could get him to talk through the chain of command that led to Logan.

She shuddered beneath my arm. I pulled her tighter to my side. "No," she whispered. "I don't want to be responsible for that."

"It could happen regardless. He's gotten himself in with some serious assholes."

She grinned. "Sounds like your sort of person."

"You think so little of my standards? I'm wounded."

"You," she jabbed me with one finger, "are an ass."

"And you are cute as hell, girl." I pulled her around, shifting her body against the front of mine and kissed her until I could barely remember where we were.

I only hoped it was the same for her.

CHAPTER TWENTY-SEVEN

JENNY

An oxygen mask hung beneath my chin where I'd pulled it off to breathe real air. Theo still hovered around me, Danny not far behind me. I caught the glares between them when I turned back to check they weren't killing one another. Danny's faux glare held a cheeky edge, typical of the big, younger cop; Theo's was his typical grumpy self. Nothing hid there, everything open, regardless how it would be taken by anyone else. That was why I loved him.

I loved him.

There really wasn't much more to say. I wanted to wake up wrapped up in his arms every morning and tend every bruise, every mark, whether a physical or a mental scar, together.

Every night.

But the chances of that being my life were slim. First, I had to get Ashley back. She needed to come before every wish I had of my own life. Without her, what was the point of anything? Especially with all the screw-ups I had made.

I'd left the team to clean up my brother's mess, heading back to their office on the back of Theo's lurid green bike. I'd clung tight as Cal objected, his face twisted in a mix of petulance and resignation, but his old partner had typically ignored the younger man.

My arms tight around his waist, the bike purring beneath us, we'd shot through Melbourne traffic. Cars hadn't been an obstacle as we'd weaved between them. God knew how many traffic violations we'd amassed, but at that point I no longer cared, trusting wholeheartedly that Theo would fix any mess we'd incurred. I'd slid off the bike, unsteady, not from his driving but from a lack of clean air.

The concrete pavement had rushed to meet me the moment I released my death grip around his waist. He'd caught me before I'd hit the ground, sliding my helmet off with the care he'd take with a newborn, the concern in his eyes giving my heart a stutter. The heat bore down from late afternoon sun until he'd lifted me in his arms, carrying me inside the cool of his building.

Up in the team's office, there'd been a clean sofa to close my eyes and let the immense stress of the day drift away as I listened to the beat of his heart against my cheek. My only wish then had been that we could have spent the time alone, together instead.

Danny picked up my mild case of carbon monoxide poisoning, had called a paramedic to watch me until I flapped the man away. One man held my focus, and he was a room away. Far too far for my liking.

Cal moved me about like a chess piece as he sorted the investigation to his liking. I supposed that's what I was; a pawn to be allocated a square somewhere in the battle between him and Logan.

Liam's absence didn't come as a surprise; I'd rather expected his distance.

After all, he'd taken my daughter. And no matter what sort of ex-military hard ass he thought himself to be, I could bet diamonds he wouldn't be willing to face me without a decent reason.

Black had no such qualms.

But then, he hadn't stolen my daughter, either.

Micah and Danny had carted my brother off, and I honestly didn't care where he went. Despite Theo's concerns, I *did* partially hope he was put in with Logan.

Though no part of me wished death on my brother, *mostly*, I certainly would love a decent scare in his direction.

Logan appeared equipped for the job.

Was it fair to throw someone as soft as my brother under Logan's wheels? I thought back to the abject fear of him entering my house. My relief that someone with a bigger view of the entire situation — my kindest words, even in my own head for everything that had happened — had thought to take Ashley and hide her.

Even from me.

My heart ached. Selfishly, because if Chad had gotten hold of her, God only knew what would have happened to the poor child.

And in her short decade of years, she'd already suffered enough.

No mother, a psychotic father by any definition, and shunted through foster families until she had reached us. Me. Her last, I had hoped.

Now, I wasn't so sure.

Theo stood at my back. I didn't need to look at him as Cal ran through a list of legalities that went over my head. I knew I could ask Theo any questions I needed — I trusted he would be there to ask. Hoped. Surely they wouldn't abandon me after all these years? Panic rose in my throat. I swallowed it back with a monumental effort, backing to a chair I gripped in a hold that would have crushed anything more delicate.

His presence behind me soothed me. My anxiety sank, letting me see the world with fewer fetters. It wasn't gone, exactly; my world still held a lot of stress, but I'd been kidnapped, my daughter taken, my brother had abused me, and I still didn't know where I stood with the man I loved.

And I had no idea if he loved me back. If he would walk away the moment he had a chance. After all, he'd had over two years with us — the length of a short marriage. I sniffled, covering the motion with my fist. Cal glared at me as I broke through his tirade of legal jargon that went well over my head, regardless of how I tried to keep up with him.

Even if Selena had been present to give me the humanitarian version, his meaning still might have escaped me.

My head had overfilled with information to take anything else in. The space between my ears buzzed as my brain finally fried. I spun on my heel and came face-to-face with Theo. He raised one eyebrow at my lack of composure, the corners of his mouth curling the tiniest amount.

I grinned fully, relieved to not be serious for a moment. My head quietened as my brain began to function again. A brief reprieve. His smile fell, and I nodded, resigned to take in as much as I could. My smile dropping, I turned back to Cal.

"Okay. When do I get to see Ashley?" It was a shot in the dark, but how could I not ask? He grimaced, piercing me with an intensity that bordered on disturbing. I pushed it back with a wave. "Seriously. I've had her with me since a year after her f– after his disappearance. I signed all the papers and waived all the risks. Why is it different now? Why can't I have my daughter back?"

Cal's face softened, reminding me of Mila. They suited each other. But that didn't sort my problem.

"Because you had Paul." Theo's warmth, his nearness brought tension across my back. I bit my tongue. Foster care had a convoluted process and required a full family. Now, it was just me, alone. That made things a whole lot harder, especially when her situation came into consideration.

Like, now.

Cal turned away, busying himself with whatever he didn't need to be looking at. I smiled at my friend's back. Tension shivered across my back as Theo's front pressed to my shoulder blades. It might have been for comfort, but my body had the opposite reaction to him, going into overdrive.

It's the situation. You're full of adrenaline.

Except that I wasn't.

His body heat pervaded me, sinking into my skin. I stilled, then leaned back against him, closing my eyes when his arm slid around my waist.

For the first time, I didn't speak. I waited for him. I'd pushed so far, so much with him, and where had it gotten me?

This time, I waited to see what would happen.

Theo straddled the chair at his desk, just behind me. Where else would he be? I sat at Cal's, my hand hovering over the mouse while dark eyes tracked my every movement. Unnerving, to say the least.

"Take it easy on her," Theo grumbled.

Contact with him had been brief. He'd retreated as soon as Cal stared him down; not out of fear of any sort, I suspected, but out of respect for me.

I gave Cal a semi-grin, and he looked unnerved.

"Pick a place on the map. Any place. Zoom in wherever you like. Pick a state, a city, a farm. We'll get you sorted." Danny stood at the corner of the desk while I stared at him, my head whirling.

"You guys will move me...anywhere?"

"Yeah." Something diminished in his usually-cheeky face, a light dimming. He nodded once, looking behind me. I knew it had to be Theo. Without another word, he walked out of the office, leaving me staring at a map of Australia.

Strong hands gripped my shoulders. I leaned back into him, exhausted.

"Take your time."

"You won't stay?" I asked, not caring if I begged. Wherever I went, it would be away from the only family I had left.

Starting again was *not* the same as starting fresh.

It was hell.

Theo's mouth brushed my cheek, pressing against my hair. "Anywhere you go, I'll watch you. I promise. But this needs to be your choice."

A shudder ran over my shoulders, the tremors leaving my wrist as his hand pressed over mine.

"Do I have to leave? Go somewhere I know no one?"

Without you?

"It would be safer, but no. You don't have to leave...here." His face shuttered, his fingers curled lightly beneath my chin. I leaned into his touch, closing my eyes, letting the promise of his haven call me away from the task they'd set. The choice. "You never have to be alone if you don't want to be."

I nodded, silent, my head attempting to process the information whirling inside it. When I opened my eyes, Theo was gone, and I sat alone with the map.

His advice was sound. I took my time, thinking over my options, working through everything I could to start a new life. All the choices I'd never had when Ashley and I had been forced to part ways with every aspect of *normal life* because of her father's actions. And now, it had become too much.

Very carefully, I zoomed right in on my preference and dropped a little pin on the map.

Then I left Theo's office, unsure if it would be the last time I would step foot in it.

CHAPTER TWENTY-EIGHT

JENNY

The house became a very empty place. No movement, no life. Remnants of glitter and unicorn parties littered the carpet. Some of that would *never* come out, regardless of how well the place got cleaned. I grinned, hovering at the kitchen bench. I still had no idea who was coming to get me, or what the boys' decision would be on where I went, and with who.

If I would ever see Ashley or any of them ever again.

The house bore my tracks in the worn carpet. Though we'd been here for several months, we'd left our mark on the place. I paced the room for the eighth time, under the pretence of checking the drive, though I did that, too.

Another wipe of the walls, a sixth trip to the loo, pure nerves had hit me an hour ago.

My meagre possessions were in one box; Ashley's in another. I wanted to keep a remnant of her life with me, short as it was, in the event I never saw her again. But my daughter — I winced at the term, unsure if it was the right one to use, now — had so few possessions, taking one of them to satisfy my own selfish needs seemed wrong.

Her unicorn compendium sat on top of the box. I nudged her crate closer to mine, finally accepting that I might never see her again. My stomach sank, grief numbing every inch of me as I stared at the boxes.

Her stuffed dugong she'd had at Cal's place poked out of one corner, covered in glitter. It looked like the unicorns had stuck again. Her backpack and all her colouring pads were stacked neatly at the bottom. Almost nothing had gone with her — what were they doing with her — getting her to watch TV? I hoped she was safe. I hoped she had glitter and unicorns and a life.

Oh, God. I hoped I saw her again.

Tears coated my cheeks. I crouched low over her box, the tiny remnants of a broken life packed into a carton. Her real family — the psychotic bastard who tried to give her his own warped version of life who never cared for her, and she had no mother.

I cried for everything Ashley had never had. I wept over my own selfishness. I cried for a kid who should have had a life and a family and a father worthy of who she could become.

Warm arms wrapped around my waist. I closed my eyes and cried harder in the safety of Theo's arms. His cheek nuzzled my back. My stomach ached by the time I'd stopped crying. He lifted me, straightening me gently in his arms to turn me to face him.

Rough fingers stroked my grief and stress away, mingled to create a monster I couldn't escape.

Except with him.

Theo studied at me silently, taking in what must have been a horrendously blotchy and swollen face. Fear and terror stared back at him from haunted eyes alive with grief, with the loss I tried but hadn't fully come to terms with yet. I knew it might never happen, and that scared me more than anything.

His hands cupped my cheeks, his thumbs brushing away the salt crusted there. How long had I been crying? Mortified, I dipped my chin, but he tipped my head back, refusing to let me hide from him.

I frowned, searching his eyes as he bent to kiss my cheeks, the corners of my eyes, my temples before engulfing me in his arms. I snuggled deep, hiccups bursting from my chest in painful tears.

"What happens now?" I asked his t-shirt, choking on a mouthful of it. He snorted, extracting the martial from my mouth.

His lips pressed in a firm line, his eyes steady on my face in his regular, intense stare. Other people might feel intimidated by him, but his frankness was his strength, and I valued his candour. I didn't force him; he held all the answers.

"You come with me," he said simply.

My breath caught in my chest, I blinked at him. "I'm coming with you?"

The corner of his mouth curled. b"Do you want to stay here?"

"Hell no." The words were out of my mouth before I could think them through fully. "But...what happens then?"

"Ashley?" His gaze never shifted from me. "You're not as large a target anymore. She...is."

I nodded, biting my lip. "Will I—" I broke off. His steady gaze told me the answer I didn't want to hear.

His arms folded over his chest, he stared down at me, suddenly one very large step closer. "You need a distraction? We've got a few hours before we need to be out of here."

I snorted to cover my fear. Was sex replacing my love for Ashley? Had I masked the loss of her with it?

But I loved this man. And he'd said we would be...I rolled my bottom lip into my mouth, biting it hard, then carefully letting it roll back, wet and swollen. It might make up for the rest of me.

"That's not very...romantic." I smiled to soften my words. "We have all the time in the world, for now," I corrected in a hurry, lest I'd misunderstood his earlier words, "surely you should be serenading me, something..." I stepped closer, into no man's land between us.

Theo didn't budge, staring at me with dark eyes filled with lust. The rest of his face was hard.

"Do you think me romantic, brat?" he growled, his arms dropping in to catch my elbows as he pulled me into him. "Is that your experience with me? Was I...lacking?"

I loved that he put that out there; giving me the chance to tell him he hadn't satisfied any of my desires when he'd more than fulfilled them. But agreeing with him wasn't his game.

I raised one eyebrow. "I might need another round to be sure."

"Do you expect me to be kind, Kitten?" His snarl was pure sin, pulling me into him as his hands caught my jaw, and he kissed me until my legs wobbled.

"Love me," I whispered. "Please."

Begging no longer felt like breaking his rules.

I leaned into him. Theo drew back slightly with victory in his eyes. His tongue traced my bottom lip, pulling it into his mouth with a nip. His hands closed on my back, letting me know there was no going back. I might not object, but I wasn't planning to make it easy for him, either.

"I don't make love, girl." He kissed me again, a little harder this time. "I fuck."

"The fuck me lovingly."

I swung my hips against his, pleased when he rolled with me, a small groan rumbling deep in his chest. Theo's hands found mine, our fingers lacing together. He towed me back to the lounge, clasping both our hands at my waist as he pulled me down onto the sofa.

I straddled him, sliding my hands beneath his shirt. Every muscle pressed taut against my hands, every inch of them familiar in a way I hadn't been with a man for years. I didn't want to *stop* being familiar with him.

Theo's fingers curled around my waist, settling me over him, pressing down to feel the shape of him beneath me. His arousal evident, pressing hard between us. I rubbed over him, tugging his shirt up to lick all those familiar places on his chest to his stomach.

His hands formed the shape of my ass, pressing me down as my fingers traced the shape of him, trying not to show how breathless he made. My hands ran between us, stroking myself and his hardened length as I held his hard gaze.

"Jesus, girl." He opened his eyes, staring into mine. "Are you going to torture me?"

He rolled me, tugging my jeans over my hips, his hands stroking along my legs. I discarded my shirt, the feel of his naked flesh against mine the greatest distraction of all.

He settled between my legs, nudging them apart. I moved but was surprised, after the way our last time together had played out.

"You don't have to—" I broke off with a small frown, not really sure what I was protesting about.

"You need some TLC, babe," he murmured, understanding lighting his eyes. He dipped to kiss the length of my throat. "I'll play games with you any night but for right now, accept that someone wants to love you."

My hands gripped his shoulders, my legs curling around his calves. "You shouldn't be so complex."

"This isn't complex. This is fucking. The sweet sort of fucking."

He kissed me slowly, letting his weight sink over me. I moaned beneath him, the promise of coiled energy in him calling me. His hands slid down to my hips, gripping hard. I found he was right. I needed something sweet from him.

"Lovingly," I reminded him with a small smile, rocking my hips.

I found the tip of him against my entrance, sliding forward once more, then undulated the length of him, sliding to the root of him until he filled me almost painfully. He groaned, my own whimper escaping my lips, though I swallowed the moan that came after. Barely.

His hips flexed over me, but I shook my head, tugging my hands free of his and pressed them to his stomach. He kissed me, then flipped us both, so I straddled him on top. His hips flexed again. I moaned, pressing my thighs tight on either side of his hips, controlling the movement with a shake of my head.

"What, I can't fuck you lovingly from here?" His smile was all cat-got-the-cream.

I shook my head again with the same small smile as before.

"Not tonight, Black. My way. Please?" I pressed my hands to his stomach. "Still?"

He stared at me for a moment, then gave a single jerk of his chin, his hands curling loosely over my thighs, sliding to my waist.

My hips began to roll of their own violation, a natural rhythm rocking me over him. A low growl began in his chest, but the hands that curved over my waist were gentle, their downward urge a wish, not a promise.

One hand caught mine, dragging our clasped fingers to my stomach and down. He pressed my hand over my pussy, rubbing my fingers in a circle over my clit.

"Touch yourself," he grated hoarsely. I nodded, heat flaring in my cheeks, but I knew I wouldn't deny him.

"Do you want to come together?" I tried to work out what he wanted, still rolling my hips over him, my fingers tracing in small circles that earned clenches around the hard length of him inside me. I paused only for a moment as he shook his head.

"No. I want to feel you come around me."

My lips tingled at his words, the flush creeping down my chest where my nipples tightened into tiny, hard buds. I continued the motion he'd started my fingers on, my clit swelling easily beneath my pads with him seated deep inside me.

My undulations became jerky as I chased the wave of pleasure, then smoothed as it began to crash over me, so fast. I clenched around him as my orgasm crested, my core hot and molten. Theo grunted beneath me, gripping my hips tight as he thrust up, deeper in me at the pinnacle of my pleasure. I screamed softly, my head tipping back, my hips still rolling and rocking the length of him throughout.

Panting, I hunched over his chest. Theo half rose on his elbows, finding my mouth with his.

"You're beautiful, Jen."

My breath caught, I hiccupped against his mouth. "Don't say that," I whispered, wrapping my hands behind his neck, stilling with him completely inside me. "This was fun. That's all. Remember? A stress relief."

"It's a relief, but not for that. Girl, if I'm going to love you right, I need to be over you." His gaze switched from eye to eye, seeking my permission. I nodded, moaning as he moved gently inside me.

"What do you mean, love me right—" I yelped the last word as he flipped us a second time, my legs wrapping about his thighs as my back hit the pillows. His weight settled over me, sinking us both deeper. I moaned, arching back to offer him everything.

His mouth kissed the exposed flesh from my collar bone along my throat and over my jaw. Our mouths met in a deep, long kiss that dropped me down into a trance where he was the only focus in my world for that moment.

"I want to love you right because I do love you, Jen."

His promise whispered against my lips, he began to move inside me. A deeper, slower rhythm than mine, our limbs entwined around each other. Not battling for domination but twisting and sliding over the other's slick skin, our breath mingling, hands tightening until it didn't matter where we were, becasue we were together.

I mouthed the words into his kiss, but his thrusts stole the sound. I arched, crying out as his body pushed deep into mine, hitting every nerve ending.

Theo's roar over me seared me, my body clenching in response to his erratic, deep thrusts. I screamed into his skin, tasting his sweat as he folded me in his arms and blocked out the rest of the world.

CHAPTER TWENTY-NINE

BLACK

Jen pressed to my side as I tugged her up the drive. The garden hadn't changed since I'd last seen it, though there were a few weeds that could come out. Whoever Liam had been paying to maintain the place in my two-and-a-bit-year absence looking after the girls hadn't done the best job.

Now there was more than one of us in the house, there was a good chance it would come back to the standard I'd had before.

When I used to care.

I'd put my own apartment on the market to sell. I didn't need it, especially as I hadn't been in it for a few years, either.

Late afternoon sunlight flickered off her hair. I stroked it back behind her ears, my fingers lingering over the soft skin at her neck, the gentle slope of her shoulders. She shivered but didn't pull away.

For the first time, I didn't have to care about how I touched her in public. Liam had made some noises, but Cal and even Danny had barked him down when he'd objected. I hadn't had to stand up for her; they'd done it for me. The feeling of being part of a larger family, one that actually gave a fuck, came as a novelty.

It had taken me aback for a long moment as I realised how long I'd actually had these men at my back. Longer than just the years I'd tortured Cal as a partner or been an intentional pain in Liam's ass.

"Theo, where are we?" she asked, looking between the house and me. Her eyes flitted between us as the cogs turned. I toyed with the idea of letting her flounder, if only for my own private amusement, then grabbed her hand as I decided to hold off being an asshole for at least a few minutes.

"Come on." I tugged her up the drive, through a kissing gate at the side of the front garden to the curved staircase that led to the front verandah. Her head turned back, she paused halfway up the stairs, looking down over the city.

"Theo, I had no idea—" She started again, her words dropping away as the view took her attention.

"I know, Jen." I pulled gently on her wrist, so she faced me, then stepped down to share her step, hating that I loomed over her at this moment. "I know you had no idea of anything about me when you dropped that pin on the map. I know you didn't check where I lived or researched what the house looked like. I knew you wanted to be here just because of me."

She stared at me, wordless for a second. "You're right, I should have checked. Oh, my God. I'm hopeless," she snorted, shaking her head. My knuckle caught under her chin, tugging her back to me.

"You're far from hopeless, girl." I leaned down to kiss her there, in front of the entire city, not caring who saw us.

"I love you," she whispered against my mouth, and my heart soared. Cradling her jaw carefully between my hands, I brushed my lips over hers.

"I love you, too."

A small hiccup burst from her mouth, then a fit of giggles. I kissed her anyway, drawing her small but strong frame into my arms.

"I want to show you my—" *Life* didn't feel fitting, seeing as I'd been living with her for over two years. "Home. Our home," I said softly, slipping my arm around her shoulders, pressing her lower back with my other hand, so she walked ahead of me up the stairs. She stopped at the top, looking, not at the view like anyone else would. Overlooking all of Melbourne, but at the door her hands clenched, the knuckles turning white. I slipped my hand into my pocket and drew out a shiny key.

"This one's yours. Why don't you see if it works?"

Her slim fingers curled around the shiny metal. She took two hesitant steps into the house, the key sliding effortlessly into the lock and turning with ease. The door swung open.

My pocket buzzed as she stared down the hall. I took a moment to read Liam's message and shoot a quick *thanks* back. There would be time to rib him about the gardening later.

"It's your home, too," I said, placing my hand on her lower back again, but with no pressure. She nodded, not moving. A doubt gripped me, my back aching in all the places she'd tended over the years. "If this isn't the right thing for you, Jen, I'll find you a safe place to live. I promise you. There's no pressure—"

She cut me off, turning oh her heel to kiss me, hard. "Shhh. I was just thinking." That lip slid between her teeth again. "Of how Ashley would love your house."

I nodded, unspeaking, and pressed my hand to her back, a little firmer this time.

She nodded, her head dipping, and I knew she hid her tears. Well, the non-asshole factor lasted three whole minutes. Jen walked down the hall, checking each room as she went.

"It's beautiful."

"I grew up here. It's my family's home. Mum's been gone for years now, and the house became mine years ago before Dad went into respite care. I looked after it in the hope that he'll come home, but that's...not realistic any more." The pain moved from my shoulders to my chest. Jen's hand wrapped around mine, her lips brushing over my knuckles.

"It's beautiful. I don't think I can invade your home, Theo."

"I haven't been in here for over two years. Since I started looking after you."

The confession stung my throat. I tugged her down the hall, pausing at an open door and ushered her inside. The wooden bed I'd used for the last few years before I'd been put on protective detail with Jen and Ashley looked brand new. The gardener might not have done the best of jobs, but Liam's maid certainly had.

"I can sleep on the sofa," Jen said quickly.

I took the bag from her shoulder, placing it squarely in the centre of the bed. "You sleep here. I will too...if you want me. Otherwise, there are a few spare rooms I can occupy."

Jen's nose wrinkled. "That's a harsh word."

"A bit." I nodded in agreement.

"What if I want you to sleep with me?" she asked, staring straight at me.

I repressed a grin with effort. Brave woman. Not many would be comfortable holding my gaze, let alone challenging me, yet here she was, in my house, doing it all the same. I loved her all the more for it.

"Then you'll never be alone at night." I leaned on the doorway, letting her process the offer. She surveyed the room, finally turning to me with a slow nod.

"Please."

One corner of my mouth lifted. "You got it." I caught her hand. "There's something else you should see."

She frowned as I pulled her back down the hall and along another, that went to the back of the house. The last spare room overlooked the backyard. High fenced and full of flowers, the place flocked with parrots at dawn and dusk.

She stared at the freshly-made bed for a moment. "I thought you said..."

I moved from the side of the room, exposing the little box sitting on the floor. A glitter-covered dugong nose stuck out from one corner. Her eyes lifted to mine, filled with hope, and the underlying fear of disappointment beneath. I promised myself she would never have to look like that ever again.

"Why don't you unpack her things, and I'll call Liam?" She nodded, her eyes full of unshed tears.

A small, tentative knock announced our last family member at the back door half an hour later. Liam had waited until dark fell, then had Micah bring her up to the house.

She stood beside the big man and his equally-enormous monster truck looking small and insignificant.

Here, she was neither.

"Ash?" Jen whispered from the hall, walking forward with quick steps.

Micah held the door open, Ashley walking into the house beneath his arm when he nodded to her. She stepped into the dim light, a big step for a little girl who had been through so much, though I hoped Micah had briefed her on the way here.

He might be a huge lump of a man, but the head on his shoulders was reasonably unique and for a bodybuilder; he managed to not cross the line on vanity or selfishness.

"Mum!" she squealed softly, tearing into Jen's arms and hanging from her neck.

Her legs lifted around Jen's waist. Jen straightened with a groan, hefting her daughter in the air.

Ashley began her usual debrief tirade of everything that had happened to her since Jen had seen her last, pausing only to hug me, then Micah as the large man waved from the shadows, reversing his huge truck quietly down the drive.

I locked the door, drawing the front curtains and flicked on lights. Ashley acquainted herself with the house while I worked out what we'd eat for dinner. Finally, dressed in red and white striped pyjamas, Ashley appeared in the kitchen, clutching every stuffed toy she owned.

"Thank you for letting us stay here," she said, very clearly, and carefully. I turned off the heat and moved the frypan full of noodles and stir-fried vegetables.

Squatting down to her level, I held out my arms. She took a tentative step, so similar to Jen's hesitation, then flew into them, a giant, stuffed toy crushed hug that took my breath away. Tears ran into my skin as she cried.

"I missed you, but I missed Mum, and I missed you and is this your house? Are we going to stay here?" she asked, the flood stopping as quickly as it had started.

I laughed. "Yes. My house." I wiped away the tears, stunned at the resilience she had despite the traumas she'd endured.

"Good. Can we stay? We both want to stay. But Mum doesn't want to tell you that."

"Your mum picked coming here, rather than go somewhere else."

My calves cramped from squatting. I wriggled my toes but otherwise kept my focus on the tiny girl in front of me. She'd come out with it in her own time, and I didn't have to wait long.

"Can you be my Dad?" she whispered, studying her toys. "I mean, like adopt me? Because without Paul, I have trouble staying with Mum and I don't want to leave her. Ever. Will you?" she asked with puppy dog eyes.

"You really want that?"

She nodded. A shadow fell over us from the side, though I knew Jen wasn't trying to pry. I stood, ignoring the cramps in my calves. "Babe, I'm probably too old to be your Dad."

Ashley hung from my hip, too long to nurse, but still wanting to be carried. "Yeah. But mine really sucks, and you do a great job. Please?"

I blinked, salt stinging my own eyes. "I'll see what I can do."

The words were out of my mouth before I knew what I was saying.

Ashley nodded and slid down, bouncing to her mum. A conversation about unicorns ensued, and a new obsession involving glitter. The two of them filled my empty house and black heart, and I didn't care in the least if unicorn dust got all over it, as long as it was filled with the women I loved.

Thank you for reading Black & Jenny's story!
I hope you enjoyed it as much as I enjoyed writing it,
and I got just a little immersed in this one.
Please do leave a review, as they feed authors.
I've made it super simple:
just click this link, and you'll travel to the Amazon review
page
for this book where you can leave your review.

Sofia xx

http://www.Amazon.com/gp/customer-reviews/write-a-review.html?asin=B08SPVMPLB

ABOUT THE AUTHOR

Sofia Aves writes fast-paced police romances, suspenseful mysteries, steamy cowboys with a Montana backdrop and the occasional cheeky god. She loves reading Indie authors and hides her collection of college romance books beneath an ever-growing TBR pile.

Sofia is a mum of three crazies and an overly large fur baby who thinks she's a teacup puppy. She loves orchids but can't always keep them alive. Sofia lives near Brisbane, Australia.

www.sofiaves.com

Join Sofia's newsletter & get a free Blue Blooded Brothers short story:

https://BookHip.com/CNMQFX

Follow Sofia on BookBub:

https://www.bookbub.com/profile/sofia-aves?follw=true

BLUE BLOODED BROTHERS

ACKNOWLEDGEMENTS

SENTINEL took on a life of its own over NaNoWRIMO — novel writing month, which is held in November each year. Black's story had been bugging me to get out for a while, but I use the stories I *want* to write as a way to end procrastination and get through the stories I *need* to write. But the biggest part of this book — the reading and editing, beta readers, critique partners and setting it all up to become readable, happened over Christmas. How dedicated are you guys? Thank you all so much for believing in Black and Jenny's story and for supporting me while I wrote the blackest heart I have to date.

This book didn't appear overnight. Beta readers, critique partners...The. Best. Editor. In. The. World. Ashley — you made all the ideas more readable, and a whole lot more relatable. A book takes a team, not a person, to be something amazing! And I'm only one person.

Because I had doubts. Doubts about this man who had such an amazing heart but who covered it all with a bluster that had hardened into armour over the years.

So thank you. Thank you to everyone who helped read, tweak, and comment on Black & Jenny, and thanks to you for reading their story, and bringing them to life too.

Sofia xx

Are you ready for MICAH'S story?

Read IMPACT here

What does the ultimate adrenaline junkie do when the stakes get personal?

Always chasing his next high, Micah Riveria makes the biggest bang he can – whether it's a new explosive to play with, lifting the biggest weights he can, or pushing the limit on the competition monster truck circuit. While the task force winds down after a big win, Micah spends more time at the track working with Jimmy, the geeky computer girl with green hair who tweaks his truck to perfection before every comp. Some of the drivers are looking for bigger highs that the pro circuit can provide, and Micah is swept up in a game of ultimate stakes — with Jimmy at the centre of it all.

There's no job, no assignment, so the team take a break — and Micah heads to the track. He's content to talk geek with Jimmy, live odd hours and get away from the expectations of the team and family. In the midst of his r&r, he finds himself suddenly part of a group of adrenaline junkies, pushing themselves and their limits — further and further.

As their behaviours become more erratic and desperate, Micah discovers theft beneath it all — and people begin to get injured. He calls it in to Cal who tells him to stay in — perfectly placed to drive the investigation. As his relationship with Jimmy heats up, he realises she might be right at the epicentre.

SNOW ON THE RANGE

Red Hart Ranch

Book 1

Every Christmas, Red Hart Ranch opens their doors, and Montana provides the perfect backdrop for good company and better food. But this year, the table won't be as full.

Eve Beaumont is a twin heir to Red Hart Ranch. She loves the land, loves the people, and will do anything for them. Christmas sees most of the ranch hands return to their own homes to celebrate. Only a few long term cowboys remain with the family.

When Eve and her brother Trav go into town to collect supplies, they each bring home a drifter for Christmas. Rhys Archer and Simon Haldon are as different as two cowpokes can be. One, rough-edged who can work the land and animals with a firm hand; the other, a smooth talker with a devilish charm. Eve finds herself attracted to both men, but when tragedy hits the ranch, romance is the last thing on her mind.

Vandalisms happen around the ranch, and Eve isn't sure who she can trust. She knows neither man is who he pretends to be — but when no one listens to her, she has to prove her suspicions on her own.

www.ingramcontent.com/pod-product-compliance
Lightning Source LLC
Chambersburg PA
CBHW010532100726
47903CB00011B/2980